The huge fireball momentarily looked like a giant luminous brain, covered with convolutions, and then grew into a mammoth glowing giant in the night. The fireball turned reddish-yellow and then blood red. The hues of the monster were of every variety, and like a garbled spectrum, glowed an eerie yellow-green-peach-purple-violet, erupting like an insane display of fireworks, only far, far more deadly. It was beautiful nature run amok.

Seconds later, the shockwave bowled over the townspeople who watched with furtive glances through slits between their fingers, fighting the pain of a light whiter and brighter than any they had ever known. The next day, hospitals in Plattsburgh, in Burlington, and in numerous small communities would resound with the kind of stories not heard since Hiroshima and Nagasaki.

Most of the initial victims were from rural areas outside Lake Placid who lived in widely separated homes in the hollows. Most of the injuries in town included blindness—temporary and permanent—for those who looked directly at the fireball, or were cut by flying shards of glass. And there were the self-inflicted

ALSO BY ROBIN MOORE

BLIND SPOT

COMBAT PAY

THE KAUFMAN SNATCH

THE TRINITY IMPLOSION

ROBIN MOORE

and

Louis Perdue

MANOR
BOOKS
INC.

All characters in this book are fictional and any resemblance to persons living or dead is purely coincidental.

A MANOR BOOK

Manor Books, Inc.
432 Park Avenue South
New York, New York 10016

CHAPTER ONE

On the morning of June 5th, 1967, as hundreds of thousands of Palestinian refugees watched numbly, Israeli Mirage jets dipped and dived to visit rockets and flaming napalm on the land. Daring Israeli commandos struck deep into the heart of Arab nations in lightning raids which Nasser and other Arab leaders were unable to stop. Soon the massed military might of Egypt, Syria and Iraq was liquidated, having been either captured or destroyed. More than a billion dollars worth of Russian hardware was fit only for the scrap heap.

A rag-tag group of rebels, whom many thought to be no more than marauding thieves and murderers, made feeble efforts to strike back. Most of them were Palestinians, who fancied them-

selves the saviors of their people. They called
themselves *Fedayeen*—sacrificers. Israeli officials
dismissed them as bandits with no particular
significance. Arab leaders such as Nasser and
Hussein saw them as a threat to their power. It was
a time of uneasy peace. After the moment of
jubilation, Israel resumed its vigilance. But for the
Arabs there was only the smouldering embers of
humiliation after their debacle.

On April 29th, 1969, a group of wealthy
merchants and oil men met on the eighteenth floor
of the Imperial Hotel in Damascus. They bore no
resemblance to the poverty-stricken masses huddled in refugee camps in Jordan, Lebanon, and
throughout the Middle East. Most of these men
wore western business suits; only one was dressed
in traditional Arab attire. And, though they were
completely different from the *Fedayeen*, they had
this in common with their violent brethren: they
had been children in 1948, and vividly remembered the dislocation, the sudden loss of homes,
when the nation of Israel was created.

It was then that they had been scattered like
spores riding the wind, in their own diaspora. They
had landed in West Germany, France, Britain and
the United States, where they excelled as university students. And all of them became members of
GUPS—the *G*eneral *U*nion of *P*alestinian *Stu*-
dents, an organization which, by the end of the
1950's, boasted a membership of twenty thousand
students in some seventy countries. They turned
out a multitude of newsletters and papers, filled

2

with angry invective that demanded, "Give us back our country!"

But on that April day they felt impotent. True, like the Israelis before they had their own nation, these Palestinians turned out to be the smartest merchants, the most skilled civil servants and engineers. But the leaders of their separate states had failed to win concessions from Israel. Indeed, they had lost three-fourths of the Palestinian lands to their Jewish opponents. Now, at last, they were moved to action.

One of their number, a GUPS member named Yassir Arafat, seemed to have a promising answer. After his years as an engineering student at the University of Cairo, he had devoted his life, not to a business and personal fortune, but to building an organization pledged to what he called *Al Fatah* (in Arabic, victor). Formed after the 1956 Suez defeat, the movement grew in vindictiveness, but not necessarily in strength.

For such movements need food and ammunition, medical supplies, time for manpower training, all of which cost money. Individually, the businessmen in the room had supported him and had urged their associates to do the same. This common commitment to the cause was the reason for the assemblage in the green-carpeted suite that April day.

And then a cotton broker from Cairo suggested that the men in the room offer a reward to any person who could supply Arafat's organization with an atomic bomb. To give his idea credence, the broker pledged half a million dollars.

In the excited buzz that followed, more than seven million dollars was pledged. They agreed that the person or group achieving the goal would receive five million dollars, with the remaining two million to be used as seed money. The money would be distributed among trusted GUPS leaders throughout the world, who in turn would seek out people in universities and industry. The majority of the money was allocated to the United States, not only because that nation had the most advanced nuclear education and manufacturing facilities, but also because their security control over everything from missile material to finished bombs was less restrictive than anywhere else in the world.

*   *   *

It was November 19th.

Alex Greely had been driving over Interstate 81 for seven hours. The foothills of the Allegheny Mountains petered out here, but were still steep enough to make the heavily-loaded semi labor. It roared downhill, crawled uphill.

Greely was proud of his rig, with its status symbol bulldog on the grill. Mack trucks had always been sought after in Caton, New York, where he grew up, and where it seemed the kids all wanted to be truck drivers because that was what their fathers did. Greely had worked for years to go into business for himself. Finally, four years ago, he had made the big step and bought his truck.

Now he was even prouder. He had made the last payment that afternoon. The truck was his.

Yet, in a way he was saddened to be the sole owner. Why couldn't his son appreciate his joy? A junior in college, the first in the family to go beyond high school, the boy had no interest in the economics of making a living, only in saving the world. Greely suspected that his son was embarrassed because his old man drove a truck.

Still, there was a ray of hope. The last few times Alex, Junior, had come home, he had expressed an interest in learning to drive the truck. It wasn't that the father wanted his son to become a truck driver, not with a degree in physics on the horizon. It was just that he wanted the boy to be proud of his profession. Yes, that was it, he had a profession. Because he did not wear a suit was no reason to knock it.

The citizen's band radio crackled and popped in the darkness, the yellow smile of its illuminated dial grinned at him. The towering tractor, with fifteen forward speeds, pulling a flatbed loaded with odd-looking oil barrels, signaled for a right turn and eased off onto the exit ramp just south of Cortland. Dusk had fallen. A white 1969 Ford van with dented fenders and rust stains below the doors also signaled for a right turn and followed the truck down the ramp. Pulling onto an older two-lane road that had been replaced by the Interstate, Alex headed for a spot he had eaten at many times before the Interstate had been

5

completed, and had spawned the plastic-and-metal monsters crowding the interchange.

The white van followed the semi into the gravel parking lot of the truck stop. Greely drove around back to park with the two other trucks on the lot. Only then, for the first time in hours, did he look at his co-driver, an older man who lived down the road from Greely in Ludlowville. Fortunately, the older man was the silent type; he had not said ten words during the entire trip.

Normally, Greely did not like to drive with anyone else. This man was retired, and sat with Greely only on these special trips, because the Atomic Energy Commission required him to travel with another person when he carried fissionable material.

Loaded on the flatbed behind the cab were twenty-seven "birdcages" of plutonium nitrate that he was carrying from the West Valley, New York storage facility.

West Valley was little more than a crossroads dropped into the middle of nowhere, thirty miles southeast of Buffalo, and fifteen miles north of the sleepy Catarraugus County town of Salamanca. The country around West Valley was still wild in many places. Even the farms stashed in the hollows of the Allegheny Hills were few and far between. Traffic throughout the section was usually light, and a traveler unfamiliar with the area would never suspect that a booming nuclear reprocessing plant and a warehouse loaded with fissionable material lurked in the region's bucolic

6

summer greenery and ski-slope hills of winter.

Stored here, half a mile off New York Route 240 at the end of Buttermilk Road, was plutonium recovered from the spent fuel rods of nuclear power plants, enough plutonium to arm the world.

The plutonium on the flatbed was in a syrupy water solution as plutonium nitrate. The ten-liter flasks of material were suspended inside the oil-drum-like containers with metal studs. The bird-cage arrangement was necessary to prevent too much plutonium from coming together and "going critical," resulting in a chain reaction which, while not exploding, would cause great amounts of heat, radiation and danger.

Greely had passed through the seven-foot-high barbed wire topped, chain-link fence seven hours before, and watched as workers loaded the squat cylinders onto the flatbed. His truck was not specially equipped, and normal routine called for him to be accompanied by another vehicle containing two armed men. But he had never had anyone riding shotgun before, and as long as the plutonium was not in the more easily used metal form, the rules were blinked.

The two men got out, Greely locked the cab, and they walked across the gravel, their boots crunching. The older man walked through a hallway into the diner; Greely stopped for a few moments in the unclean rest room to urinate and wash his hands, wiping them with his own handkerchief, then joined his companion.

Outside, three men leaped from the white van

and set to work on the cab's door. A hastily-fashioned key did not work, and one of the men broke the window to get in. Nor did the makeshift key work in the ignition. All three sat along the seat taking turns twisting the key, sweating, cursing, to no avail.

Greely, meanwhile, studied the menu, decided on the chuckwagon steak and took a sip of water. He patted his pockets.

"Damn. Forgot my wallet," he said to his companion. "It's in the truck." He rose from the seat and went to retrieve his wallet.

The three in the truck were momentarily paralyzed by the nearing footsteps on the gravel, then, as fear thawed paralysis, they got out of the cab on the other side of the approaching Greely, diving under the flatbed. They saw his feet coming toward them, then stop as he obviously saw the smashed window.

The largest of the three leaped from under the flatbed, grabbed the startled Greely from behind, shoved his forearm across Greely's Adam's apple. Greely gagged and groaned as the second man, a small, swarthy Palestinian, leaped on him, kicking out at his groin. The third man crouched by the rear wheels of the cab, sickened by the violence.

"Get the hell over here and help us get this finished!" the large one screamed, as one can scream in a savage whisper. He was kicking Greely about the head, as the downed driver lay on the gravel, doubled up in a fetal position, kicked gashes on his face and head staining the ground warm red.

Slowly the third man crawled from his hiding place. The keys to the truck were still tangled in Greely's limp fingers, and the third man reached down to retrieve them. As he grasped the keys his eyes met Greely's, and for a brief instant they locked, and he could see the expression of pain, sorrow and anguish in Greely's eyes, the tears that crawled like snails down his cheek, mixing with the blood oozing from a gaping wound. The third man quickly straightened up and climbed into the cab.

The third man did not see the other two drag the inert form of Greely behind the rear wheels of the cab. He shoved the key into the ignition and the engine roared into life. The other two climbed in beside him and he began to back the truck away from its parking place near the diner. Then he felt the jostling bump as the cab's wheels ground over the body of Greely, and an involuntary sob ripped from his throat, but he shifted gears resolutely and drove off the gravel.

He was unfamiliar with the controls, and the engine strained as the semi moved along the level road in gears designed to traverse steep hills. The truck roared away into the darkness.

Greely's companion did not see the truck leave. The food had arrived, and, while he wondered what was keeping the driver, he decided to eat while everything was hot. He would look for him in a little while, if necessary.

The semi pulled onto the entry ramp for Route 81 and pulled into the right-hand lane. The driver was still shifting into a median gear when it was time to pull off at the next ramp.

The road narrowed. The truck passed through the hamlets of Marathon, Virgil, and entered Dryden, then crept along asphalt streets, past the old Dryden Victory Supermarket with its peeling white paint, stopping for a red light beside the Methodist Church. Its white clapboard sides and steeple bell made it the beautiful cliche of every small town church. Across the street, on one corner, the lights were going out in the Mobil station, and on the other corner, high-schoolers, some in athletic jackets, others in colorful shirts, crowded into the Brooklyn Diner. Friday nights after a high school football game, the diner would be packed with kids, parents and teachers. Later, after midnight, the diner's clientele would change. State policemen were attracted to this oasis in the countryside, rubbing shoulders with truck drivers and college students out on dates. Cornell was about ten miles south, the State University at Cortland the same distance north.

The light changed and the semi, with its strange load, turned left, moving past the fire station and down the maple-lined streets, the leaves fiery with fall colors. They crossed the railroad tracks about a quarter of a mile from the light and soon were out of town.

Next came a series of country lanes for another five miles. Finally, the semi came to a halt, its engine idling. The large man got out and opened a half rotted wooden gate, partially obscured by tall weeds, which blocked a rutted dirt road. The third

10

man maneuvered the truck, trying to get it onto the narrow road and in a half dozen attempts he failed a half dozen times. Once a car came over the rise and the trio bolted into the woods, certain that it was a police car. It wasn't. Finally, after aiming the trailer diagonally across the road, the driver succeeded.

In low gear the semi whined along the path, shearing off low branches, lumbering, growling, until it reached the end of the path, confronting a now unused barn, like hundreds of others dotting the dairy farming region. The semi crawled through double doors into the bowels of the barn; its lights were doused and it settled into silence as the big diesel's supercharger hummed to a halt. The rust-encrusted hinges screeched in protest as the other two men slammed the doors shut, and an eerie darkness descended inside the ancient vastness of the old enclosure.

The smaller man struck a match and touched its flame to both mantles of a propane lantern. The weird flowing shadows cast by the kinetic match flame dissolved into the lantern's glare, a light reassuring to the third man. He leaned on what was left of the broken side window, staring impassively at the black walls of the barn, covered from the inside with black particle insulating board, to cover knotholes through which prying eyes might examine the interior.

The other two men set to work with a chain hoist hung from stout rafter timbers. One by one the birdcages were unloaded, carried to the sides of the barn, and hidden behind stacked bales of hay.

Then all three waited in silence. When finally there was a knock at the barn door it came like a thunderclap. The small man rushed to the door and unlocked it.

Outside was a huge black man, standing beside the white van, its engine running. Inside sat a blindfolded man. The small man ran to the truck's cab and nudged the driver. The semi's engine was coaxed back to life, and the rig was driven, empty, out the other end of the barn, around it, and back onto the road.

Followed by the white van, the semi drove along the main highway for about forty-five minutes, then slowed and pulled off on the shoulder, the van right behind it. The black man led the blindfolded man out of the van and helped him into the cab while the driver got out. The van drove off, its original three occupants inside.

The man in the semi removed the blindfold, removed the handkerchief and rubbed his eyes. He had never seen the black man, never seen any of the others, and had only the vaguest idea where the white van was now. But that was none of his business. He started the truck and drove south. Soon he would find his way back to Binghamton.

After that his job would be finished. His employers would pay him and the truck would be sold. They were in business to merchandise that sort of thing. No doubt they already had a buyer, some poor sucker with bad credit who never dreamed he could own so handsome a rig.

Probably the slob would never be able to repay his debt to the organization, and would end up working for them. It had happened before, so often.

The white van drove back to the barn and pulled up alongside it, near the weatherbeaten farmhouse. The black man looked at his watch; it was 11:30. Less than two hours had passed since the truck was driven away from the diner. The plutonium was secured, the truck disposed of.

And this area was so remote, so sparsely populated, that the chances of someone seeing them were practically nil. Even if they had been seen, so what? Nearly everyone in the poverty pockets sprinkled throughout the hills and hollows was either a truck driver or knew one. One semi, more or less, was a common sight.

The third man opened his door. He had been leaning on it since leaving the semi. He stepped out, put a shaky leg on the ground, and collapsed, leaving him lying there with scratched face, soiled from the dirt and the tears streaming down his cheeks. The black man lifted him up and helped him into the farmhouse.

The third man wept until fatigue captured him and sleep overpowered his grief. He dreamed fitfully, seeing the bleeding face of the truck driver, seeing the pinched agony etched in the lines and gashes of his face, seeing the terror and sadness in the almost-dead eyes.

The third man was a Cornell student, a physics major in his third year of studies. His name was Alexander Greely, Junior.

13

CHAPTER TWO

Alexander Greely, Jr., writhed and tossed on the metal frame bed as the nightmare of his father dying replayed itself over and over in his head. His body quivered convulsively in his tortured sleep, playing a virtuoso performance of squeaks and groans on the cheap bed's gridwork of springs and wires.

In the next room were the hulking black man, Jean Lafayette; the barrel chested Irishman, Tom Flaherty; and the swarthy, slightly-built Algerian, Amhad Ismael. The Algerian and Irishman drank beer from cans, the black man sipped instant coffee. His eyes gleamed brighter than the others'.

Like so many others who were fanatical for political, religious or ideological causes, Lafayette was almost ascetic in his self-discipline. He did not smoke, drink alcohol, or overindulge in eating, and took a dim view of those who did. His only vice was women, and in his own mind this minor weakness did not detract from his determination to affect the course of human events. He wanted power, but not in the egotistical sense, only to free the victims of various world political systems. In a single breath he condemned capitalism, communism, fascism and all their variations.

Lafayette's parents had emigrated to New York City seven years ago when he was still in high school. They had lived in Haiti, and Jean's father had known the sting of being a black colonial. The bitterness had led him into communism with its utopian ideals, with which young Jean's mother concurred. But the fanatic devotion to communism left them with little time to show their son the usual parental love and devotion. Jean grew up hating his parents, colonialism and communism. He became a nihilist. Sartre became his ideologue, and the destruction of all forms of imperialism his life's goals. He thought and spoke in the cliches of the New Left.

Unlike so many with the same overt goals, he was, in a sense different. Yes, he cared about people very much, but only those he classified as good. For all the others he had nothing but hatred. For him it was a clearly defined black-and-white world, with no grey areas. His caring reached out to his companion restlessly tossing in the next room. It did not reach out to the broad shouldered, vulgar Irishman.

Tom Flaherty was a product of South Boston, Massachusetts, presently a Cornell University civil engineering student. He had served eight years as an explosives and demolition expert in the army during the Indo-China War, and had kicked around at various jobs since then, mostly working for highway and tunnel contractors who needed his skills with high explosives. He had grown tired of the endless stream of jobs which paid comparatively little. He saw civil engineering as a chance to open up the more profitable side of contracting, and looked forward to the day when he could own a company that hired people like himself.

Flaherty was not a kind man. He delighted in taunting smaller people, and earned a reputation in the army as a sadistic fighter, the type who continued to beat his antagonist long past the point of unconsciousness.

Tom Flaherty and Jean Lafayette were antagonists, but they did not come to blows. Rather they looked upon each other with thinly veiled scorn.

The black man was in this caper because of his beliefs. Tom was there because, as he liked to boast, there was nothing he would not do for a lot of money. The black man saw Tom as someone to be used in order to accomplish a moral task. Tom saw him as a raving ideological idiot. These disparate views often caused sparks to fly, but both also realized that muscle for muscle they were evenly matched, and a fight between them would not end easily.

Flaherty and Amhed soon arose and retired to their rooms in the farmhouse and slipped into the kind of alcoholic stupor which can be caused by chug-a-lugging a six-pack of half quarts of beer each. Lafayette continued to sit at the table, rising only to make more instant coffee. He stared intently at the fitfully tossing figure of Alexander, wondering in his heart what devils drove this man.

Three years earlier, Alexander had entered the sprawling university perched on a hill overlooking the town of Ithaca and its 20,000 residents, and Lake Cayuga. He commuted to classes, driving a white van from his home in Ludlowville.

But the snobbery of a basically plebian school trying to be Ivy League wore heavily on him, as social friction exposed his very proletarian background. He was an introvert, and his circle of friends remained mostly those with whom he attended high school. That is, they remained his friends until he met Jean Lafayette, whose spouted cliches found a warm reception with Alexander.

Alexander listened and believed, as Jean explained the ills of the world in his usual trite, dogmatic doctrines. The endless sessions, with Jean talking and Alexander listening, gradually fed his resentment and it grew, like Jean's, into a bitterness against society.

At home Alexander's life became intolerable. His attempts to convince his parents of the world's injustices invariably led to shouting matches about patriotism and America, about oppression and imperialism, and they always ended when he stalked out and drove away in his van. Only Jean could cool him off. His former high school friends felt as his father did. They wouldn't listen either. He was grateful when Amhed made it possible for him to move out of the house. But that came later.

Meanwhile, Alexander and Jean bounced like ideological billiard balls, from Trotskyite to Maoist groups to Marxist groups and back again, oscillating around the left perimeter of the campus political factions, encouraged by one meeting, discouraged by the next, and always disappointed by all the groups' willingness to talk but their reluctance to take any sort of action. All the meetings did was fuel their prejudice about the American political system.

Another frequent visitor, particularly at the more violence-oriented groups, was an Algerian electrical engineering student, Amhed Ismael. He had taken note of the two students at several meetings, because they always raised questions about the groups' indifference to take action. Like them Amhed was disgusted by the students' purely academic interest in destroying imperialism and oppression. He was intellectually nauseated by these empty-headed offspring of wealthy bankers and stockbrokers, who joined the leftist groups because they were fashionable at the time.

One evening, as a Maoist group met to be bored by a dry talk on Russian revisionism, Amhed spotted the pair at the back of the activity room in Willard Straight Hall. He sat down quietly next to Jean.

"I'm Amhed Ismael," he said, offering his hand to Jean. All three shook and introduced themselves. "I have noticed you two at these meetings," his clipped accent might have passed for French to a careless ear. "I think you may share my frustration with this sort of atmosphere, and perhaps might like to learn how to start doing something."

Jean and Alexander were delighted to leave the boring lecture and join Amhed for refreshments in the Ivy Room downstairs in the "Straight" Willard Straight Hall, the Student Union. They entered the cafeteria and sidled through the turnstile into the serving area. The turnstiles were set at a point below waist level, and Jean muttered something about their being designed to castrate people. They got coffee and seated themselves at a dark wooden table with benches.

"I was a small child, no more than five, when the legionaires killed my father," the slim, swarthy man began. "My father settled in Algeria after being shoved out of Palestine by the Zionists, and soon became part of the resistance during the Algerian struggle for independence. He became a strong follower of Ben Bella. He was a scholarly, meticulous man, and these traits made him the best letter-bomb maker in the country. He also helped run a series of 'safe houses' through which passed every notable Algerian rebel, including Bella himself. It was for this activity that the butcher legionnaires killed him."

Amhed told how he had huddled in a corner,

watching, horrified, while the legionnaires tortured and finally killed his father, and then gang raped his mother.

"She committed suicide six months later, carrying the offspring of one of the beasts." The small Palestinian spat out the sentence as if the words were acid. "My father's friends came for me after they heard of my mother's death and carried me with them as they fled legionnaires and their own explosions."

It was an exciting life for a youngster, and Amhed loved it. He was about seven years old when he began running errands and relaying messages for the men who built bombs, the bombs that forced *Le Grand Charles* to give Algeria its independence. Afterward, it was time for Amhed's schooling. He completed his secondary education in Algeria, and was sent abroad to college by an uncle who was a merchant in Algiers. He had excelled in his electrical engineering studies at Columbia University, and was now a graduate student at Cornell.

"The most important thing in my life, then as now, was the Palestinian student organization," he said earnestly. He then explained the background of the group.

"Now, my friends," he said, "I would like to learn about you."

By the time they had finished, Amhed knew he had the ideologically right people. He appreciated the black Haitian because they shared a common hatred of French colonialism, and he liked the shy

American, whose cool exterior, he felt, harbored an abiding hatred that could be unleashed to his advantage. As they walked out of the huge stone Willard Straight building, he told them of the reward.

"A group of my countrymen, Palestinians, not Algerians, have pledged a huge sum of money, five million dollars, for a particular item they feel would assure them of regaining their native land now occupied by the Zionists," Amhed said. "I think you two might like to help them get that item."

"What is it? What must one do to win the prize?" Jean asked.

"The person or group must deliver an atomic bomb to the *Fedayeen*. Either that, or they must use a nuclear bomb to destroy an approved target."

"Jean and Alexander stared at each other, shocked. "You've got to be kidding!" Alexander shook his head.

"Not at all," Amhed assured them. "The money is there for the taking, by anyone who can meet their terms."

"But why an atomic bomb?" Alexander was still not sure he had heard right. "There are other things that can be equally disastrous, without having to fight the enormous technical obstacles that would present. It wouldn't take much space or time to manufacture enough meningitis virus or bubonic plague to wipe out a country. I could name a dozen other avenues equally as practical."

"I know that. So do my countrymen," Amhed

explained. "But they feel that the mere possession of a nuclear weapon is of sufficient psychological value that it may not have to be used at all. We can negotiate from a position of strength as never before. Arafat knows that to reach the goals of Al Fatah, the *Fedayeen* cannot remain a loose guerrilla force. We must become warrior statesmen, bargain from a political position. But Egypt, Syria, Jordan and the others are afraid of us. If they gave us too much aid, we might become too powerful, a threat to their own vested interests. No, there is no substantial help to be expected from those quarters. Our greatest sources have been private individuals throughout the world. But, unless we show results soon, even those contributions will dry up. We need that bomb, quickly."

Amhed was disappointed that the pair would only promise to consider the proposition, and give him an answer the next day. They arranged to meet at the Pub in downtown Ithaca at 7:30 the next night.

Alexander dropped Jean off at his apartment on Eddy Street in College Town and drove home, his thoughts far from driving. He ran a stop light and narrowly missed being broadsided by a green sedan. He twisted on the radio, punched the buttons, and finally settled on WVBR, the Cornell student FM station.

A panel had just begun discussing the new Bell nuclear power station that had finally received approval after years of controversy. The power station's opponents had contended that the reactor safety systems were inadequate, and the enormous amounts of cooling water would alter the ecology of Lake Cayuga, on whose shore the power plant would be located. The people of close-by Ludlowville were concerned about radiation hazards.

Alexander had heard the story a dozen times. He was only half listening when one of the panelists, a professor in theoretical physics from Cornell, who had worked on the original Los Alamos *Manhattan* project raised an objection he had not heard before. The professor said that the power station's operation would be one more source of plutonium, and since security safeguards against thefts of fissionable material were so light, no more reactors should be built until safeguards against theft were beefed up.

Chance and happenstance play an enormous role in human events. A stop light might mean a person arrives at an intersection too late to be killed by a drunk driver. Or, he can keep his date with death a split-second later by gunning through the yellow. So it was that night for Alexander. The laws of possibility had decreed that he learn of a huge prize for the delivery of an atom bomb. Now he heard that security surrounding the vital fissionable material was relatively light.

It was at that instant that he knew the atom bomb could be built.

Actually, the controversy about adequate safe-guards for nuclear material had been widespread during the late 1960's. Originally, American security organizations were set up to keep other countries from gaining the knowledge to build the bomb, giving the United States a nuclear monopoly. That was a foolish hope at best. Despite the valuable information transmitted to the Soviet Union by American communist sympathizers, Russia would have had a bomb eventually. Their technology could not long be denied, which was proven by the fact that their Sputnik got off the ground years before American astronauts went into orbit. The same could be said of other nation's nuclear capability; the nuclear club was growing steadily less exclusive.

With nuclear monopoly thwarted, many American security measures were dropped, and much technical information about the bomb was declassified. But that posed no problem until the advent of large scale nuclear reactors for power purposes. These reactors produced vast amounts of fissionable plutonium as a result of the chain reaction, and what had once been a rare man-made element became available by the ton. And each ton was not as well guarded as a few thousand dollars. Whereas the dollars went by armored car, the plutonium usually went by truckline, train or freight plane, sometimes mingled with the usual cargo.

Alexander, his brain a jumble of thoughts, did not sleep much that night.

Nor did he attend classes the next day. He and Jean spent most of the day wandering about the campus, discussing the risks and rewards of accepting Amhed's offer. Would it really benefit their cause to team up with the Palestinians? And could they build the bomb in the first place? Both were majoring in physics, and both were in the top ten percent of their class, only their political pursuits preventing them from spending more time at their studies and doing even better. But an atom bomb! It seemed such an unattainable goal.

It was only 7:00 p.m. when Jean and Alexander arrived at the Pub. Amhed was not there yet. They walked to the rear and took a booth in the left corner. The door was visible from there. Jean noted with distaste the people blowing cigarette smoke out of their mouths and noses, looking for all the world like poorly tuned automobiles spewing pollution.

Alexander ordered a beer and Jean a root beer. They sipped, exchanging few words. The enormity of what they were about to become involved in weighed heavily. To be caught would certainly mean a lifetime in prison, perhaps death. Alexander remembered Julius and Ethel Rosenberg, and decided that their crime would be almost insignificant, compared to turning over a workable atomic device to a terrorist enemy of the United States.

What worried both men was the fact that this bomb would certainly be used against Israel. Neither was anti-Semitic. They looked upon Jews as another oppressed race, deserving of liberation.

Amhed, too, had professed no hatred against Jews. "It is the Zionists I am against," he had said last night. "They are the ones who took our land

and turned us out, homeless and poor. They did this with the help of the United States, and that is why the United States and the Zionists are our enemies."

He added that because America had stepped up its military assistance to Israel, he felt the Palestine consortium might pay the prize if the first bomb went off in Washington.

At 7:23 Amhed came through the door and looked around, searching for his friends. Jean saw him. He picked up the empty mugs and walked to the front of the pub, sidling up beside Amhed.

"Can I buy you a drink, friend?" he asked, his mouth an inch from the Arab's ear.

Amhed started. He saw Jean and looked relieved. "You frightened me a bit," he said. "I hadn't expected you to be here yet. Is Alexander here?"

"Back in the corner," Jean pointed with one of the mugs. "Why don't you join him and I'll bring you a beer if that's what you want."

Amhed nodded. He walked to the booth and slid into the seat beside Alexander.

"Jean and I have done a great deal of thinking," Alexander said. "We hardly slept last night."

"Good," Amhed nodded. "I would hesitate to get involved with anyone who would rush into such a serious thing. But I will wait for your answer until Jean returns."

Soon Jean was back. He slid two frosted mugs of beer onto the table, and, holding his own root beer, took a seat facing the other two.

"There's no use beating about the bush," Jean said simply. "We'll do it."

"A toast," Amhed grinned. "To the three of us." They clinked mugs, beer and root beer spattering together on the table.

The conversation grew intense as Amhed explained how much money would be available for the project, and what arrangements could be made for their future escape. During the course of three more filled mugs, it was decided that the three should room together, preferably wherever the bomb would be made. Their new location had to be isolated, and have a structure large enough to house all the needed equipment. After some discussion, Alexander suggested that they find an abandoned farm with a barn and rent it.

"Excellent," Amhed smiled. "Who would suspect what we are up to? The 'in' thing among students now is back-to-nature. And we are renting a farm. Except that it will be our own private little Los Alamos."

It was also agreed that Alexander and Jean would spend the next three weeks seeking information about nuclear bombs, and at that time they would determine what the chances were of building it, and how many, if any, additional people would be needed to finish the job.

*   *   *

Anyone working in Washington might well follow a set routine getting to work in the morning.

27

Suppose an individual drove along the south-west freeway, past the monolithic designs of L'Enfant Plaza, and down through the short tunnel exit to South Capitol Street. Another right turn would take the individual to a red light at South Capitol and D Streets. Two left turns later, he would be pulling into the underground garage behind the Rayburn House Office Building. Above him is a fountain and a flower garden maintained by the Botanic Garden.

After parking his car, the individual might walk to the Longworth House Office Building, and only a weary veteran would cease to be amazed at the intricate system of tunnels and underground chambers that honeycomb Capitol Hill. An atomic bomb might take out all of Washington, but whoever was in the tunnels would at least survive the blast.

And the individual would walk on, past the printing offices, that churned out billions of brochures, posters, newsletters and other para-phernalia which Congressmen need to call attention to themselves in order to stay in office.

A right turn and up two flights of escalators would bring the individual into the Longworth Building. Had he turned left, he would have reached the Rayburn House Office Building, and straight ahead was one of the tunnels leading to the Cannon Building. There were also tunnels and subways to the Capitol from all these buildings, and, through the Capitol basement, other tunnels and subways to both Senate office buildings.

These tunnels were for people and only minor features of the tunnel system. More elaborate and numerous were the steam and utility tunnels connecting just about every building in the federal enclave.

But, what the individual would *not* see, if he came to work on a certain morning in October, was two Cornell University students, sitting on the steps of the Library of Congress, waiting for it to open.

Alexander and Jean had scoured the stacks of the mammoth libraries at Cornell, and within a week had found about three-fourths of the information they would need for the bomb. The rest, they believed, would be in Washington.

They had discovered that there are basically two ways to make a nuclear bomb. Both involved the process of putting enough fissionable material together to make it "go critical" and explode. The idea of a *critical mass* had been known several years before any nation embarked upon the building of an atom bomb. The idea was relatively simple.

Radioactive atoms give off radiation primarily by splitting up into two different atoms. The splitting is accompanied by a tremendous amount of energy. Some of the fragments strike other atoms and cause them to split also. Depending on the type of material and its size, fragments are thrown out by the billions, causing the simultaneous splitting of billions more atoms. Then these atoms throw out fragments, and the process accelerates until an explosion occurs. Naturally, the larger the piece of fissionable material, the greater chance any fragment has of hitting an atom. And so it is, the textbooks told the two would-be bombers, that to sustain chain reaction, every fissionable material had to be of a certain minimum size.

The idea of a chain reaction was demonstrated shortly after World War II, when the American people wanted to know what a chain reaction was. To demonstrate, many set mouse traps were enclosed in a glass cage, and each trap delicately "baited" with a ping pong ball. Then, one ping pong ball was dropped into the enclosure. It struck another ball and bounced, then both balls struck and bounced, each time triggering a mouse trap. In split seconds the glass enclosure was filled with flying ping pong balls going off every which way. It was crude, but the public got the idea.

In making a nuclear bomb, the basic idea is to take a barely subcritical mass and use some method to make it suddenly go critical. One method for doing this is to take one subcritical mass, then fashion a "bullet" out of another subcritical mass, and fire the bullet at the first mass. When they meet, the two pieces together are greater than the critical size and it explodes.

This was the "Little Boy," the type dropped on Hiroshima.

To aid the explosion, the masses needed an *initiator*, a substance that would emit neutrons intensely at the right moment. It couldn't emit them continuously, since that might trigger a premature explosion. Scientists finally settled on a lithium-polonium initiator. The lithium was non-radioactive, and the polonium was not intensely radioactive. But, when mixed together, the mixture sprayed neutrons with an incredible intensity. Thus the solution was simple:

Put your sample of non-radioactive lithium on the target piece of material, and the polonium on the bullet piece. When they meet, BANG!

The "gun type," they figured, was by far the simplest type to make, but it required Uranium 235, which was much less common than plutonium. But, plutonium emits so many neutrons of its own, that neutrons leaping off its surface at or near the speed of light would cause the approaching mass of "plutonium bullet" to go critical before the two pieces actually met. This would result in a "fizzle yield."

The other method, they found, while not as simple, is more efficient: *implosion*. Rather than increasing the mass of the material, implosion squeezes the material suddenly and increases its density. This has the same effect on neutrons as increasing the mass. So, the idea is to take a sphere of plutonium, with an initiator in the center, and compress it into a critical mass using ordinary high explosives.

As they sat on the steps, the great cast-copper doors behind the outer glass doors swung open, and a custodian stepped forward to unlock not only the doors to the Library of Congress, but also the doors to nuclear nightmares.

To most people, the architecture of the Library of Congress building is awe inspiring, wondrously beautiful. The two Cornell students saw none of that beauty. They saw instead a magnificent edifice built while people starved, a monument built on the backs of the poor and oppressed. They walked on through the marble archways, past gilded walls and cut-stone steps and floors, straight back and through the doors of the main reading room. READERS ONLY, the sign read, VISITORS PLEASE USE VISITORS GALLERY. They stopped at a bulletin board to the left of the door and examined the instructions on how to borrow books from the library. They were not permitted to take the books from the building, but decided that smuggling them out would be no great task.

Of course, they already had some tracts. They had purchased declassified technical bulletins from the National Technical Information Service and the Atomic Energy Commission which were pretty exhaustive in their treatment of every phase of bomb construction, except in the arrangement of the high explosives. For, despite the complicated technical and construction problems, the group had decided to build an implosion bomb.

Uranium 235 was not only less readily available than plutonium, but a bomb needed about three times as much Uranium 235 to achieve a critical mass. So they needed information on how to arrange the high explosives around the spherical nuclear core. They had learned that as little as a millionth of a second's delay in firing some of the explosive charge could result in an uneven implosion, with the result that the core was blown to bits instead of being squeezed into a critical mass. The shapes, the strength and the placement of the explosives were the most ticklish problems they faced. They also knew that of all the information concerning the atom bomb, the bulk of what still remained classified concerned the explosives.

The rotunda of the vast reading room was impressive, but not to the Cornell students. They walked around the massive circular request desk that occupied the center of the rotunda. Radiating in concentric circles from the request desk were long numbered lamp-lit desks for readers. Around the huge desk the card catalogue began. They split up the subjects they had to check and began to search through the millions upon millions of cards that filled up four rooms, more space for the cards alone than a small city would allot to stacks of books on shelves. They got their desk numbers beside each other and took their requests to the desk, three by three, that being the maximum number.

They looked up "Los Alamos," "The Manhattan Project," "Atomic Bombs," "Plutonium," "Explosives," and a dozen other related subjects. By noon their eyes were swimming through a sea of words, some helpful, many interesting, most redundant since they already had that information. By the end of the first day they knew much more than before. They smuggled four books out, tucked into their belts, covered by the navy blue windbreakers they wore.

In Alexander's van, which had been used for the trip to Washington, they drove back to the Quality Inn, Capitol Hill, across from Union Station, where they were staying. The trip had been paid for by Amhed. In fact it had been agreed that everything they did or obtained would be financed by Amhed's cash, or simple larceny.

They ordered supper sent in, then settled down to try and absorb the thermodynamic and hydrodynamic equations relating to explosions. By nine o'clock they had scoured their stolen books and added immensely to their understanding of the technical problems involved in building the bomb. But they were still unclear about the arrangement of the explosives. Wearily Jean slammed shut a book about the use and manufacture of shaped charges.

"Alex," he said slowly, "I think we're going to need someone to help us with the explosive end of this business. I mean, so much has to be done, in such a definite way, that even if we could figure out the exact shape of the explosives, we might blow ourselves up trying to make them."

Alexander, also weary of reading, nodded. "Maybe Amhed can get somebody with that kind of expertise."

"Well," Jean grunted, "we'll give it another try." Within an hour both were fast asleep.

The walk from the hotel to the library was not an unpleasant one. The route took them some couple of hundred yards from the Union Station through one of the many parks spread throughout Washington. They passed by the Russell Senate Office Building and the Dirksen Building. Crossing Constitution Avenue, they walked past the Supreme Court Building with its classic Greek proportions and columns, finally arriving at the library. This time they went to the lower entrance under the main stairs, then past the guard on duty and up the marble stairs to the main level.

"You know, Jean, if I could just get some sort of an idea about the basic shape of the explosives, maybe it would be valuable to whoever Amhed finds to help us," Alexander said.

Jean thought for a moment. Then he said, "How about the testimony at the Rosenberg trials?"

They agreed that they might possibly find a clue that way. The main prosecution witness, David Greenglass, had been a machinist at Los Alamos and had fabricated the high explosive charges for the scientists. Indeed, the sketches of those lenses, which he passed to his brother-in-law, Julius Rosenberg, were pieces of the evidence which ultimately led to the electric chair for the Rosenbergs. Greenglass had escaped with a jail sentence.

Alexander filled out three slips for books dealing with the Rosenberg trial and placed them in the wooden box on the request desk. It took considerable time for the request to be filled, and only one of the books arrived. The other slips were marked NOS—Not On Shelves.

Invitation To An Inquest was the book they needed. It had been written in 1965, and in the picture section, between pages 228 and 229 were three sketches of the high explosive lens molds David Greenglass had fabricated. The sketches were crude and showed little detail, but the principle was there. Someone who knew his way around explosives and could also handle all the hydrodynamic equations in their other books could come up with the right configuration. They were sure of it.

Each of them stuffed a book under his belt again and walked slowly past the uniformed policeman at the door, chatting amiably. The policeman's job was to catch people like them. Perhaps he saw the bulges, perhaps not, or it might have been that his thoughts were far away at the moment. Jean and Alexander walked out the door with no questions asked.

Second guessing is so easy. If a knowledgeable observer knew what to look for, and if he happened to look at the list of books reported missing or stolen even two weeks later, he might have guessed what the thieves had in mind. The missing books included:

Invitation To An Inquest, by Walter and Miriam Schneir; *The Curve Of Binding Energy*, by John McPhee; *Sourcebook On Atomic Energy*, by Samuel Glasstone; two texts on high explosives,

36

The Effect Of Nuclear Weapons, by the Atomic Energy Commission, and *The Plutonium Handbook*, by Gordon and Breach. By themselves, no one of the books had enough clues to help anyone build a bomb, although the McPhee book would be most helpful. But, together, combined with an education in physics, and exposure to the academic advantages of a large university, the package might be sufficient.

Jean paid the hotel bill with cash. He and Alexander grabbed a cheeseburger for lunch and left the city, heading onto the Southwest Freeway toward Shirley Highway and the Beltway. Traffic flowed smoothly across Fourteenth Street Bridge and past the Pentagon. Traffic was light as the van sped past exits for Springfield, Fairfax and Vienna, the commercialized bedrooms for the bureaucrats, congressmen and their staffs, who flowed like a tide each day, filling Washington in the sunshine hours, deserting it and its crime by night. It took only half an hour during the early afternoon to reach the Rockville, Maryland exit; at rush hour it would have taken an hour and a half. Up Interstate 70S they drove, through Civil War country, whose towns read like a page from a history book: Antietam, Gettysburg; no battle in modern warfare had equaled the carnage at Antietam: 22,000 dead in less than three days. Past Hagerstown, the van went north on Interstate 81, through Amish country, with its anachronistic horse-and-buggies, carrying black-shrouded riders from near Harrisburg, Lancaster, and the hundreds of hamlets sown like seeds through the aging mountains.

They stayed on Interstate 81 through Binghamton. Their business would bring them back to that city in several weeks, in contact with the Mafia family whose influence pervaded every facet of commerce worthy of a second glance. Twenty miles south of Cortland the van turned onto New York Route 79 and headed west through the sleepy town of Richford and continued on toward Ithaca. By 8:30 they were home, to chat briefly with Amhed and tell him of their finds. Afterward, they slept soundly.

*   *   *

It took Amhed and his cohorts less than two weeks to find an ideal setup and less than two days to move in. The house and barn were typical of those left behind, as hundreds of dairy farmers called it quits, unable to make it financially, or lured to jobs in industry which paid better for less effort. The house, barn and about six acres rented for three hundred dollars a month.

The house had a kitchen and two rooms on the first floor, two rooms and a bathroom on the second. Jean had one room on the first floor, Amhed and Alexander used the two upstairs. The second room on the first floor was a common room. Alexander would move his bed in with Jean when the fourth man arrived. There was a full cellar with fieldstone foundation and crumbling cement walls. The house had been built during the depression of the 1930's; from the look of the hand-hewn timbers in the house and barn, the hand-split lath strips in other walls, the structures obviously had been made from natural, readily-available materials.

The barn was in fairly good shape. It did not leak and had a concrete floor, the result of the owner's futile attempt to modernize. That was perfect, they told the realtor, since they wanted to open a ceramic and pottery studio in the barn, thin justification to the electric company for installing the heavy-amperage line, supposedly for a kiln.

Privacy for their work was assured. A little-used drive connected house to barn, about fifty feet of cracked asphalt. A dirt path, heavily overgrown with weeds, ran from the barn some seventy-five feet to the blacktop road that ran by the house.

All that was needed was some carpentry work on the inside of the barn, to convert it from bovines to bombs.

For three weeks the three men hammered and sawed and soldered and painted and dug, to turn the barn into a nuclear factory. By the end of the second week, Amhed had found the fourth man, Tom Flaherty.

It was during the third week that Alexander began to grow weary of the task. It wasn't that he was lazy; but all he could see stretching ahead was work, work and more work, with no guarantee that their labors would meet with success.

"Why don't we just steal an atom bomb from the army?" he suggested. "I'm sure they've got bombs stashed away all over the place, here and in Europe."

"Funny you should mention that," chuckled Jean. "A few years ago, some Green Berets on maneuvers managed to get into one of the storage sites without tripping any alarms and without being spotted by guards. They could have walked out with whatever they could carry."

"I remember the incident," Amhed added. "It was pretty embarrassing. They've beefed up security a lot. I'm sure if it was as easy now as the Berets made it look then, Black September—the *Fedayeen*—would have tried it long ago."

"We've got to keep working," Jean said grimly. "When we're finished with the barn, our next step is to figure a way to get our hands on plutonium."

"I have an idea about that," said Alexander. But he did not elaborate at the time. There were some preliminary steps he had to take before that could happen.

"And even when we do that, our bomb will be much cruder than the military bomb. It'll weigh about three or four tons, be about the size of a typical office desk. We've got to find out how to position the bomb without its being discovered."

"And we've still got to determine its critical mass," Alexander mused. "We can use a table of critical masses for different configurations—cubes, spheres, different shapes—but the critical mass will vary, depending on what materials we

40

pack around it, and how pure the plutonium will be. I don't know how pure a core of plutonium we can make in the barn."

"Well, you can leave the explosives part of it in my hands," growled Tom Flaherty. "What we need is a well-equipped machine shop and metallurgical lab. That kind of equipment isn't cheap. And the way I figure it, the explosives will eat up most of the money Amhed's got." He thought for a while. "Of course, we could steal the equipment."

"No, that won't work," Jean said.

"Why not?"

"If anyone looked at a list of the things that were stolen, he would recognize that it adds up to a shopping list for an atom bomb. We need the stuff in a hurry. Someone might get suspicious about the unusual thefts. People don't go around stealing plutonium, a half-ton lathe, a drill press, at least not very often."

"Are you talking about the FBI or the local fuzz?" Tom sneered. "The only thing the cops around here know how to do is set speed traps."

"Tom's right, Alex," Jean said. Amhed agreed, and, reluctantly, so did Alexander. And Alexander knew where the plutonium, at least, would be coming from.

Through information gleaned from an Atomic Energy Commission booklet, Alexander had learned that there were two privately owned plants which processed fuel rods and separated the uranium, plutonium, and the useless fission products. One plant was located in Morris, Illinois;

the other at West Valley, New York.

In 1944, the first large atomic reactors were set up at Hanford, Washington. Their sole purpose was to produce plutonium for the Los Alamos bomb project. Plutonium, before 1940, had existed only in scattered atoms, when the first microgram quantities were manufactured and "discovered" by Glenn Seaborg at the University of California at Berkeley.

The Hanford reactors were incredibly inefficient compared with those used by power companies today. In comparison with the grams-per-day production of the Hanford Plants, today's reactors produce the element by the pounds and tons. Indeed, a new generation of reactor, the *breeder*, is designed so that it produces a greater weight of plutonium than the uranium which is used to produce it. In other words, it produces more fuel than it uses. The plutonium, however, is dangerous to handle, and not economical to use in other power plants, so it has piled up in warehouses.

As long as plutonium is not economical, the workhorse of the atomic reactor will continue to be a form of uranium called U-235. This is a relatively rare form of uranium compared with the more common U-238, a slightly heavier form. However, U-238 does not split easily. It would rather remain inert and absorb neutrons; this can slow down and stop the chain reactions. For this reason fuel rods must be "enriched" with U-235, the more fissionable isotope (or weight) that provides the punch in the chain reaction.

But the chain reaction continues, and more and more U-235 splits into smaller atoms, things like Krypton-85 and Cesium-137, and other radioactive elements called fission products. These fission products "poison" the reaction and cause it to slow and become less efficient. At some point, the amount of U-235 becomes so small that the fuel rods have to be replaced with fresh ones.

However, all is not lost. The neutrons that were ejected when the U-235 fissioned, had a variety of uses. The majority of them were used to strike other U-235 atoms and cause them to split, continuing the chain reaction. But some of the neutrons were captured, absorbed by the U-238 atoms, causing them to become another isotope, U-239. This is an unstable element, and after giving off radiation, it changes into Neptunium-239, which is also unstable. In less than two hours, most of the neptunium has decayed into Plutonium-239. The power of the reactor and the length of time the fuel rods are left in the core determine how much plutonium is produced. Rods left in high power reactors for a long period of time produce small amounts of an unstable form of plutonium-Pu-240, which gives off radiation as it decays.

Uranium and its refining processes are extremely expensive, so power companies send their fuel rods to be recycled, not to obtain more plutonium the way the military does, but to obtain more uranium for remanufacture into more fuel rods. The plutonium is looked on as a byproduct and is stored for the time it may be economical to use as reactor fuel.

The chemistry used at Morris in Illinois and West Valley in New York, for processing the fuel rods, is very straightforward, simple enough for a college sophomore to carry out the operations, except for one fact: the intense radiation given off by the fission products would give a person a fatal dose of radiation poisoning in a matter of seconds.

For this reason the processing is carried out by remote control, by giant mechanical hands with television monitors and periscopes for the eyes, all run by a human being, protected by huge thicknesses of lead and concrete.

The fuel rods arrive at the processing plant in huge steel-and-concrete drums, which are emptied into a vat of water and allowed to "cool off." The water is first demineralized, lest the intense radiation create more radioactive fission products among the elements that are impurities in the water.

Ironically, the new fuel rods which have not been used in a chain reaction are safe to handle by hand. Their radiation, while greater than background radiation, would have to be handled for long periods of time to induce radiation sickness. The potent materials are the fission products.

The water around the fuel rods glows an eerie blue-white. Shielded by the water, people walk around the edges of the water vat and look at the Cherenkov glow, caused by the effects of radiation on the water. The glowing masses are picked up by mechanical arms and taken into what the workers call "the canyon," where the rods are cut like butter by sharp steel blades. They drop into a churning vat of nitric acid, which dissolves the steel jacketing as well as the uranium, plutonium and fission products inside. The result is a chemical solution that is hot with radiation as well as hot from the chemical reactions.

Chemical processes convert the uranium into its hexafluoride form. Through separate systems, the processing plants collect the uranium hexafluoride gas and the plutonium nitrate solution. By the time they reach this stage, they can be handled once again by unshielded humans. They are then bottled and shipped to other plants for conversion to uranium oxides or metal or plutonium oxide. The plutonium nitrate, however, is most often stored as a syrupy green nitrate solution, since plutonium oxide is the most powerful poison known to man, far more potent even than cobra venom. As little as a millionth of a gram can be fatal. Because of this potency, millions of kilograms of plutonium are piled up in warehouses, its only use: a bomb.

The liquids left from the conversion process have no earthly use yet. Their deadly radioactivity will last for thousands of years, yet it is impossible to discard it where it will not contaminate the environment. In tanks in New York, Washington State and a dozen other sites, the seething liquid of which nightmares are made boils from its own radioactivity, and has to be refrigerated or cooled with water. Man will have to cool these materials practically forever, for if their deadly assortment of chemical poisons and inescapable radiation were to break loose on civilization, only the wildest fabrications of science fiction could predict the outcome.

Alexander wearily put aside all his notes and reflected on the steps to come. He already knew where the plutonium would come from: it would be stolen from his father. But that was no big deal in and of itself. Stories of lost shipments of fissionable material, sent via truck or airline, were common knowledge. In 1969, for example, the AEC received word that a shipment of weapons-grade uranium hexafluoride had disappeared. After a good deal of searching, it was finally located in a freight room at Boston's Logan Airport. Estimates that one or two percent of all trucks, carrying all sorts of goods, are not disputed. It was only a matter of time until a truck carrying enough plutonium for a bomb met the same fate.

Alexander decided to spend some time at home, hoping his father would tell him about the truck shipments of plutonium from West Valley. He swallowed his ideological outrage at his father's ideas. Alexander spent three nights that week eating dinner with him, being careful not to bring up the subject abruptly. His patience and self control had been rewarded the third night.

It was after dinner. Alexander and his father were in the living room, while Mrs. Greely was in the kitchen happily doing the dishes. It had been so long since father and son had been on good terms. Perhaps the boy was coming around at long last.

"Yeah, I was picking up this load at West Valley one night back in September, gonna make a run with it to the nuke lab in Syracuse and then down to Columbia, South Carolina, to a processing plant there. I was talking with one of the guards that was watching while the boys loaded the truck. He told me what a Mickey Mouse thing he thought the regulations were. 'Hell,' he says, 'If I was gonna steal something, I sure as hell wouldn't waste my time on the pee green junk in those things. Who needs it?'

"I'd gone the whole way that night," the older Greely explained, "and I had old Tompkins with me. You know the old geezer from down the road?" Alexander nodded. "And I had two rent-a-cops following me. It sure cost a bundle. 'Don't worry about bringing those guys again,' this guard says to me about the cops. 'Just bring another guy with you in the cab and you can load it up.'

"Seems the Atomic Energy fellas made a rule that you could do away with cops following you if you had what they called a specially equipped truck. But they never defined what 'specially equipped' meant. So," he concluded with a snicker, "if anyone asks, I've got me a specially equipped truck."

"When are you making the run again, dad?" Alexander managed to sound off-handed.

"In a couple of weeks, the 19th. Say," the father

47

suggested eagerly, "old Tompkins ain't much company, but he's free. Think you could swing it? I could even let you drive some if you learned a little about a truck before then."

"Sounds interesting," said young Alexander. "I'll try to arrange it. But you know what school is like, something could come up at the last minute."

For the next two weeks Alexander came to the house repeatedly, learning how to drive the monster Mack. It was a difficult task, and Alexander wasn't that skilled, but finally his father told him he was good enough to drive on the open road at night, with little traffic, on the trip to South Carolina. First, though, they had to drop off another load at the Syracuse University Nuclear Center.

After the second lesson, Tom had handed Alexander a wad of soft wax and told him to make an impression of the truck keys. Tom said he would have a key made so that the truck could be driven away while his father ate or slept.

Alexander made the group promise there would be no violence. "After all," he pointed out, "he might be an enemy of the people, but he's still my father." All but Tom agreed.

On November 17th, Alexander phoned his father. "Pop," he said, "I can't make the trip. A sudden exam. Can you still get hold of old man Tompkins?"

"Yes," said his father, the disappointment evident in his voice.

Then came the highjacking of the truck. And the

murder of his father. And the frantic flight. And now the hideous nightmares.

He was driving the truck, alone, and suddenly, standing in the road was his father, waving his arms, but the truck would not stop, and Alexander could not steer away, and the truck smashed into his father, driven by his own hands, and the truck bounced as it ran over the body of his father, and...

Alexander screamed in his sleep. Jean arose from the table swiftly and strode into the next room, grabbed Alexander by the shoulders and shook him awake. He sat up, rubbed his eyes, looked around wildly. Then he remembered, and the tears would not stop.

"Control yourself, man," Jean said softly. "You're going to make it."

"I didn't want the old man hurt," sobbed Alexander.

"Yeah, I know, man," said Jean. "But you've got to think of it as another one in the cause of freeing the people." He could not speak of "the cause" except in cliches.

"Freeing the people, hell!" shouted Alexander. "Did you see the way that Irish sonofabitch kicked him in the balls? Kicked him in the head? Kicked him in the face? There was no reason for that!" His voice cracked and he began to sob convulsively.

The black man gave him a sedative. When it took effect, he too lay down on his cot in the same room and slept.

CHAPTER THREE

While Alexander slept, his father's mangled form, almost severed at the waist by the giant steel semi tires, had been discovered.

Old man Tompkins had only started to eat his greasy hamburger when another driver dashed up to the cashier and asked to use the phone to call an ambulance. Something the man said about a mangled body in the parking lot caused him to bolt out the door.

Sliding on the uneven, slippery gravel, he found Greely's body. He stood transfixed, his body rigid with horror. The air smelled of death, of blood and tissue, it smelled of the woods he knew after he had killed a buck. He fell to his knees, his senses reeling, nauseated. His insides retched, his mind retched, knowing that what had only minutes before been a walking, alive human being was now so much meat.

He fainted.

The ambulance came to take away the meat, accompanied by three white Plymouths with the dark green markings of the New York State Police. The oscillating red beacons punctuated the glare of headlamps and spotlights which cast their harsh illumination across the grisly scene like so many miniature suns.

The troopers made the ambulance attendants wait until a photographer arrived to take pictures of the scene. One young sandy haired trooper walked behind his car and threw up. He had seen corpses before, but never so mangled!

The photographer came. His face was emotionless as his strobe flash winked again and again, taking closeups, backgrounds, pointing his camera in every direction, and he too was trembling when he had finished.

Tompkins regained consciousness, lying on a stretcher. Someone had cleaned his face, but his mouth was full of acid, rancid taste. He asked for water, and a trooper brought some from the diner.

"Did you see anything at all?"

"Nothing," Tompkins said weakly. "I was inside, eatin'. Greely forgot his wallet in the cab. That's the last I saw him alive."

"Where'd this Greely live? You know his phone number?" the trooper asked.

Tompkins gave him the information. Another trooper went inside the diner and dialed, but there was no answer. Greely's wife had gone to stay with a friend in Ithaca, as she always did when he was going over the road and would be gone a couple of days.

"Any other relatives you know about?" the trooper asked.

"He's got a hippie son," said the old man querulously. "Doesn't live at home. Don't know where in blazes he lives. But he goes to college. Cornell."

All but the hardiest spectators were driven back when the attendants loaded the remains of Greely into a rubber body bag. The gawkers dispersed, and no one was left when the last Plymouth showered gravel with its rear wheels and hummed onto the two-lane highway.

By then teletypes had started clicking in state police barracks all across New York and in their Pennsylvania counterparts. The truck's license number and description were condensed into electrons and spread like lawn seed to local police, sheriff's departments and police in half a dozen states.

The state police barracks in Ithaca, New York, was a white structure with a rail fence in front, looking for all practical purposes like a typical tract development home in some suburban community. The Ithaca barracks controlled state troopers in Tompkins, Cortland and Tioga Counties. It was the central communications post, and the district commander, Lieutenant Leslie Atkinson, had his office there.

Atkinson could not remember being called out of bed before. He was further surprised that the wakening call came from Jerry Deming, the chief of the Bureau of Criminal Investigation for the district.

"Les, we've got something, and I think it's too big for us to handle," Deming explained. As Deming went over the details, Atkinson grew more frustrated and angry, listening to Deming while he went over the gory specifics.

"Dammit, Jerry, it's two o'clock in the morning!" Atkinson exclaimed. "You woke me up with a chicken-shit thing like that? Sure, it's horrible, but you've handled a fatal before without calling me. Why'd you do it now?"

"Chief," Deming said quietly, "the truck was loaded with plutonium nitrate. Somebody can make an atom bomb with that stuff."

Atkinson sucked in his breath. He felt as if he'd been slapped across the face with a cold, wet towel.

"I'll be right there," he said, and hung up.

Leslie Atkinson was fifty-three. He had been a New York state policeman for thirty of those years, having started as a recruit, after finishing a post-college stint in the Marine Corps. He had worked his way up to district commander, and he was proud of it. To him, physical conditioning was a fetish. With his flat belly, a salt-and-pepper sprinkle in his brush-cut hair, he could still pass for a hard-ass Marine.

Five minutes after he received the call, Atkinson was driving his Galaxie toward the barracks five miles away. His gut feeling, which never failed him, told him there was big trouble coming.

He recalled reading magazine articles about the proliferation of nuclear power plants, and how that would mean security problems. He assumed then that the AEC, or someone, would see to the guarding of the material from terrorists or foreign powers who might seek the material to make a bomb. He knew about some special standards of safeguarding materials in transit, such as having two drivers in a truck, and an armed guard following, but what bothered him most was the fact that these safeguards were designed to foil anything but a "Significant Armed Attack."

And what was a "Significant Armed Attack?" Two gangster highjackers armed with hand guns? A dozen commandos with machine guns? Why the vagueness? But this was the AEC; surely they knew what they were doing.

Also, take that regulation that processing plants could not have more than one percent MUF—Material Unaccounted For. That was a good regulation in 1946 when there was little fissionable material available. Now, one percent could arm a small nation, or a small war, for that matter. In 1945, all the plutonium in the world was in a cigarbox in Los Alamos, New Mexico. But by the year 2000, nuclear electric power generation would have produced more than ten million kilograms of the man-made element. It was inevitable that, sooner or later, some terrorists would get their hands on enough material to make one or more bombs.

As the Ford glided through a tunnel of trees that blocked out the stars of the moonless sky, Atkinson passed the brightly-lit transformer stations of the New York State Electric and Gas Company's Ithaca headquarters. Six miles to the west was an old coal-fired plant that supplied power for the entire area. Soon it would be supplanted by a new nuclear power plant that had finally been approved, over the violent objections of environmental groups. The Bell power station, in a few years, would become another mass of the radioactive tar-baby he was about to grab.

*　　*　　*

Alexander's mother contacted him through the dean's office at school. The morning after the highjacking, Alexander had awakened with a sleeping pill hangover whose dimensions overpowered even his remorse. Jean had manhandled him into the shower.

"You've got to go to classes today," Jean yelled at him through the glass shower door in the remodeled bathroom. "If you're not in school, they might send out a trooper to notify you about your father. We can't afford to have the cops nosing around here."

Alexander went to classes. He had no sooner taken his seat along with a hundred other students when he heard his name being called.

"Mr. Greely."

"Here, sir," Alexander stood up. He slowly walked down from the twenty-third row of the amphitheatre, feeling as if a hundred cameras were focused on his face.

"Please call this number," the professor said, handing him a yellow telephone message memo sheet on which was written the number of his parents' home in Ludlowville. "I understand there has been a death in your family. Please feel free to take all the time you need. I shall see to it that all your absences in your other classes are excused."

"Thank you," Alexander replied. The professor's obvious sympathy was wasted on him. He walked away to call his mother. Mrs. Greely did not answer the phone. He spoke with the woman with whom she had spent the night. Alexander promised to attend the funeral. He could hear his mother sobbing in the background.

Alexander walked out into the bright sunlight, strode on between Olin Hall and the Gannett Medical Center, heading toward the Engineering Quad. He had a specific destination.

Cornell was built, for the most part, around three main quadrangles. The oldest, the Arts Quad, was surrounded by buildings devoted mainly to the College of Arts and Sciences. The Engineering Quad comprised the engineering section, the Ag Quad, the College of Agriculture. Other units of the giant university worked their buildings into or between one quad or another.

He walked along the sidewalk and looked up at the sky through the yellow leaves of a line of elm trees that had not yet succumbed to the Dutch disease. Something inside him wished he could get

56

rid of the hatred that was eating him up. He jogged across the street and into the glass and stone edifice called Carpenter Hall.

The basements of all the buildings ringing the quad were connected. Alexander walked through the front door of the engineering library in Carpenter Hall, into the basement and past they myriad of workshops, where the equipment included high power lasers and the activities included fusion experiments.

The heels of his shoes clicked on the linoleum floors and echoed through the bare halls. It was Friday, and many of the grad students and professors had already left. He walked slowly, looking into one room or another, without giving the appearance of searching for anything. But he was searching for something, and soon he found it.

An induction furnace.

The furnace was part of the materials application lab, and was used to experiment with small samples of metals, by inducing in them an intense magnetic field, which in turn caused the metal to heat and melt.

He kept walking. Room 12, Thurston Hall. He walked another fifty feet and came to a loading dock that opened to the outside through double doors. Checking to make sure no one else was in the hall, he examined the door to see if it had an alarm. There were no wires connected to it, none of the silver tape one often sees on store windows. Satisfied there were no security devices on the door, he pushed at the horizontal bar on one of the doors and it clunked open. He walked through and jumped off the four foot high dock, then continued on across the asphalt parking lot and over the bridge spanning Cascadilla Gorge. The Gorge was one of two parallel gashes that slashed across the campus at its northern and southern ends. The Fall Creek Gorge, because of its greater depth and width, was a favorite launching spot for despondent undergraduates to finalize their suicide plans.

Alexander found the white van parked outside the Chef Italia. He entered, and saw Jean sitting in a corner booth talking to three coeds, all of whom were better-than-average looking. Jean saw him, too, smiled, and excused himself from the three ladies. He joined Alexander in another booth.

"How'd it go?" Jean asked.

"Okay. I called my mother and promised to attend the funeral. She's taking it pretty hard. I can't understand it," he shook his head. "All those years she's been put down by him, she was never allowed to do anything as a person. Now somebody's gotten rid of her troubles and all she can do is cry."

Alexander studied the menu and ordered a plate of spaghetti. Jean ordered an expresso.

"I found something we've been looking for," Alexander winked at his companion. "An induction furnace."

"No shit! Where?" Jean was delighted.

"In Thurston Hall. It's a cinch. No alarms, and there's a loading dock not more than fifty feet from the room it's in."

58

Jean pulled out a small notebook and wrote down the details.

*   *   *

The doorbell rang, and at the same time there was a sharp knock at the door of Vito Orsini's home in Appalachian, New York.

Orsini, aged thirty-seven, was a mediocre hood with half a dozen arrests on his record. He had served one and a half years at Attica on a manslaughter charge in 1967, was paroled, and started to work with Triple Cities Transport, a firm headquartered in the Binghamton-Johnson City-Endicott area. The firm itself was legitimate; at least the police could never prove anything wrong. However, its owner, Matthew Miano, had barely escaped capture during the famous raid on the Mafia Summit in Appalachian. One of the state troopers who participated in the raid claimed he had seen Miano there, but there was again no conclusive proof. The company's books and Miano's personal income tax returns had been audited several times, and all was in order. The police suspected him of numerous shady dealings: transporting goods stolen in the rackets by members of the "families" in the triple cities area, acting as broker for trucks stolen during highjacking, and that even some of his own trucks had been stolen in other parts of the country, their engine numbers altered, and pressed into service by Miano. Once more, they could prove nothing.

Vito Orsini was the blindfolded man who had

59

driven away Greely's Mack truck. He had delivered the semi with its empty trailer to the Triple Cities Transport warehouse about one o'clock in the morning and had gone straight home to bed, his pay stuffed securely in his Jockey shorts.

It was now not quite eight o'clock in the morning. Vito Orsini awoke, groped his way to the door, and was confronted by two men. He knew at once that they were federal agents.

"Mr. Vito Orsini?" asked the balding man, flashing his ID.

"Yeah," Orsini grunted. "Whaddya want with me?"

"May we come in?" asked the slim, dark haired agent. Orsini shrugged and stepped aside to allow them to enter.

"Mr. Orsini," the slim man said, "a truck driver was murdered last night and his rig was stolen."

"Too bad," replied Orsini slowly. "I didn't have nothin' to do with that."

"We're not accusing you of the crime, Mr. Orsini. Normally, it would be a case for the local police. However, in this case, the highjackers made off with a load of weapons' grade plutonium. That makes it a situation for the FBI."

Orsini scratched his head and stared at the floor. Plutonium? That was atom bomb stuff, wasn't it? For sure he hadn't known what the load was.

"You kiddin'?" he snorted at the agents. "I'd be afraid to go near that stuff. Look, I'm going straight. You guys got nothing on me."

"We're not accusing you," repeated the slim man. "Would you mind coming downtown to answer a few questions?"

Orsini knew he had no choice. The fed fuzz could make his life miserable if he refused to cooperate. He decided to play it cool.

"Look," he said reasonably, "this is my day off when I can sleep late. Gimme a break, huh? Let me get a little more sleep, and we can meet at the Athens Restaurant about noon. Okay? I'll tell you whatever I know, and that ain't anything much."

"Of course," said the balding agent, and both men left. Orsini watched as the car, with its U.S. Government tags, drove away. Then he promptly called Miano and told him of the visit by the agents.

The Athens was a small clean restaurant in the industrial section of Binghamton, the kind of place workers patronized when they forgot their brown bags. The two agents were waiting for Orsini when he arrived. He sat down at their table.

"I tell you, I don't know anything about that murder and the highjacking," Orsini insisted, taking a large gulp of water. Lunch was ordered, Orsini's plate containing greasy fried things the menu said were shrimp. The agents had hamburgers and ate practically none of them.

"It would be worth a lot of money to us, to find that truck and its payload," said the balding agent.

"Yeah?" Orsini tried to keep his renewed interest hidden.

"Yes. Perhaps as much as fifty thousand dollars."

Orsini digested that bit of information as quickly as his cast-iron insides digested the shrimp. But he shrugged. "I still don't know nothin'. But I could ask around."

"You do that," said the slim agent. He paid for the lunches and the three men left the diner. Outside, he pressed some money into Orsini's hand, then both agents walked away through the haze that filtered through the smokestacks across the street.

Orsini unfolded the money. In his palm were three fifty-dollar bills. He stuffed them into his pocket and went home.

*   *   *

Even as the FBI was questioning Vito Orsini, Lieutenant Leslie Atkinson received a call from the Atomic Energy Commission. The person on the line didn't seem at all concerned about the loss of enough material to make twenty-five bombs. She had called to check whether there were any results yet, and to warn him about one of the containers, which contained not plutonium nitrate, but plutonium oxide. The container, she explained, had been stored in the facility by mistake, and was being shipped to the conversion plant with the nitrate.

She did not tell Atkinson that plutonium oxide is a deadly poison, which, if inhaled directly, caused death from massive fibrosis of the lungs in a matter of hours, or at most, days. Or that smaller doses (less than a thousandth of a gram), when inhaled, follow the same path as calcium, and once in a person's system are deposited in the skeleton, where radiation slowly destroys tissue, and causes incurable bone cancer.

All she said to the police was, "Be very careful with it. It is extremely dangerous."

"Aren't you worried about the possibility of someone making a bomb out of that stuff?" Atkinson asked.

"Oh, no sir," was the reply. "Someone would need their own Manhattan Project to build a bomb. We don't feel it's anything to worry about, although we will assist you in every possible way in recovering the material."

The rationale, somehow, was not reassuring to Atkinson.

Nor would Atkinson have been reassured if he had known that the FBI was not yet concerned about the hazards connected with the missing material.

Their primary concern was that the stolen matter might be a new business venture by the Mafia, that of selling nuclear materials to foreign countries. And then it would become a concern only if those countries had the capability of fabricating a bomb from the stolen materials.

So, as things stood, the AEC was not concerned about the possibility of some American terrorist group constructing an atom bomb. Neither was the

FBI. Only Lieutenant Leslie Atkinson felt a strange sense of foreboding.

*   *   *

The funeral services for Alexander Greely, Senior, were simple and religious. About two dozen people came by to visit at the funeral home on Green Street in Ithaca. The top of the casket was sealed shut. Mrs. Greely had insisted on seeing the remains two days before, and was still under heavy sedation.

The funeral procession was small. A handful of cars followed the motorcycle policeman through the leaves covering the narrow Ithaca streets. A half dozen stop lights later, Alexander Greely, Senior, was covered with earth after a short graveside ceremony.

His son wept, but his agony of the murderous night was gone. He was re-convinced that his father was an evil man because he supported an evil government, and evil men deserve no tears.

He drove his mother home, but wouldn't stay. He went back to the farm and cried again.

CHAPTER FOUR

To his neighbors in Cos Cob, Connecticut, Eric Hoskins was one of the friendliest people alive. He lived alone at the end of a tree-shaded circle in a comfortable three-bedroom home with brick veneer siding.

There was much about Hoskins that was likable. For one thing, he loved children, and made a big hit with women who had small children, since he often volunteered to baby sit when the local high school girls had heavy dates. For another thing he was well educated, erudite, and polite to a fault, but he never flaunted these qualities. Third, he was financially secure at the age of fifty-plus, the owner of a consulting firm. The men in his neighborhood envied his bachelorhood, while the females insisted that a catch like that had no business being single, and frequently tried introducing him to an available divorcee or widow. He remained cordial but elusive.

What none of his neighbors knew was that Eric Hoskins was an explosives connoisseur. Whereas people may collect fine wines or art, and become experts in the more esoteric details of their collections, Hoskins prided himself on his knowledge of explosives.

He had started at Dupone in 1942 as a chemical engineer fresh out of college. As one of the few scientists there with a strong background in physics as well as chemistry, he was immediately put to work designing various types of explosives for use by the armed forces.

Hoskins contributions to the war effort were staggering. His advances in the design of shaped charges and the formulation of optimum compounds for shaped-charge used heightened the destructive powers of weapons greatly.

He also turned out to be an able and effective team leader, his natural gregariousness and organizational ability immediately recognized by upper management at the company.

After the war, Hoskins was put in charge of military explosives development, and later transferred to head commercial explosives sections, and finally was made division president, with the responsibility for all plants manufacturing any sort of explosives.

Hoskins missed the manual work in the laboratory. Management was dull, unchallenging. He longed to be back detonating charges and watching the ballistic pendulum shove upward because of the invisible shock waves. But he enjoyed the kickbacks from companies he dealt with.

Seven years after assuming control of the explosives section, the company changed suppliers of nitric acid for the manufacture of explosives. The new company refused to kick back anything. When he squeezed them a bit too hard, they took their case to his superiors. They offered to help Hoskins find a new position with another company, even agreeing to pay him all the money due on his contract. They were nice because they were a big corporation, with not only an image to protect, but thousands of secret contracts in the explosives field, and wanted no publicity with this sort of controversy. Hoskins gave them no trouble. A deal was made, to pay him a "consulting" salary for the next twenty-five years. The contacts he had made while at the company allowed him to develop his enjoyment of explosives and to add to his considerable income, too.

He did go into business as a consultant, working with contractors and tunnel builders whose needs for explosives were often specialized. His business prospered. But he was restless. He found himself drawn to others who liked the loud explosions and the destruction they wrought. More often than not these people were hoodlums or would-be terrorists, but that didn't matter to him. Now, as before, he was responsible for ordering vast amounts of every type of high explosive manufactured. The "leakage" from this volume was more than enough to supply his fellow connoisseurs at a tidy profit to himself.

And his expertise was part of the sale. He showed the gangsters how to detonate their purchases, advised them on what kind of explosives to use for a particular job. The hoods appreciated him as much as they did their explosives.

To Hoskins, explosives had a vintage. Picric acid had a nostalgic aroma about it, invoking images of bearded Prussians clumsily attempting to utilize the new chemical, with foolhardy and often fatal boldness. The only proper use for this old fashioned chemical was in fun, for the pure enjoyment of mastering an antiquated art, the same reason that leads grown men to spend small fortunes renovating classic automobiles.

TNT or trinitrotoluene, was the table wine of explosives, the workhorse that mined coal and blew up cities with equal versatility. It could end up as dynamite sticks in an annoying tree stump, or as a shaped charge penetrating a solidly constructed bunker.

There were a hundred other explosives and combinations. C-4, ah, that was the equivalent of fruit-flavored wines so popular with the young. This was because C-4, plastic explosive, could be molded like putty into an infinite number of shapes, and therefore was in demand by terrorists and rebels, who wanted an explosive equally at home in a manila envelope letter bomb or to take out a bridge support.

Once he had confided his love of explosives to one of the engineers whom he thought shared his appreciation. Hoskins saw the look of disgust on the man's face and promptly fired him, and never thereafter did he tell another person of his bizarre fetish. And yet, he often wondered, how could he make people understand that every explosion had, for him, an almost orgasmic effect?

It was to Eric Hoskins that Tom Flaherty and Amhed Ismael went to secure the explosives for their implosion bomb. Tom knew that he needed an explosive that was pure, could be heated up and cast like plastic. It would have to be relatively stable to withstand the heating, and rugged enough to take much handling and vibration. It had to be dimensionally stable and not subject to wild fluctuations from size induced by temperature changes. It should exert the greatest possible explosion pressure within those confines in order to compress the nuclear core with sufficient force to produce a nuclear blast.

Tom had toyed with the idea of covering the bomb's core with a two-foot thick layer of plastic explosives. It would make the job easier, but the problems with air bubbles and the difficulty of achieving the exact thickness all around were overwhelming. He ruled out C-4.

In addition, Tom knew that most explosions produce a more or less spherical shock wave. A group of spherical shock waves impinging on the core would do nothing more than blow the bomb apart before it went critical. So, he would have to resort to shaped charges. But, what shape? He would have to fabricate a system of charges that would develop concave wave fronts all around the core of the bomb simultaneously. He knew he could figure out the right shapes, but first he wanted to see if he could obtain the right materials. Otherwise all the work, the planning, would be pointless.

While Alexander was attending his father's funeral, Tom and Amhed purchased Allegheny Airlines tickets on the 2:10 flight to LaGuardia, from which point they transferred to an air taxi that landed them at a small, one-runway field in Westchester County. From there they drove to Hoskins' house in a rented Vega.

Tom had met Hoskins three years before during the construction of I-64 in western Virginia. Tom had been one of the few explosives men working with Hoskins to notice the discrepancies between the amounts the company paid for and the actual amounts used. He spoke about it to Hoskins privately, and they saw eye-to-eye at once. Tom received what Hoskins called "a monthly stipend" to keep his mouth shut.

Tom had called Hoskins the day before, to set up an appointment. Hoskins was waiting for them when they arrived.

"Tom," Hoskins peered at his visitor through thick rimless glasses. "What a pleasure to see you again. I didn't think our paths would cross again." He grasped Tom's thick hand and shook it with a genuineness that surprised the big Irishman.

"Who's your friend?" Hoskins looked at Amhed.

"His name's Amhed Ismael. He's from Algeria.

And don't worry, he's on our side. I can't tell you what we're involved in, except that it's big, and when it happens, you'll know who did it. I can tell you that much of what we need is being paid for by some of Amhed's friends."

"Come into my office. We'll be comfortable there." He ushered them into the cozy converted office-den. Hoskins offered them some refreshments, which they politely refused.

"I think that we have an opportunity for another mutually profitable deal," Tom said, his words reminding Hoskins of the past.

Hoskins nodded. "What did you have in mind?"

"I need a large quantity of explosives."

"My friend, you have come to the right place," Hoskins said, his eyes lighting up. He knew that Tom was a kindred spirit where explosives were concerned. "What are you going to use the explosives for?"

"I can't tell you that, but I'll describe what I need. First, it has to be stronger than regular TNT, and nearly as resistant to shock."

"Something like cyclotol or ammatol," mused Hoskins, already lost in thought.

Tom continued, "It must have a high detonation velocity and the brisance must be as high as possible. Last, but equally as important, it must be stable enough to be heat cast, since it will be formed into shaped charges."

Hoskins opened his mouth to say something, but Tom quickly added, "And I'll need a ton of the stuff."

71

Hoskins sat back and regarded his visitors for a moment. Most of the people who came to him needed only a few pounds of plastic or six sticks of dynamite. Simple enough.

"A ton? You mean two thousand pounds?" Hoskins repeated.

"Yes, as nearly as I can figure out. I think it should be something like pentalite or torpex or something of that nature," Tom said.

The older man fell silent. He sensed something ominous in the request, but it ignited in him a challenge, a feeling of excitement.

"Yes, it can be done," Hoskins said slowly, pensively. "But it will take time. I can't afford to drain off too much too quickly from any one customer. And I'll have to convince a few of my clients that it would be more profitable for them to switch from TNT and dynamite to pentalite. Yes, pentalite might be your best choice. Torpex is more powerful, but it's primarily a military explosive and we might arouse suspicion by starting large orders for it. Yes, pentalite is superior in strength to TNT and yet not as unstable as pure PETN."

The words were coming out of Hoskins faster now as he solved problem after problem in his head, as if he was a child reciting multiplication tables in school.

"If we make out pentalite mixture half PETN and half TNT, you can melt-load it without trouble. For very powerful shaped charges, this is about your best choice. But can't you tell me more? Shaped charges have always been my favorites. I know it's been a while, but I'm certain I can help you with your design."

The big Irishman shook his head. "Thanks, but I've got a good idea of the shape the charges have to take. All I have to do is derive a couple of more equations and I'll have what I need. I have access to a computer with a graphic plotter that will speed the process."

"Well," Hoskins said, the disappointment clear on his face, "I'll get it for you. But it will take time."

"How long?"

"If I pushed things, I think I can accumulate that much explosive in about a month."

The delay worried Tom. He needed to begin the long and tedious process of casting the charges and X-raying them for flaws. The resulting recastings could eat up more time than they had.

"Couldn't you make it quicker? How about three weeks?" he asked.

Hoskins rubbed his chin thoughtfully. "Maybe," he said, "but it entails a lot more risk. As much as I regret it, I'd have to charge a premium."

"How much total for delivery in three weeks?"

"Under the circumstances, the price has to be twenty thousand dollars. In cash. You understand how much risk this entails. I've never undertaken an operation quite so large, and it could jeopardize my entire business. It could also result in criminal prosecution for all of us. Actually, if I were in my right mind, I'd say it's no deal."

He saw the look of apprehension on Tom's face and smiled.

73

"But, since I've known you for a long time, and since I'm anything but in my right mind, I'll say yes. Still, I must ask for a deposit. Not that I don't trust you, but I will have certain expenses when ordering the material."

Amhed, who had not spoken a word, pulled an envelope from inside his windbreaker. Inside the envelope, Hoskins saw, were fifty one-hundred dollar bills. He nodded patronizingly at Amhed.

"This will do. And might I say, Tom, it's always a pleasure doing business with professionals."

"There's one more thing we need, Eric," Tom said. "I need two thousand electric detonators. Not the standard detonators, but precision types. They have to have the same detonation time within a couple of microseconds, and there can be no failures."

Hoskins smiled a knowing smile, and in that instant Tom knew that Hoskins knew.

"I know exactly what you mean," Hoskins said. "I worked on one such model at Dupont many years ago. They were for the Manhattan Project, and were used to detonate the high explosives for the first implosion bomb. That was the only time such precision has ever been demanded. Luckily, those fuses are now commercially available. Some explosives experts feel they need the extra reliability. No trouble. Just tack on an extra five thousand to the deal."

Tom looked at Amhed, who nodded.

"We'll be back three weeks from today to take delivery," Tom said.

Tom and Amhed arrived at the Ithaca Airport on Allegheny Flight 310 at 11:07 that night, after hopping on every two-plane airstrip in upstate New York. It was almost midnight when they arrived at the farmhouse. Alexander and Jean were already asleep.

*　　*　　*

"How much money do we have left out of the allotment?" Alexander asked Amhed.

"About three thousand."

"Is that all?"

"That's all. And we've still got to pay for the explosives."

"Why do you have to buy it?" Alexander wanted to know. "Couldn't we steal at least half of it?"

Tom pointed out the risks involved in stealing explosives. Such storage facilities were usually well guarded. They had to pay for the explosives, but much of the rest of their needs could be stolen. Beginning with the induction furnace.

That Saturday, the day after the funeral, was their best opportunity. The Cornell Big Red football team was playing a night game against Penn at Schelonkopf Field, and the intense Ivy League rivalry would keep every member of the campus security force busy handling the crowd. No one figured to be in the building where the furnace was housed.

The rented yellow van made its way along the brick-paved road of State Street and up the incredibly steep hill toward the Cornell campus. It turned left up Eddy Street and immediately became locked in the crush of spectators on their way to the game. The four occupants could see the glow of the stadium lights like an aura above the old homes along Eddy Street.

The clog of vehicles crawled slowly past the numerous stores and fast food places, through the narrow brick archway that had been the original entrance to the campus, then across Cascadilla Gorge on College Avenue. No one paid the slightest attention to the van. For all anyone knew, its occupants were going to the game. The sides of the van had been decorated with "BEAT PENN" banners, painted on long strips of white butcher paper taped to the sides of the truck to hide the rental company's name. Poster board signs with other spirited slogans covered the front and rear, effectively blocking off the license plates.

Tom, who was driving the van, backed it against the loading dock, and the other three climbed out. Alexander counted windows; the fifteenth from the door was dark. The induction furnace was in that room. Tom concentrated on the locked door, and it seemed an eternity before they heard two dull clunks and Tom could pull the door open. Alexander had brought a wooden dolly with hard rubber wheels, which he could pull with a length of rope. They all walked quickly but quietly through the circles of illumination cast by the ceiling lights; only every third one was lit in the interests of saving energy.

They stopped at C-12. Tom tried the door with a gloved hand. It was not locked. Three of them flitted inside, Jean staying behind to act as lookout, his lean body blending into the semi-darkness.

The furnace and its stand were bolted to the floor. Alexander and Tom pulled adjustable crescent wrenches from their pockets and set to work on the bolt heads while Amhed held a flashlight, whose lense was covered with red cellophane. The red light would provide enough illumination without being as noticeable as a naked beam. The electrical connection was a thick black cable that led to a three-phase, 440-volt junction box. Alexander noted the amperage marked on the circuit's fuse.

The furnace was not extremely heavy, but the small swarthy Algerian grunted as he lifted, the weight obviously more than an equal match for his 135 pounds. The furnace was gingerly placed on the dolly. Alexander then grabbed the light from Amhed's hand and scoured the room for any other material he might find useful. He was not disappointed. Within twenty minutes the trio had accumulated a pile that included a tall canister of argon gas, a half dozen ceramic crucibles of assorted sizes, an alternating current arc welder, and a full case of welding rods, flux, and other accessories, plus an optical pyrometer used to measure the temperature of samples on the furnace.

They had loaded everything but the main unit of

77

the arc welder onto the van and were just opening the door into the hallway preparing to wheel it out when they heard footsteps. Suddenly there was a gagging sound, followed by a muffled but sharp crack.

Alexander peered around the door. He saw Jean dragging the body of a young man dressed in a red pullover sweater. The student had stopped by to check on some experiment before going to the game. Jean had stepped out of the shadows behind him, reached around and caught the student's neck in the crook of his right arm. The young man had gagged as Jean had brought the hand all the way around the neck to grasp the biceps of his left arm, placing his left hand on the back of the student's head. Then Jean jerked upward, hard, standing on tiptoe, his left hand explosively smalling forward, his right arm closing like a pair of pliers. The sudden massive strain was too much for the cervical vertabrae and ligaments that protected the thin young man's spinal cord at the neck. The ligaments ripped, and as they did, so did the spinal column. The man was dead in seconds.

Now Jean dropped the body to help Amhed and Alexander with the material. Tom lifted the dead student in a fireman's carry, moved swiftly to the edge of the gorge and dropped his burden in.

No doubt the body would be discovered in a day or so and reported to the authorities. The fire department would be called to recover it. Parents would be notified, and a two-inch column would

78

appear on an inside page of the *Ithaca Journal*. It was no big deal. Nearly a dozen or so Cornell students disposed of themselves this way every year. Other students would talk about it for a couple of days and the incident would be forgotten.

It was 7:50. Game traffic had thinned. No one had bothered about the van with fight slogans plastered over it. The van eased out of the parking lot toward College Town, up Dryden Road and back to the old farm that was rapidly becoming an atomic laboratory. The material was unloaded, covered with black plastic throws; bales of hay were stacked around.

The school slogans were removed and the van driven back to Ithaca, Alexander driving his own van while following. The rented van was parked in the lot by an old service station, the odometer reading was filled out, keys and papers dropped into the rental station's slot.

The rest of the night was spent commiserating with other Cornell students, who had watched Penn win, 17-13. The bell tower tolled to announce that November 23rd had arrived.

As they drove back to the farmhouse, Tom suggested, "Why don't we give our operation a code name? Just like the government does."

"Not a bad idea," chuckled Amhed. "At Los Alamos, they called it 'Manhattan Project'."

"Yeah," said Tom. "But didn't they give that first atom bomb a code name too?"

"Trinity," Alexander remembered.

"Good enough," said Jean as they drove up to the farmhouse. He pointed grandiosely at the barn where the bomb would be constructed.

"Gentlemen," he said, "I give you the Trinity Implosion!"

CHAPTER FIVE

At dawn on November 23rd, Lieutenant Leslie Atkinson sat at the desk in the tiny cubbyhole that was his private office, his puffy eyes mesmerized by the dance of falling snow. He had slept little since being called out of bed the night of the Greely murder.

For three days, troopers all over New York had been stopping trucks of the same year and description as Greely's. Even though road blocks had been set up within an hour after being notified of the highjacking, they had come up with nothing. Troop cars had been placed on Interstate 81 at the Preble and Pennsylvania line south of Binghamton; along Route 17 at Oswego; on the thruway at Syracuse, Henrietta, Utica; on major truck routes running through Geneva, Auburn,

Albany, Oneonta and Elmira. The net result was one false alarm. A semi, a Mack like Greely's, was spotted, but the load turned out to be oil drums filled with machine shop metal wastes on their way to Buffalo to be reprocessed.

"Coffee, lieutenant?" Trooper Hoover stuck his head through the door. Atkinson nodded, although the coffee from the night before had left a sticky, rancid taste in his mouth.

"Hey, Darcy," Atkinson called out to a trooper in the next room, "what's the weather going to be like?" Continued snow, Atkinson realized, would complicate the search.

"Not too bad," Darcy called back. "It's just a flurry. Temperature will climb to 40."

Trucks don't just disappear, Atkinson kept telling himself. Of course, Greely's rig could have been driven into a warehouse in Cortland, or even Ithaca. There was no guarantee it had been moved out of the area. Indeed, he had a gut feeling that it wasn't that far away.

Trooper Hoover came in with the coffee. He could see the weariness etched into the lines of the commander's face, under his eyes, the slackening jaw. In three days Atkinson had managed to sleep some six hours total.

"Lieutenant," Hoover said, "do you think the Mafia is involved?"

"Mafia?" Atkinson blinked.

"They could make a truck disappear real easy."

Hoover went over in detail the Triple Cities Transport case out of Binghamton. Anderson remembered it vaguely, although at that particular point in time he would not have sworn to the spelling of his own name. The files at the barracks indicated generalized suspicion of illicit activities, but no concrete proof.

Their slick operations had been brought to police attention when a local truck driver had purchased a semi from them and agreed to Triple Cities financing. Without knowing it, the driver had signed a contract calling for a huge final payment, which he could not meet. When the company's collector had knocked on his door demanding the final "balloon" payment of ten thousand dollars in cash, and learned—not to his surprise—that it couldn't be met, the driver was coerced into a usurious loan. When he fell behind in his payments, the company threatened to take the truck away from him.

The driver, a former infantryman, got his hackles up. He went to his neighbor for advice. The neighbor, a state trooper, read the ultimatum letter sent to the driver: "JOIN THE ORGANIZATION." He recognized it as a thinly disguised version of involuntary servitude (which Orsini was serving). The agent who sold him the truck was indicted and convicted of loansharking and extortion. But still the Bureau of Criminal Investigation agents were stymied when it came to getting the goods on Miano.

Hoover pulled the file on Triple Cities and placed it on his commander's desk. A chilling thought crept through Atkinson's brain. What if the Mafia dealt in contraband plutonium, or even had a bomb already! Oh, dear God!

It was Sunday, and the Albany office of the Organized Crime Task Force would be closed. He would have to wait until the next day to follow Hoover's suggestion.

No, wait. Better yet, he'd let Hoover himself have a crack at it.

He summoned Jerry Deming and Hoover via intercom. "Jerry," Atkinson said to the Criminal Investigation Bureau head, "Hoover has come up with an idea I think we ought to follow up." He outlined Hoover's suggestions. "Since he's been busting his ass doing detective work, I can assign him this part of the investigation if it's all right with you."

Deming was pleased. As head of the State Police Investigative unit in the Ithaca district, he never had enough men and was grateful to have the bright young trooper assigned to him even temporarily.

Leaving Hoover to study the Triple Cities file, Atkinson got into his car and drove home, for the first real sleep he'd had in three days.

*　　*　　*

Slim, dark-haired FBI agent John Langley, and balding agent Dale Russell sat in the Athena Restaurant on Water Street in Binghamton waiting for their ham-and-eggs breakfast to arrive, quietly sipping coffee and looking out the window, as if expecting someone to join them.

The previous night, Langley had received a call from the nervous Italian named Orsini, who told him that he would turn informer, but also demanded additional compensation besides the promised fifty thousand dollars. The agents had agreed to a breakfast meeting.

John Langley had been an FBI agent for almost five years, and liked to think of himself as unobtrusive, the typical stereotype of an FBI man. He was fairly familiar with some sections of central and northern New York State, having been born and raised in Liverpool, a tidy suburb of Syracuse. He had graduated from Syracuse University, where he majored in business and accounting, and had a modicum of success as the baseball team's left fielder. At loose ends after college, he joined the army; in one of the atypical bureaucratic non-blunders they assigned him to the base comptroller at Fort Belvoir in Virginia as an accountant. His circle of friends at the base included a few attorneys who were advocates in the military justice system. He grew interested in their work and managed to be transferred to the office of the Judge Advocate General.

From the army, it was just a step to the George Washington University Law School in Washington, D.C. With his army and legal background, it was inevitable that he become one of the many agents of the Justice Department. The Bureau was his life; he never married.

Russell was older by ten years, and had been

recruited into the Bureau after outstanding service in the army's investigative division. He had broken up a gang which was engaged in highjacking truckloads of goods ostensibly meant for distribution to overseas PXes.

Thus it was only natural that the two be partnered for this case, Russell because of his experience with trucks that mysteriously vanished, and Langley because he knew a little about the central New York area.

Idly they watched the waitress going about her duties. She looked to be a worn thirty-six or forty-year-old woman with straggly hair and a thickening waistline. She was friendly enough, especially with the regulars who made up the usually light Sunday morning clientele.

"Where's our man? What's keeping him?" muttered Russell, consulting his watch.

"He'll be here," said his companion. "Maybe he's figuring out new ways to make us sweeten the pot."

"Can't blame him for trying," chuckled Russell. "If his boss finds out, he may not survive to spend the money." Russell kept his loathing for informants to himself. Such people were extremely useful to law enforcement agencies, but he was disgusted with those who sold out their trust.

Orsini arrived, and walked to the back booth where the agents were seated. Russell got up, and Orsini slid into the booth with his back to the wall while Russell sat beside him. The waitress came over and took the additional order.

"We were starting to worry about you," smiled Russell.

"Yeah. I'll bet you were sweatin' about my health," Orsini said sarcastically. "Look, I could get killed doing this. I got to talk to you before I spill. Like if I get hit, I want my wife and kids taken care of. If I don't get that, I walk out of here."

"We can't guarantee anything like that," said Russell slowly. "I mean, your boss isn't exactly the *capo de grosso capo*. I don't know how valuable your information is, and I don't know how bad Washington wants him."

Orsini saw then that he had no way out. He would have to literally manhandle the agent in order to step over him and leave the diner. This was no time to create a scene, for then Miano would surely get wind of his meeting with the FBI.

"Don't worry," the informer grunted, "the stuff I spill would wreck all the families in a couple of counties. You'll get your money's worth."

The agreement was pegged at the original fifty thousand dollar offer. Orsini and his family would be guarded until after the trial, and then they would be relocated with new identities. After breakfast, they went to their office in the Post Office Building.

With no stenographer available on Sunday, Orsini talked and answered questions while the agents took notes and kept the tape recorder working. He told them how stolen trucks from all over the state were funneled into Miano's Triple Cities Transport, how many of the drivers were paid off by the highjackers, getting an additional percentage after the loot was fenced. All the Mafia families in the state—Buffalo and Binghamton being the strongest—sent their trucks to Miano. New York City was the only mob that handled their own, although they sometimes sent the particularly hot ones upstate.

The trucks from the other mobs arrived without cargo, and all Miano had to do was repaint them, and, in some cases, replace identification plates with forged ones. Binghamton highjackings, which included all those done within a hundred miles of the city, were usually driven straight to the Triple Cities loading docks and either unloaded and repackaged, or simply transferred to another semi. In the case of flatbeds, the tractor was simply switched. Miano usually had "orders" for everything before he ripped it off, Orsini emphasized. The person who ordered the freight got it.

"Sometimes a guy is forced to renege on a deal, and Miano ends up with the stuff on his hands," Orsini said. "It could be a load of television sets or cameras, stuff like that. Miano turns it over to his uncle. In fact Miano doesn't handle anything if his uncle says not to. His uncle's a big man, Democratic party ward chairman, he's the accountant for a lot of big wheels."

Orsini named the man. The FBI agents were duly impressed and made a note of his firm's address.

Additional questioning centered around the

theft of the plutonium. The FBI had contacted the Atomic Energy Commission to determine how critical the theft was, and what the chances were for someone to build a bomb. The AEC memo had read:

(1) Assuming an 85 percent yield in extracting plutonium metal from the nitrate solution, enough material could be obtained to make five bombs. This is assuming a relatively inefficient system which would need a nearly critical core to begin with. A more efficient design would make possible the construction of more nuclear devices.

(2) The likelihood that a terrorist group could construct a functioning nuclear device is remote. The highly technical nature of the construction, and the quantity of personnel and equipment needed to build the device would preclude the necessary secrecy, and could not exist without attracting the attention of law enforcement agencies. Considering that the Manhattan Project cost the United States billions of dollars, and taxed the brains of the finest scientists in the world, we believe this project beyond the capability of any terrorist group.

(3) In view of the highly improbable nature of the situation, there seems little need to try to estimate damage from an improbable bomb.

(4) The great harm resulting from the theft of this material stems from the possibility that it might be sold to a foreign power, to accelerate their attaining of nuclear capability. However, any nation that has the capability to build a bomb

would also possess the capability to produce its own raw materials for the core.

(5) Should a group attempt to construct a bomb, several factors should be noted by law enforcement agencies attempting to locate the group. The project involves great quantities of high explosives and the consumption of enormous amounts of electricity. Either of these facts would be helpful in an investigation. Also, we have had extremely good results contracting with a Las Vegas firm called Aerial Radiological Measuring Surveys (ARMS). They specialize in using airplanes with sophisticated equipment to measure radiation level changes on the ground. In addition to monitoring radiation level changes near nuclear power reactors, they have successfully located missing radioactive shipments lost through error (or fallen off trucks, an actual case history, June 21, 1968; a capsule containing radioactive Cobalt-60 fell off a truck between Salt Lake City and Kansas City. Ground searches were negative. ARMS located the capsule in some weeds on Route 36 just east of the Missouri River). End of memo.

Russell had mailed the report to Lieutenant Leslie Atkinson in Ithaca.

Orsini knew nothing of plutonium, and soon he grew tired. His talk petered out. He said he would talk with them again later that week, and if they wanted the truck that he had delivered for the mysterious young men, they would have to act quickly before it was repainted, re-registered and resold.

The agents returned Orsini to his car parked near the waterfront, a couple of blocks south of the Athens Restaurant. Then they returned to the Post Office, rewound the tapes and placed them in a safe with a notation to have transcripts made. A copy would eventually be given to the Organized Crime Task Force, who would forward their Xeroxed copy to Atkinson's office in Ithaca. The bureaucratic delays in exchanging information would be a damning key factor in weeks to come.

"You think we've gotten it all out of Orsini?" Russell asked wearily.

His partner shrugged. "Maybe. Hard to tell with a guy like that. But whatever he does know, he'll tell us now. He's got no choice. He's scared."

But Orsini was no longer scared and would no longer talk. He was dead.

It would be three days before a farmer, driving through the hills outside Binghamton, would finally stop to look inside the auto he had seen parked beside the road since Sunday night. He would find Orsini's body on the front seat. A vacuum cleaner hose ran from the exhaust into the window on the passenger side. The Broome County sheriff's men would come by accompanied by the coroner, who would pronounce the death a suicide. Only two FBI agents would note that the gas tank was still nearly full, and the battery still charged, and they would conclude that Miano had found out Orsini was singing and instructed his enforcers to take the gentleman for a nice, long ride. They stopped at an isolated lane before with Ace bandages to avoid leaving rope burns, covered his mouth with porous adhesive tape which also left no marks, and stuffed him on the front seat while the engine's exhaust did its work. After their victim was blue from asphyxiation and quite dead, they turned off the engine, removed the tape and bandages and fled the scene. They would note with satisfaction that the *Binghamton Sun* would report the death as suicide in its November 28th edition.

The FBI had investigated only because the man was an informer. Finding some evidence of foul play, they turned over their evidence to the sheriff whose men had found Orsini, and also notified the state police. From that point they worked exclusively on the problem of a highjacking syndicate and almost completely forgot the stolen plutonium.

In a few cruelly short months they would be sorry.

CHAPTER SIX

The snow had cleared, leaving only traces of itself in the wrinkles and folds of the land where it gathered, resisting the effects of rising temperatures. Trooper Hoover had already absorbed the files on Miano and Triple Cities, and now he stared out the window, looking at the cars passing the station on Route 366. The sun was trying to break through grey clouds, and the bleak leaveless trees and withered grass and weeds painted a monochromatic picture.

It was Monday. Hoover had drawn the 7:30 a.m. to 4:00 p.m. shift. And he had been busy. Already he had spoken to the BCI investigator who had originally handled the Miano case, and had been given the name of a man who worked for Miano and had been helpful to the authorities in the past.

He could usually be found at McHale's Tavern in Binghamton. His name was Dutch van-der-something or other, the agent wasn't quite sure.

Hoover's relief arrived and he headed home, where he traded his grey uniform and wide brimmed hat for a pair of olive green, rough work pants held up by a leather belt. He slipped into a heavy woolen shirt, put on a knit hat and shoved a worn pair of gloves into his back pocket. He was dressing down because he didn't want to attract attention.

Closing the door to his bachelor apartment just north of Triphammer Road, he climbed into his Datsun 260-Z and made his way out of the parking lot up Route 13. It was 5:07 and the winter sun was beginning to set. He traded cars at the substation for the same reason he dressed down, and drove away in a Plymouth sedan belonging to one of the other troopers. The car was three years old and showed signs of an acute case of children: ice cream stains, fragments of broken plastic toys, a litterbag stuffed full of used Kleenex, and the unmistakable musty odor that bespoke changing of diapers on the back seat. Not that he had anything against kids; he enjoyed them, as long as they belonged to someone else.

Hoover steered the Plymouth past Cornell and turned onto Route 79, and changed roads with the precision of someone who knows every inch of the pavement. He reached Binghamton shortly before 6:45, taking it easy all the way, his mind preoccupied with the task that lay ahead. Only once did his attention waver, when he saw a striking brunette in a short coat and a micromini dress. The gusts of wind blew up the side hem and Hoover was rewarded with an eyeful of upper thigh.

"Must be freezing her twat off in that outfit," he grinned.

Market Street, where McHale's was located, was a drab stereotype of a factory area. Long lines of empty stores indicated that many businessmen had fled the decay. Remaining were an occasional bar, a discount store, a second hand shop, an auto supply emporium.

McHale's was almost empty. Most of the patrons were rough, middle-aged men nursing beers, bar rye and some kind of emotion, probably anger, sadness, frustration or loneliness, sometimes all of those emotions simultaneously. A group of four men were over at a bowling machine, and another group played a round-robin match on the electronic pingpong machine.

Hoover straddle-sat on a stool at the bar. "Beer," he said to the bartender, who drew a brew into a stein and slid it over to him.

"Seen Dutch tonight?" Hoover asked. The bartender's eyes showed no recognition.

"Dutch, one of the guys who works for Miano," Hoover repeated. "You know him." It was a statement, not a question.

"Sure, I know Dutch. But I don't know you."

"I have to get in touch with him. It's important."

"You a cop?"

"Do I look like a cop?"

95

"What's a cop supposed to look like?"

"Hey, no more games," Hoover snapped. "I've got some money for him." Hoover was lying, but he made it sound convincing.

A flicker of understanding moved in the bartender's eyes. He gestured toward the group at the bowling machine. "The one in the red shirt."

Hoover took a deep gulp of beer, paid for it and walked over to the group. He waited until the man in the red shirt finished his turn and tapped him on the shoulder.

"Dutch?"

"Yeah," the beefy man smiled. "What can I do for you?"

"I was told I could find you here. I need a truck."

Dutch surveyed the young man. A cop? Maybe, but he's pretty young. Also, pretty young to be wanting a truck.

"Sure," he said, "I work for Triple Cities, and sometimes we have something to sell. Why don't you come by to see me tomorrow?"

"No. I need a certain truck, a particular year and model, and I was told you could help me."

This, Dutch knew, was a cop. Young or old, he was a cop. Yeah, sure, a "certain truck." And the guys were always "told" by someone that he could help. He was getting tired of it, and one of these days he'd stop, and let's see where it left the cops then.

He arose and steered Hoover over to a corner booth. Both ordered fresh beers.

"What kind of special truck you looking for?" Dutch asked off-handedly.

"I want a Mack truck, about three years old, fifteen speeds, electric transaxle and a sleeping compartment behind it."

Dutch shook his head and grinned. Hoover had done everything but give him the serial number.

"How'd you know?" Dutch asked.

"Never mind. I want the truck."

"It's not there."

"What's that supposed to mean?"

"It means they unloaded it already. It went out of here yesterday afternoon."

"Who bought it?"

"I don't know," Dutch said honestly.

"Repainted?"

Dutch nodded. "Light blue, I think. That's all I know." The tone of Dutch's voice indicated clearly that the interview was over.

Hoover paid for the beers and left the tavern. He drove the Plymouth back to the substation, retrieved his own car and went back to his apartment.

Tuesday was Hoover's day off, but he came in anyway. He telephoned the Organized Crime Task Force's center, but was refused information.

"No offense, but we have to be careful. A syndicate man could mess things up if he found out how much we know, or who our informants are. You'll have to be cleared through security first."

"But I'm a police officer," Hoover protested.

"So are a few of the syndicate boys," was the reply. "It'll take a week to ten days for your clearance."

Hoover hung up and walked into the glass-walled booth that housed the computer terminal and teletype machine. He sat down, and after typing in all the proper codes, he asked for a list of all Mack trucks registered in the past four days in New York State. Luckily, the past four days included Saturday and Sunday, confining the list to seventeen.

Nine of those were new and he crossed them out immediately. Two had no sleeping compartments, and one had a ten speed transmission. He was left with five possibles.

He fumbled through a telephone directory, found the number he needed and dialed the Mack factory. He identified himself and was connected with the records department. A polite girl answered, and said that she would be happy to check out the date of manufacture of the five trucks he was interested in.

They went through three on the list, but when he read the identification number on the fourth, the girl sounded disturbed.

"The truck with that number does not match the description you gave me," she said. The color, the engine, the size of the cab and the weight of the tractor were not the same as Hoover had gotten from the DMV.

Hoover knew then that he had found what he was looking for. The truck was registered to a man from Coventryville, a small town on Route 206, about twenty-five miles northeast of Binghamton.

*   *   *

98

The man in Coventryville was greatly upset when the troopers came and took his truck away. It was his, he insisted, he had the papers to prove it and a big lien on top of that. His protests were useless. It would be two years before he would get it back.

The truck's windshield had been removed to allow Miano's workmen to drill out the rivets that attached the original serial number tag. A false one had been pop-riveted into its place. A check on the engine's serial number proved it was definitely Greely's truck.

The BCI literally tore the cap apart trying to find clues left by the highjackers, but the cab had been very well "detailed," as the used car dealers put it. New mats, touch-up paint and minor repairs changed a lot. They had just about run into a dead end when Jerry Deming crawled under the tractor and scraped off the caked mud and dirt that adhered to the underside of the fenders. The scrapings were carefully packed in plastic bags for analysis by the crime lab in Albany.

By the end of the week Deming had a puzzling clue. The lab at Albany told him that the samples were glacial soil, which covered most of the state. The interesting find was fructose—fruit sugar. And fragments of apple skins and seeds.

He took the information to Lieutenant Atkinson. "Looks like someone went bananas and ran over a fruit stand," Deming grinned wryly at his own attempt at humor. "Crime lab said their analysis showed fruit sugar, bits of apple. What's that mean to you?"

"Damned if I know," sighed Atkinson. "Maybe an orchard. A food packing plant like the big A & P in Horseheads, maybe the garbage area of a supermarket. Can't help you on that, Jerry."

A call to the widow Greely gave no further leads. Her husband did not work for groceries or food processors, and he never loaned the truck to anyone else. Deming came to a temporary dead end.

Atkinson had not meant to pass off Deming so lightly. He was more concerned with the cargo than the truck. He could not accept the disappearance of a load of plutonium, and he felt in his bones that the dangerous material was still somewhere in the vicinity. He had already decided to request funds from Albany, to hire a company that searched for missing radioactive material by air. He knew that would take time, and he was worried.

His phone rang. It was an old friend and former state trooper, Richard Flowers. Flowers had taken over as head of the Cornell University Safety Patrol, a campus police force whose personnel were better paid, better trained and better equipped than many public forces in other areas. Flowers was having trouble with some strange thefts. Could Atkinson lend a hand?

Although there are no formal contracts of laws requiring cooperation among police departments in upstate New York, they usually work together very closely. Atkinson agreed to drop around.

Atkinson found CUSP in the basement of Barton Hall, the all-purpose gymnasium-basketball court-ROTC drill field-880 yard track and haven for indoor jogging maniacs. He knew the department was mainly concerned with parking and traffic violations, petty thefts, drug usage by students, and safeguarding the university's property.

"What'd you lose?" Atkinson asked, after he shook hands with his old buddy and eased his frame into a chair.

"A lot of stuff," Flowers said, sliding a list across the desk. "I can't find a pattern to it. I called the sheriff's office, and the campus security forces at Ithaca College and Cortland State. They reported some losses too."

Atkinson looked at the list. It contained a number of disjointed, seemingly unrelated items: high pressure steel spheres used for oceanographic equipment, radiation measuring equipment, chemicals and expensive quartz labware, X-ray equipment, television cameras and monitors, a furnace, and almost an entire machine shop— lathe, drill press, milling machine, dies and taps, and a hundred other tools. The list went on.

Atkinson was equally puzzled. "Anybody taking this stuff would sure have a hard time trying to get rid of everything. A potential buyer could pick up such things in good used condition almost anywhere, without resorting to stolen goods."

"And those things are damned heavy, Les," Flowers pointed out. "Like that furnace. That's why I think it's a gang operation, like maybe three or four men. And I agree that the stuff would be difficult to fence, which leads me to the conclusion that maybe the gang wants to use the equipment themselves. But, for what purpose? What could they do with it? What would they make with it?"

Vague, uneasy thoughts rattled around in Leslie Atkinson's brain, thoughts of lab equipment mixed up with missing plutonium. Was somebody *really* going to build an atom bomb?

Somebody? Who? Terrorists, in central New York State? Impossible! No, why was that so impossible?

Flowers had a Xerox copy made of the list for Atkinson's use. The troubled policeman folded the pages neatly, went out of office and drove home. He felt alone, frustrated.

Trooper Hoover too would come to know frustration. He would be tied up presenting his information to the grand juries, and after that to the District Attorneys, and then to another string of grand juries. The subsequent indictments would be returned as true bills on all counts. But the homicide indictment would be dropped before the trials due to lack of concrete evidence. On the other charges, Miano and five of his employees would be convicted, and promptly enter will-financed appeals. It would take more than a year before the case was reviewed.

And then the case would be thrown out for technical violations. The family counted among its kin some very good lawyers and jurists.

CHAPTER SEVEN

"Uncle, this is your nephew," Amhed said into the telephone, although the person to whom he was speaking was no relative. Indeed, the two had met only once, when Abu Amani had visited GUPS groups in search of recruits.

"Which nephew, my son?" Amani responded. "Ours is a large family." He hoped the conversation would have little meaning to anyone who might be tapping his phone.

"Abu Ali," Amhed replied, giving the common name assigned him at their original meeting. "My grades have been very good, and I think I will even win a prize for my performance." Amhed had rehearsed the conversation before telephoning. He knew that Amani was a careful, meticulous man, to whom even a slight mistake was unforgivable.

Abu Amani had worked as a middle level manager in an energy transportation firm in Damascus. He was surprised one day to receive a message to report to the office of the company's president. Very few at Amani's level had ever come in contact with the top man. As he ascended to the twentieth floor suite of the steel and glass building that sprouted out of refugee squalor, he tried to find a reason for the summons. It wasn't his work which he knew to be exemplary, nor were his habits to be reproached. Nervously he identifed himself to the receptionist and cudgeled his brain to find the reason. Then the answer sneaked up on him. Of course! He was not a Palestinian. He was Syrian.

This company employed many people who had been evicted from their homeland. Usually, these Palestinians did well, and were open in their support of the PLO, especially to the man named Arafat. So that was it! They must have complained about him because his loyalty was to Syria, not this nebulous PLO organization. How dared they!

His anger and loyalty would change before another hour had passed.

Sitting next to him, the company president, through flattery and the promise of pie-in-the-sky, had described Palestinian ideals and hopes, the search and reward for the building of an atom bomb. Other militant Palestinians had been dispatched around the world and were searching for people who could win the five million dollar reward.

104

"What we need now is a trusted Syrian, one not identified with the PLO. You are such a man. I know, I personally have watched you. I know you can contribute to the success of our mission," the president said smoothly.

Amani was properly flattered. "What must I do?" he asked eagerly.

"First, I must discharge you as an employee," said the president. "The reason will officially be inefficiency." He saw Amani's crestfallen look. "Do not worry," he assured him. "We both know that is not the true reason, and we both know the need for secrecy in our work." He emphasized the word "our" to further impress Amani.

"I have used my influence to place you in a diplomatic post in Syria's United Nations delegation," the president continued, and he saw the gleam of satisfaction in Amani's eyes. "Naturally, you will discharge your duties faithfully to the Syrian delegation, but in actual fact you will be working for me and the Palestinian cause."

Amani nodded.

The president went on, "You are being assigned the most important area in the world and thus can rely on great resources. You will maintain a lifestyle commensurate with that of a junior officer. All your expenses will be paid by our consortium. You will be given the number of an account in a Zurich bank, which will contain one million dollars. Your primary source of manpower will be drawn from carefully screened members of the General Union of Palestinian Students, and you will have a list of them. They are your responsibility.

"But, understand that should your operations be revealed, the Syrian government and this company will disavow any responsibility for your actions. And do not permit the large sum of money at your disposal to become a temptation. There are people who will take a most terrible revenge if you do. Carry out your mission and you will be well rewarded."

Amani understood and accepted the terms, with one reservation. "But why must I be discharged for inefficiency?" he complained. "My work has met all standards."

The president laughed. "If your work had been below par, you would not have been chosen," he pointed out. "But the inefficiency reason will allay suspicion. And soon that record will be destroyed, I promise."

Now, a well entrenched Amani was listening to a young voice on the telephone, saying, "I think I'll need additional money besides my tuition if I am to complete my degree successfully and earn the prizes I am capable of winning."

"Of course, my nephew," Amani replied. "I will be happy to send you additional support. None of my other nephews or nieces have been able to achieve as much. I am proud to contribute to your scholastic success."

They both hung up. The next day Amani would send a package of currency in assorted denominations to a trusted GUPS operative in Kent, Ohio, who would rewrap and remail the package to Amhed. Amani would also write a letter to his former employer, that he had spoken with his "nephew" and that he was about to win an award for his "achievements" in college.

Amhed pushed open the door of the phone booth. He knew he had recited the correct ideological phrases at the right time, but he didn't really care about the whole mess. What mattered were the fat Swiss and Belgian bank accounts he knew the top Arab leaders had. Even the tinplate dictators, who were the kamikaze radicals of the Arab movement, whose every rhetorical utterance was devoted to bettering the lives of the oppressed masses, had millions of dollars stashed away, money derived from bleeding off funds from United Nations relief money, or by taking the food and medicine donated by international charitable organizations and selling it all on the black market. They were all opportunists, mercenaries, using their ideology and political power for the sake of their bloated egos and bursting purses. Amhed wanted to count himself in.

But he was different in one respect. He didn't long for power, only a life of leisure purchased by money. For that reason he could get along with Tom Flaherty, for he detected the same reasoning in the big Irishman. Otherwise, Tom, like the Arabs, was using whatever ideology was expedient at the moment. Tom could just as easily have worked for Israel, doing exactly the same thing, just as the ideologues in most Arab countries could have fit into the mold of a Portuguese dictator who loved colonial wars, or as a communist party boss. The link between them all was megalomaniacal despotism.

Amhed's greatest worry was his cut of the reward. How much, if anything, would he receive? True, the consortium, through Amani, had kept him supplied well, if not lavishly. He had repeatedly tried to find out if he would share in the five million dollar reward, only to be reprimanded for thinking of himself and not for the good of all Palestinians.

"Bullshit!" he said, half aloud. Everyone who fed him that line was not exactly living on an austerity budget. He walked down Campus Road past the floodlit tower of the Uris Undergraduate Library, and decided then and there to make his own preparations. The plan sprang into his mind almost full-grown.

The group would demand a huge ransom for the bomb, not from the consortium but from the United States! After all, Washington, D.C. should be worth *something* to the Americans.

"We'll have to build two bombs," he told the group that night.

"Two?" Alexander was stunned. "That means twice the risk, and twice the chance we'll get caught."

"Orders," Amhed lied. "Either we do it their way or they'll stop supporting us. If we back out now, think of all the work we wasted. And we'll all be security risks. You know the PLO will find some way to guarantee our silence. It won't be pretty."

The room fell silent. Amhed realized he would have to spring his plan, but only part of it.

"The consortium also outlined a kind of ransom plan," Amhed lied again.

"Ransom?" Alexander's face had a blank expression.

"I don't know all the details yet," Amhed said glibly, "but here are the general terms. America will have to see to it that all Arab prisoners are free. They will have to stop all military aid to Israel. And they will have to pay a great deal of money."

"I understand all that," Alexander said slowly, "but why the need for two bombs?"

"I'm getting to that," Amhed was irritated, knowing in his heart that the guiltier the person, the more irritated he becomes when accused of his guilt.

"Look, for the ransom idea to work, they have to know we are capable of carrying out our threat. We set off the first bomb in a relatively isolated place, so that there is minimal damage to life and property. Then they'll be convinced."

Now Tom spoke up. "Well, we'll have one more thing working for us. It'll give us an idea how powerful the bomb is, or even if it works at all. I sure as hell would hate to turn over a dud to the people fronting all this."

Jean said, "What the consortium wants has merit. Besides, we have no choice. Either we do things their way or we get tracked down and eliminated by the PLO."

"Exactly right," Amhed put in.

109

"We should be able to set the test shot for about the middle of February, and if the ransom isn't met, the real one a couple of weeks after that," Tom said.

"Will the core be ready by then, Alexander?" Amhed asked. Alexander nodded.

"The second shot should be scheduled as close as possible to the first," Jean said. "The minute that mushroom cloud clears, every security force in America will be on our tails: FBI, CIA, the army, everybody."

"Well," Alexander reasoned, "in that case we should have the second bomb in position to detonate before we make the first test."

Tom rubbed his chin thoughtfully. "What if something goes wrong with the test bomb? What if we must make some adjustments? We might not be able to get near the second bomb once it's positioned."

"Tom's got a point," Jean noted.

Alexander noted Tom's look of triumph. Damn, the cunning of that bastard! Sure he had a point; it wasn't what the Irishman said as the way he was saying it, anything to make him look bad.

"First things first," Amhed said. "Where can we make the test?"

"How about Canada, or somewhere in the far west?" Tom suggested.

Now Alexander could return the compliment. "Sure," he observed, "both areas are almost unpopulated. But we'll be hauling a heavy load, which means we need good roads. Good roads into

110

Canada past customs. How do you propose sneaking an atom bomb through customs?

"Out west would be fine if your name is Robert Oppenheimer and you want a place where you can build and explode an A-bomb without anyone knowing about it. Oh, it can be detected after a while, but according to Amhed, the first blast is supposed to make a good show, not just tear a hole into some wide, flat piece of real estate. Remember, it's got to be far enough away not to hurt too many people, but close enough to impress the hell out of everyone."

"You little turd," Tom murmured, without anyone but Alexander understanding.

"So the best place seems to me to be somewhere in the Adirondacks."

The Adirondack Mountains were the closest thing to wilderness south of the Canadian tundra. There were few centers of population, and hundreds of thousands of acres that remained wild, preserved by the New York State Legislature's "Forever Wild" laws. It was only about eight hours' drive from the farm.

"That's not nearly as far away as the other sites," Alexander said, feeling no particular need to defend his choice now, judging from the expressions on the faces of Amhed and Jean. "There are no borders to cross. We have fine access from there to an Interstate that will take us straight to Washington. Most important of all, we'll also be fairly close to New York City, the biggest section of urban sprawl in America, counting places like Yonkers, Jersey City and Newark. You can make a lot of people awfully jittery setting off a nuke that close to The Big Apple."

He had regained his confidence now, and as he spoke he could see Flaherty glower.

"I think we can find a depopulated area so no one will see us come and go. We can place the site on a ridge over from a town, so that the light and mushroom cloud can be seen, and the shock wave can rattle a few windows. The world will know about the blast and the reporters will flock in, but by then we'll be long gone."

Alexander's plan seemed air-tight, and although Flaherty seemed sullen, he offered no objections.

"Now, as to the second bomb," Alexander went on, "I was doing a bit of reading, and I think the best place for it would be somewhere outside the Capitol Building at a time when the President of the United States is delivering his *State Of The Union* address. Presidents used to deliver that speech in January, but the trend now is toward later in the year, especially for new Presidents, who say they have to be on the job a while before making the speech. For the past few years it has been made in March or April."

"Why the *State Of The Union* address?" Amhed asked.

"Because," Alexander said coolly, "if it's not a dud, the bomb wipes out just about the entire federal government with one blast. Present

112

during a typical *State Of The Union* address are: the President, the Vice-President, all the Senators, all the Congressmen, the entire Cabinet, all the Justices of the Supreme Court, the Joint Chiefs of Staff, and many others. Anything but a fizzle wipes them all out, and levels the Capitol area. The whole Federal bureaucracy is kaput!"

Even Tom had to admit that perhaps he had underestimated Alexander. He had disliked him since his father was killed. He didn't like the compassion in Alexander, which he mistook for weakness. But this proposal indicated no such faint heart.

"I think I know where to put the bomb," Alexander said. Alexander left the room and returned with the Capitol floor plans he had purloined from the Congressional Handbook in the Library of Congress.

They passed the plans around, and decided that one of them would have to return to Washington, and figure out the exact spot, the best route and method of getting the bomb into place.

"You do it, Alexander," Amhed said. "You look like the typical all-American boy. You'd attract less attention. Besides, you've already been there."

"I'll go," Alexander said.

* * *

The December wind blew grey clouds and drizzle from the Atlantic, west across Long Island Sound and over the winding roads and stone fences of Connecticut. If it had been colder, Eric

113

Hoskins thought to himself as he sat in his Greenwich office, it would have snowed. Perhaps it was snowing in upper New York or Vermont. He rose from the overstuffed leather chair and walked over to the only luxury he allowed himself in his rather Spartan office, a fireplace. It wasn't a stone hearth, merely a free-standing black sheetmetal unit, but it provided the radiant warmth so much more than the modern central systems. He grabbed a poker, slid back the spark screen and poked at the embers, adding another piece of split applewood whose dry splinters immediately flamed and sent fruity fragrances through the office.

He stared at the kinetic images of the dancing fire, which seemed to accent his basic loneliness, the impossibility of reaching people on his own mental level, of making good, true friends. Perhaps he was incapable of really loving anyone, and in that case being loved in return. The closest thing to an intimate, over many long years, had been the Irishman, Tom Flaherty, whose love of explosives nearly equalled his own. It had been one basis, of a sort, for communication between them. Now the petulant Irishman was coming to pick up his order, an unusual one, even for the expert Hoskins.

Hoskins knew that the material would be used to construct an implosion bomb. The ultimate explosion, he thought, and the mere mental images of the bomb sent shivers of anticipation through him. He was envious, but thankful that at least he'd had a hand in it, just as he had in helping design the shaped charges that resulted in the first American atom bomb.

He had not seen the first one go off at Los Alamos, and he was disappointed. Did he want to see Flaherty's bomb? Sure! Wait, on second thought, no, not really.

In his business a man had to be careful. He recalled telling Flaherty years ago, "When you live by your wits, you can't afford to trust anyone but yourself, and be sure to trust yourself only half of the time." Good philosophy. How did he know the Irishman wouldn't get caught in the act? If he was caught, and if Hoskins were present, oh, God! No, he didn't want to be anywhere near him, except to deliver the shipment today.

Careful? Take the people he dealt with as a consultant, they were downright careless. The fools trusted him completely, to order and plan their explosive needs and procedures. He had no trouble convincing them to switch from their present explosives to pentolite. Since they all used him as auditor for the amounts of explosives, there was no way to put the finger on him, as long as he stayed within the reasonable tolerance allowed him. He skimmed off limited amounts from each shipment. As the shipments came to his Greenwich warehouse, he repackaged them, minus about seven percent less than stated on the shipping label. Each foreman who oversaw the shipments at the sight of the explosions was given his "stipend," just as Flaherty had received. It was a tight, easy routine. And highly profitable.

Hoskins went to the window, just in time to see the white van coming toward the building. He saw Tom and a black man. Hoskins was opening the door before they had a chance to knock.

"Welcome, Tom," Hoskins greeted Flaherty warily. "Who's your new friend?"

"Eric, I'd like you to meet Jean Lafayette, one of our little group," Tom introduced them.

They shook hands and Hoskins closed the door. "Can I get you something, gentlemen?" he asked, still keeping his eyes on Jean.

"Yes, the explosives," said Tom. "And I believe we owe you this." Tom handed over an envelope, which had been given to him by Amhed only the day before, after he in turn received additional funds from Amani. Hoskins opened the envelope and began counting the tens, twenties and fifties, adding up to the agreed-upon twenty thousand additional dollars for explosives and timing devices.

"Don't you trust me?" Tom asked sardonically.

"Haven't I taught you anything?" Hoskins said with a little smile. "It's all there. Now, Tom, you follow me into the back while your friend drives the van around to the side door so you can load up."

He was looking directly at Jean, who grunted and went out the front door as Hoskins and Tom walked through the door to the warehouse area.

"Why'd you bring someone else here?" Hoskins hissed when Jean had left. "Are you trying to get me arrested? Don't you know how dangerous this is?" The older man's face was red, the blood vessels at either side of his neck stood out like thick pencils.

"Calm down, Eric," Tom tried to soothe him.

"Calm down? Calm down? You parade a black stranger through my business like I was dealing in lollipops and you want me to calm down?"

"Look," Tom's Irish temper was heating up, "that little Arab I brought last time couldn't make it. And he didn't trust me with the twenty big ones, so he sent Jean along to look after things. I didn't want to bring him, but if I didn't, you wouldn't get paid. It's the Arab's money."

"Okay," Hoskins was mollified to a degree. "But remember, all it takes is one person who can't keep his mouth shut and we're all in jail. You're young, but I'd get my parole sheet slipped into my casket."

Hoskins walked to a junction box on a wall and pressed a red button. The warehouse door opened and Jean backed the white van in. Hoskins pointed to a large stack of cardboard boxes labeled "Mimeo Bond Paper," and the young men immediately began ferrying the shipment into the van. When they had finished, the body of the van was almost all the way down on the springs, and Tom was just hoping it would make the trip back to Ithaca without breaking down.

The men said their goodbyes and the van labored across the gravel portion of the lot out to the blacktop street. As they drove off, Hoskins calmly made a note of their license plate.

Six hours later, they rolled up to the barn, which

had nearly been converted into a lab by then. Only a couple of weeks more would put it into running condition.

* * *

A brown letter-sized envelope was among the hundreds that arrived at the executive offices of Syroco, oil transportation brokers, located in Damascus. Om, the executive secretary-receptionist, came in early and began to open the mail for her boss, as she had done every morning for more than twenty years. Her boss was a pleasant man to work for, a Palestinian, who had built a conglomerate with little more than the knowledge he carried out of Palestine back in 1948. But, as much as she liked him personally, she found his politics repulsive, and had years ago given her allegiance to someone else.

In addition to her generous check from the company, each month she received additional money from a friend in the office of the Directorate of Operations (Clandestine Services) United States Central Intelligence Agency (Near East Area Division).

She felt almost guilty about taking the money, since she had put information into the "dead drop" near the airport only twice in recent months, and then she had no idea how useful her information had been.

Om had been befriended by American service-men as a small child, before the end of World War

118

II, and since then had harbored a feeling of good will toward Americans, a feeling shared by few in the Arabian world, particularly since the rise of the Palestinian terror groups, and the wars with Israel.

That morning she picked up the brown envelope mailed from New York City and examined its contents with curiosity. It was from a former employee who had been fired some time ago. She now remembered his nervous politeness as he sat in the reception room, waiting to speak to the president of the company.

She read the letter: "I spoke with my nephew, and he tells me that he is doing exceptionally well in his studies. He says that he may be a prizewinner for his academic studies. I hope that his success will earn the respect of all who know him."

The letter was signed Abu Amani.

She pondered the letter, puzzled as to why a man summarily dismissed, and who, according to his record had not left on good terms, would now write to the president about his nephew. Why would the president want to read something like that? But it was the president's letter, and rather than arouse suspicion, she put it in a stack with other letters on his desk.

His reaction seemed odder than the letter itself. The president sent a letter of congratulations to Amani, and additional copies of both letters to the presidents of several companies, some scattered across the mid-East.

Om sent the telegrams and typed the letter to

119

Amani; she Xeroxed Amani's letter and the president's replies and placed them in a plain white envelope without the company's return address.

Ordinarily, Om took her lunch break at her desk or in the company cafeteria, but that day she left the building and made her way through the crowds jamming the narrow streets to a nearby taxi stand. The cab was an American Plymouth, air conditioned, a welcome barrier against the intense noonday heat. She settled into her thoughts, and was surprised at how short the trip to the airport seemed. After paying and tipping the driver, she pushed her way into the cool interior of the terminal and made for the locker section. It had been so long since her last drop that she almost forgot which locker was the one for the drop, but she remembered the right locker rack, found the empty one and placed the envelope in it. Depositing the correct change she re-locked it and put the key in her purse. Apparently, the mysterious man who had originally contacted her had a duplicate key. When she had gone back, in the past, to see whether or not her material had been picked up, she found the locker empty.

She knew that the CIA recruited people in all walks of life, they paid handsome sums even though the information they gained seemed trivial to those passing it along. But she did have some vague idea that all the small bits and pieces sometimes were fitted together to make a large chunk of vital intelligence. But even she had no real idea of the enormous meaning those letters had hidden in their innocent small talk.

Nor did Om's material make much sense to the courier who found the letters in the drop. Both were given a cursory examination, microfilmed and sent, with a hundred other items, from the Syrian capital to the monolithic building in Langley, Virginia.

Located about eight miles from downtown Washington, the building was a monument to secrecy. People met other people in the building, but dared not talk about their work. Neighbors who lived close together and worked in the building couldn't pay social visits to each other because of the security systems within the building that not only barred outsiders, but also barred members of the agency from learning about any other department unless a "need to know" was established, and the proper codes appeared on their identification badges.

Once arriving at this building, the microfilm was sent first to the Foreign Intelligence Staff. They found little significance to the letters from Om in that section, but since the letters mentioned a relative presumably living in the United States, and since the person originating the first letter, one Abu Amani, also lived in the United States, the material was forwarded to the Domestic Operations Division. The DOD was ultrasecret even by CIA standards, a very special component of the Clandestine Services Branch. They compiled information on possible foreign financing of dissident groups, and the activities of militant foreign student groups, among other things. They were forever stepping on the toes of the FBI, but that, to them, was just another occupational hazard. They thought of the FBI as an unimaginative police force, who would trip over a nest of spies without recognizing them.

CIA agent Byron Greenberg had been through those CIA-FBI arguments a hundred times before. He remembered in particular one hassle with a special agent from the FBI division of Internal Security, about the relative merits of the two agencies. Greenberg called the FBI amateur gumshoes. The FBI man called the CIA a flock of dilletantes, whose cleverness got everyone in trouble sooner or later.

Greenberg had the complete files pulled on Abu Amani, plus files on the General Union of Palestinian Students, the Syrian Delegation to the U.N. and the Syroco Oil Transport Company.

He found little suspicious on Amani. He had no nephew listed as a relative, but that was inconsequential, since the children of friends often adopted that term when referring to friends of their parents. Amani, he saw, had worked for Syroco and was fired for substandard work and personal traits. He had then worked up, from a minor communications job to head of the communications section for the Syrian diplomatic delegation in New York City. That alone made him suspect, since people in his position were usually in the employ of their country's intelligence service.

But it was doubtful that he would send anything important in a personal letter, when he had the well-secured code systems at his fingertips. No, there was obviously nothing there for the CIA this time. But, as an afterthought, he decided to send the information to the FBI. It wasn't worth anything, and might show a degree of cooperation. It would look good on the record.

When Byron Greenberg went to bed that night, he had already forgotten about the messages from Damascus. Four hours after he dropped into a dreamless sleep, another strand of the web was being woven.

CHAPTER EIGHT

The ghostly blue illumination from the mercury vapor lamps carried by the group etched the honeycomb pattern of the chainlink fence into the blacktop drive which led to the electronics company. There was no moon. The street lights, and the lights from nearby homes served more as isolated beacons than means to see.

Jean, Alexander and Tom crouched near the fence. Amhed was in the rented car, behind the wheel, about a block away, ready to come on call. Tom carried a scanning police band radio with an earplug, a receiver which had all the proper crystals for the sheriff's department, the state police and the Ithaca police. The electronic circuitry automatically scanned the crystals in sequence, and would "lock in" on channels sending any kind of conversation. This eliminated the need to turn the dial in order to monitor the various bands. If they were detected, they would have time to escape.

For three weeks, Amhed had visited several electronics supply houses in the Ithaca area, trying to find one that had the right components needed for the timing and detonation mechanisms.

He knew a switching mechanism was needed that would route the same amount of current and voltage to each of the detonators within a time period measured in microseconds. Because of the tiny tolerances involved, the device couldn't be mechanical; Amhed figured they had to be silicon controlled rectifiers, SCR, which were triggered by a pulse of the right waveform and size. The right circuits were in his lab books from earlier electrical engineering courses. He could have designed his own circuits, but that was too much trouble, especially when he could make minor adaptations to circuits which had been tested out reliable. Why build when he could buy, or preferably, steal? He went from one store to another, looking for the right materials, or trying to find out where he could acquire those materials.

Most stores carried only stereo equipment and other consumer gadgetry. A few carried a limited line of electronic components, but not quite what he needed. The Consolidated Electronic store, on the corner of Prospect and Cayuga Streets had what he wanted. Now he could get the quantity and quality of SCRs which were not otherwise available. It was the group's target for a ripoff.

On the pretense of looking for a certain thermistor for his television set, he walked into the stockroom with one of the Consolidated clerks the week before. The thermistors which vary their electrical resistance with the temperature, usually bear no value markings, and as a result thermistors with greatly different values may look very much alike. As they walked through the narrow passageways, among the bins of electronic components, Amhed took note that each bin was clearly marked with its contents. It was a logical system that would allow Amhed to find anything he wanted, unaided.

While Amhed examined thermistors with mock concentration, the clerk was called to the floor to wait on a group of people. Ahmed walked quickly through the aisles, drawing on a pad a crude map of which components were where. He located the bins with the SCRs, and was confident that his particular type was there because it was very common.

Carrying out his pretense, Amhed purchased a thermistor that looked similar to the one he came in with, then browsed a bit more, noting the locations of additional material he needed. Leaving the store, he noted the silver tape decorating the doors and windows, and decided entry would have to be gained through the roof, to circumvent the security system.

The three at the gate signalled for Amhed to

come. He was the vital cog in the theft, since he knew where everything was. Jean and Tom carried loops of rope over their shoulders, Alexander had two pairs of huge metal clippers that looked like bolt cutters. The four men looked around, shivering, partly from the cold and also because they knew that the Ithaca police station was only a block away.

"Why the hell did you pick this place so close to the cops?" Tom complained.

"It's the only one that has everything we need," Amhed retorted. "Like this is a one-stop shopping center for us."

They skulked around to the poorly lit back of the building. The structure was covered in sheetmetal panels, protected by baked-on enamel. The roof was also metal. There were few juttings from which to hang a rope. Tom scanned the roof and vent pipe for a rope hold, and the toilet pipe facilities caught his eye. It was a three-inch pipe and should hold their weight.

Expertly tying a bowline on one end of the rope, he whirled the coil around his head and tossed it up. On the fourth try the loop quoited over the pipe. Using his arms only, Tom pulled himself up onto the sloping roof and helped Amhed up. Alexander and Jean remained as sentries; both were armed with compressed-air pellet pistols. The hourglass-shaped steel pellets had been coated with succinyl choline hydrochloride stolen from an anesthesiologist's office. It was a potent nerve poison, used in minute doses as an anesthetic. Unscrupulous bow-

and-arrow hunters tipped their striking heads with it to inspire a kill. Their pellets were coated with the poison for the same reason.

Up on the roof, Tom pried up the edge of a metal roofing panel with a screwdriver, and in less than ten minutes, using Alexander's shears, had completed a C-shaped cut, and used his foot to push the cut down. He paused, his belt radio crackling, then nodded to Amhed. He lowered the slim Arab down inside the store. Amhed used the red-beamed flashlight so valuable in the past weeks and began his search. Fifteen minutes passed, twenty. Amhed gathered his booty by the armload and put it into a sack tied to the rope. Each time the sack was filled, Tom pulled it up and lowered it to the waiting pair on the ground.

And still no cops. Oh, he had seen them in the cemeteries and behind schools and construction sites, "cooping," two to a car. One would sleep and the other stay awake in half hour shifts. Sometimes both slept, relying on the desk man at headquarters to wake them by radio. Some cops even carried alarm clocks in the car.

As Tom was pulling up the final bag, Alexander suddenly stiffened.

"Listen," he hissed. Jean heard the noise too. He signalled up to Tom, who dropped flat on the roof. The irregular shuffling grew louder. Alexander's hands shook from cold and fright, and he pointed his pistol toward the corner of the building. A shadow fell on the road, followed by its maker. His bowed head came into view first. It was Jean's target.

Coolly he raised his air pistol and squeezed off a shot. The phuut! was barely a whisper in the darkness. A small dot appeared on the man's forehead, and he fell as the gun spat again.

Who was it they killed? Nobody knew the man. Actually, he was an alkie who spent his weekends almost as a pet in the city jail. The city judge and prosecuter, court clerk and the *Ithaca Journal* reporter would notice in a couple of weeks that good old Freddie hadn't been busted for public intox lately, and would wonder what happened to him. His body would be found, well preserved by the cold, under the bridge abutments running over Six-Mile Creek.

Tom pulled Amhed up, lowered him to the ground outside and followed. Each man grabbed a sack and ran to their vehicle. The rope, the shears, products of an earlier burglary, were left at the scene, minus fingerprints, and of no further use to the conspirators. They drove north on Prospect Street, turned on Aurora Street, then up the hill past the Cornell campus and to the farmhouse out in the sticks. Not once did they see any sign of a policeman.

*   *   *

A courier stepped out of the green American Motors Ambassador with a thin attache case handcuffed to his wrist. He showed his ID to the guard and passed into the building. A special agent on duty in the Division of Internal Security signed for the documents, unlocked the handcuffs and waved goodbye to the delivery man from the CIA.

"Thanks for a lot of crap," the FBI agent said softly as the CIA courier walked out of earshot. Without opening the case he took it to the head of the division.

Inspector Bill Hawkins, for five years the head of Internal Security, was down in ballistics examining the slugs removed from the body of a special agent who had been fatally hit during a shoot-out with a terrorist group he had startled as they were attempting to place a bomb in the basement washroom of the Russell Senate Office Building. Hawkins knew the agent, and his death made him sad and angry. The martyr's list, he thought to himself, could have done without another name.

Nor was his anger eased by what he found on his desk. Inside the case dropped off by the CIA was a jumble of papers and microfilm cards. As usual there was no explanatory letter.

"Stupid pinhead bastards," Hawkins muttered. "Every time they want to clean out their files, they unload it on us, thinking we should be eternally grateful."

He sorted through the pile, and except for a handful of papers and one microfiche card, he put the whole lot into the waste can to be shredded.

"Wish I could stick a few of those CIA shitheads in the shredder," he thought with a grim smile.

He punched five numbers on the green desk phone and spoke to the assistant director in charge of training.

"Look, I got another load of garbage from the spooks at Langley," he said. "The junk isn't much use to me, but I thought a few pieces of it might be good as an exercise for some of the new agents. I'll send it over."

Two agents, in about their third month of probationary training, were given the assignments. One got the pile of papers, the other the single microfiche card.

"Check these to see if we have a file on any of the subjects named," he instructed the fledglings. "Determine where they are now, and what, if any, illegal activity they were involved in. Since these came from our Internal Security Division, be particularly thorough with regard to any connection with subversive groups."

Alan Perry, the man with the microfiche card, was from the tiny upstate farming community of Bath, New York. He was jealous of his companion who had received a healthy stack of papers, while all he had was a single piece of microfiche, with photographs of perhaps half a dozen pieces of paper on it.

He ran checks on Amani and found the usual personal histories they had on diplomatic personnel stationed in the United States. There were no remarks to indicate he was engaged in subversion or espionage. The dossier did indicate he had been active in the General Union of Palestinian Students, a militant, during his years at the University of Cairo. Perry made a note of that. He did not know yet that Amani had become disillusioned temporarily, transferred his loyalty to Syria, and then back to GUPS again at the behest of an oil transportation tycoon.

Perry read further, of his job at Syroco, which he lost because of inefficiency, his job at the Syrian U.N. delegation as communications aide, his rise in status. Perry noted that the CIA had infiltrated some of the GUPS groups in several foreign countries, and the FBI had informants in a dozen GUPS groups in the United States.

He replaced the folder in the files and received permission to review other files in the Foreign Intelligence Division. Soon Perry located a file folder on the Syroco Oil Transport Company.

The Foreign Intelligence Division was one of the bones of contention that often stuck in the throats of the CIA, just as the CIA's Domestic Operations Division stuck in the FBI's craw. Each stepped on the toes of the other, and neither ever got used to it. Even as a green recruit, Perry could feel the animosity generated by questions dealing with the CIA. The CIA practice of infiltrating domestic student organizations was one of the sore points. The CIA rationale for poking its nose into these groups in the U.S.A. was that they suspected the groups were receiving foreign financing. There was one near disaster when the CIA operative in a group suspected an FBI infiltrator was an agent of the Russian KGB. Three CIA Special Operations goons were assigned to kidnap him, and one of them was wounded by the FBI agent before it was established that he was definitely not a KGB spy.

The Syroco file was thick, and Perry scanned each page carefully, to find any mention of Amani. "There was a suspicion," the report stated, "that Amani might be doing some work for his former employer, and the firing was a front to cover up this work. A source in the Syrian U.N. delegation declares that Amani received his position through the influence of Syroco's president. That fact alone makes it likely that Amani is still running errands for his former boss, although the nature of that work is not known."

Another item caught Perry's eye. It was written by an unnamed student at New York University, a Palestinian who was paid to be an informer on the activities of the NYU chapter of GUPS.

"Agent was approached by a member of the Syrian U.N. delegation and told of the existence of a reward offered by a consortium of Arab business- men for the delivery of an atom bomb to the Palestinian terrorists. The diplomat did not identify himself to him. Agent was told the reward was five million dollars for the person or group delivering a working nuclear bomb to Yassir Arafat. Agent agreed to cooperate. Diplomat subsequently identified as Amani. Further searches through informants in other groups did not add data. For that reason we feel the plot is probably nothing more than subtle propaganda, and the money pledged does not exist."

Agent Perry read on. He noted Amani's letter to the president of Syroco, concerning his nonexistant nephew, and the prize he would win. The information began to fall into place in the young agent's head. It became frighteningly clear that there was now indeed a taker for the prize, unclaimed for so long. Someone was going to give the terrorists the bomb they wanted so badly.

Alan Perry took copious notes. He returned the Syroco folder to the records clerk in the Foreign Intelligence Division, then strode back to his desk to type up his report.

*   *   *

From the sketches Alexander and Jean had brought with them from Washington, Tom was able to ascertain the principle of the shaped charges developed by the Los Alamos scientists. As he sat at the kitchen table in the farmhouse and leafed through the book on explosives they had also obtained, he knew that he had one great advantage over the groping scientists back during World War II: he had access to a high-speed computer.

The advent of the computer brought a new analytical tool to scientists and engineers. It could solve in seconds problems that would have taken hundreds of man-years using a slide rule. As computers proliferated in numbers, every university worth its educational salt made them available to its students, not only for training to use after graduation, but also for solving homework problems. Indeed, the problems assigned for outside work were so complicated that they would have been almost impossible to solve without a computer.

As an engineering student, Tom was allotted a certain amount of computer time for his studies. There were more than a dozen time-share terminals in various buildings of the engineering school that gave students access to the IBM 360/60 computer.

One of the big Irishman's better grades had been achieved in his FORTRAN course. FORTRAN was a particular "computer language" that was designed specifically for scientific, mathematical and engineering application. Had he been a student in other schools of study, he might have learned ALGOL or COBOL or some other computer language.

As a doctor must be fluent in medical language, so must a good engineer be fluent in FORTRAN. And Tom was not only fluent, he had progressed to a point where he could write the most intricate subroutines, which could truly make a computer work wonders. The development of the proper subroutines could allow the computer to draw pictures, plot curves and construct drawings of buildings from the proper numerical matrixes. Although they required special permission to use, the college had several plotters and the appropriate subroutines that would allow the computer to make orthographic projection drawings of three-dimensional objects. The orthographic projections would also present the three-dimensional forms as three two-dimensional drawings: a front, side and top view.

Tom pushed his way through the doors of Hollister Hall and walked down the stairs to the basement where the time-share terminals were located. A student was working on one terminal, but the other four were unused. With the Christmas recess, now just getting into full swing, Tom knew he and the other student would probably be the only ones there.

Tom typed in his access codes and pushed his pile of program and data cards into the machine that would interface his punched card information with the circuits of electrons of the computer.

Since Alexander and Jean had brought the sketches and books back from Washington, Tom had devoted most of his time trying to determine the configuration of the explosives, trying to derive the proper equations that would give him an explosion wavefront of the right shape, to compress the plutonium core to its maximum. He had the drawings of the high explosive lens that had been introduced at the Rosenberg trial; he reduced them to a series of mathematical equations and fed this data into the computer. These, combined with the hydrodynamic and thermodynamic equations governing explosions enabled the computer's plotter to draw for him a picture of the explosion shock wave that would have been produced by the explosives in the diagrams. Tom saw that they were off. The waves were not spherical enough to do the job properly.

Greenglass, who merely manufactured the molds for the high explosive lenses, did not know which lens was the one ultimately used. Most likely all of them had the same basic shape, and he simply drew a diagram for the Rosenbergs that closely approximated them. Also, from the trial transcript, Tom knew that the original bomb had thirty-six lenses, each with two detonators. After many long nights working with the computer, Tom had completed his method that would allow him to test the entire system in the computer—all thirty-six lenses—instead of just a single one. Finally, working from the opposite end of the equation, the one that determined the shape of the explosion's wave front, he had the computer alter the dimensions of the lenses to produce a perfectly spherical explosion.

While the FBI debated the usefulness of the information delivered by the CIA, Tom was settling down in the computer room for the final stage of his computer engineering of the explosive lenses. He turned on the plotter and instructed the computer to draw for him the shape of the lenses. He had written the proper subroutines that would allow the computer plotter to draw an ortho-graphic projection complete with dimensions and angles, and five perspective drawings from different viewpoints. He was using up an enormous amount of computer time. He had exhausted his allotment two weeks before, and knew that once the new semester began the department would be down his throat about it. But, hopefully, by that time, he would have no use for the department.

The other student paid no attention to Tom, being preoccupied with his own work. The only intrusion was by a campus security guard, who stuck his head in the door and made some wisecrack about working during the holiday. By noon Tom's work was completed. He took his punch cards and blueprints for the explosive lenses and went out to have a pizza for lunch.

*   *   *

With the exceptions of the old wino they had to shoot at the electronics store, and the student whose neck Jean had broken, the thefts had gone without a hitch. They knew all along it would be relatively easy, since they were taking things which weren't ordinarily ripped off. As a result they were all in buildings that had minimal security. Often they merely walked through an unlocked door and helped themselves.

The drill press, metal lathe and other machine shop tools were unbolted and carried off from a metal shop in Cortland.

The neutron counter, as well as a standard geiger counter and matching X-Y plotter, turned up missing from the reactor lab, only a few yards

138

from the building which had once housed an induction furnace.

A small television camera and monitor weren't missed right away at the television studio at Ithaca College because the students who used them for training were away for Thanksgiving.

The holiday also made it easier for them to raid the Cornell chemistry supply rooms in Baker Hall, and carry off an assortment of chemicals and reagents, ranging from metallic calcium and hydrogen fluoride gas, to pieces of quartz glassware, the latter obtained by dismantling a grad student's apparatus that used the hydrogen fluoride gas. They had even walked out with a small X-ray machine, used by the metallurgical lab to examine metal castings for hairline cracks invisible to the unaided eye.

The thefts had taken several weeks, but the materials were put to use by Jean and Alexander as they were brought in, assuring that no time would be wasted.

For the sake of safety, two labs had been constructed, one in the barn, the other in the farmhouse basement. Tom would cast his high explosives in the basement. It was too risky to put the explosives operation together with the core construction, since a mishap with the explosives would wipe out everybody and everything. Placing the explosive in the basement had additional assets. An explosion would mean only Tom would be killed or injured. And it would be easier to explain a basement explosion; they could tell investigators that it was caused by leaking gas lines that exploded from an electrical short. With any luck, whoever investigated the accident would not find the materials and the other laboratory in the barn. They could, conceivably, locate another explosives expert and go on with their work.

They had little trouble adapting the concrete-floored barn to their purposes. At the rear of the structure they constructed a room out of two-by-fours, about thirty feet square and ten feet high. The inside was paneled with sheetrock, and every joint was taped and plastered. There were no openings to the outside, save two doors, one behind the other, with a small anteroom between. The double doors acted as a sort of airlock, to keep foreign matter from entering the room. On the roof of the room they mounted large ventilator fans, which, like so much of their building materials, had been stolen from construction sites. The fan was mounted with its ductwork reversed, so that the huge centrifugal blower would pump air into rather than out of the room.

The planning done by Alexander and Jean allowed the stolen equipment to be installed as soon as it reached the barn. They were ready to begin the actual construction of the bomb almost as soon as the last burglary was pulled off.

It was bitterly cold before Christmas, and the snowfall of the week before still clung to the land. Alexander pulled on his wool shirt and rubber overshoes and walked quietly out of the farmhouse while his comrades slept. The silence lay heavily on the hills. In the distance he could hear vehicles on the main road, and he thought how much farther sound carried when the noises of the world were dampered and covered and cushioned with snow. Even the noises themselves were somehow different, muted, yet quite clear.

It was fifteen degrees below zero. As his boots squeaked through the cold, dry snow, Alexander thought it unusual to be so cold so soon. Usually it waited for February. New powder had fallen that night, adding about two inches to the eight-inch base. The snow loved the tops of hills like the one on which the farmhouse was situated.

Alexander had been unable to sleep, and after a couple of hours of restless tossing in bed, he decided to inspect the nearly finished lab.

He reached the front door of the barn, and inserted the steel key into the padlock with its case-hardened clasp, and a body that was machined out of a single block of bronze-looking alloy. Had he been an intruder, it would have been easier to knock a hole through the door or side of the barn, than to defeat that lock.

He swung the door open on its antique hinges and groped in the darkness for the light switch. Tripping on a scrap of wood he cursed himself for not bringing a flashlight. He found the switch and flicked it up, illuminating the fluorescent lights supposedly installed to light their ceramics shop. Pulling the door shut, Alexander looked around.

To an uninformed visitor, the room looked like a well-equipped ceramics workshop, exactly the impression the conspirators wanted to create. On the right were two wheels to throw pots, one a kick wheel the other electric. Jean and Amhed both knew a bit about the craft and could produce a few items if a surprise visitor asked them to. Then there were the kilns, three of them, the principle reason for the ceramics camouflage. The electric company would have asked too many questions had they requested the installation of special high power lines they needed for the bomb. The kilns, which used a lot of power, were the perfect front.

To the left of the wheels and behind the kilns was a table used for "wedging" the clay before using it. Above it was an electrical junction box used for the kilns. The box's huge cartridge fuses said a lot about the amount of electricity the workshop would use.

The rest of the floor was broom clean, except for a half dozen sealed buckets of clay and a set of shelves resting on concrete blocks, containing samples of the ceramics.

Directly facing Alexander was a massive wall of hay bales, from one side of the barn to the other, reaching two stories high. The hay could be explained simply to a snooper: they rented out space to a farmer up the road so that he could store his hay, thus making the unused part of the barn profitable. But the bales had really been stolen and were used to camouflage the lab behind them. Actually, the "wall of hay" was only two bales thick.

Alexander reached down and pushed against the bottom row of hay bales on the left. A section of the hay wall, two bales high and eight wide, slid slowly back, as they were set on a wooden flat with hard rubber casters. There was the double doorway leading into the lab. With the movable hay bales pushed back into position, no one would suspect the presence of the lab.

Rigid standards of cleanliness had to be maintained to insure the purity of the processes in which they would be engaged. Alexander once had a summer job as a production worker in the cathode ray section of the Westinghouse plant in Horseheads, New York, making picture tubes for television sets. He was required to wear a coat over his street clothes, nylon gloves and a white nylon hood over his head. A positive pressure was maintained inside the production room to assure that dust borne in the air could not be brought into the room. The ventilation system in the room was what scientists called laminar flow, fashioned so that streams of air would be directed down from the ceiling in layers, to sweep dust particles to the floor. Even that floor had perforations through which the dirt would be trapped. This was called a "clean room." And workers had to go through an airlock device to enter the clean room. On the floor of the airlock were mats covered with an adhesive which would clean the dirt off the bottoms of shoes. Some *ultra clean* rooms required changing into special shoes before entering.

In designing the lab where the bomb would be constructed, Alexander remembered the Westinghouse lab, and he felt a surge of pride now as he gazed around the room.

He had entered the washing room. Along the walls were a series of racks on which were hung white lab smocks and hoods, like the ones worn at the plant. Two vacuum cleaners were used to clean their clothes before the men entered the clean lab. Since the outside surroundings were barnyard dirty, defying shoe cleaning, the men stepped out of their shoes and into bedroom slippers kept inside the airlock. Making doubly sure, before passing through the second airlock door and into the interior of the lab, they walked across an area Alexander regularly sprayed with contact cement from an aerosol can.

Inside the clean room, the floor was a series of slats about six inches from the concrete floor, similar to those behind soda fountains and snack bars. He and Jean had finished the ductwork for the room two weeks before. The ventilator fan would draw air from under the eaves of the barn, through a series of seven filters before it was distributed through six grills located around the walls of the room where most of the equipment was located. Slotted vents around the bottom of the walls allowed the air to escape.

In the clean room itself were the drill press, the metal lathe and milling machine, welding equipment, a workbench, signal generators, oscilloscopes, digital voltmeters, the induction furnace, the cylinder of argon gas, the optical pyrometer. At the right side was a concrete block wall, composed of a triple thickness of concrete blocks, whose interior spaces were filled with more concrete. Behind the wall was an X-ray machine and the bench on which they would perform the critical mass experiments.

Alexander had read dozens of accounts of how the scientists at Los Alamos determined the critical mass of plutonium, the amount needed for the chain reaction that was the mechanism of the bomb. The only reliable method, the one ultimately used at Los Alamos, was aptly called "tickling the dragon's tail."

In this experiment, a young physicist, Dr. Louis Slotkin, manipulated two subcritical hemispheres of plutonium by hand, listening to the changes in clicks of a geiger counter. The radiation from each piece of plutonium was not harmful during short exposures, but the gamma radiation and blasts of neutrons from a chain reaction could be fatal. Fairly simple calculations using the separation between the two hemispheres gave him the answers he was looking for.

In the lab now, Alexander knew he had to tickle the dragon's tail himself. From his reading, he knew that the critical mass in pure plutonium was about five kilograms, or a sphere about the size of a small grapefruit. But he had no way of determining how pure the metal would be when it was refined. Any impurities, he knew, would absorb neutrons and slow down the reaction. Therefore, he would probably need more than five grams of the material.

But he had no intention of repeating the procedures of the late Dr. Slotkin. One afternoon, while demonstrating his procedures to six other physicists at Los Alamos, the daring Dr. Slotkin slipped and allowed the two spheres to contact each other and form a critical assemble. The spheres heated up from radiation, and Slotkin knew he had a disaster imminent. Reacting quickly, he pried the two pieces apart with his bare hands. He had saved his six colleagues, but not before he received a fatal dose of radiation. He died nine days later.

Alexander wanted none of the martyrdom bestowed on Slotkin. He would perform his critical mass experiments just as thoroughly and accurately as Slotkin, but only with the material on one side of the concrete wall and him on the other side. He would view the experiments with the television camera, the neutron detector and geiger counter as his eyes. He would trace the increase in chain reaction activity through the use of the X-Y plotter, which would trace on paper the imputs of both instruments.

Alexander surveyed the interior of the lab with great satisfaction. Except for a minor change here and there, it had been built exactly to his specifications. He walked over to the electronics bench with its composition board work surface and the strips of 110-volt outlets along its rear side and eased himself up to sit on it.

There had been moments of doubt for him, but always the idea of skulking around the countryside, plundering legitimate establishments of society like a revolutionary Robin Hood had smothered those doubts. As he stared moodily at the slotted floor, many images flooded his mind, the image of his dead father, the image of the wino and the unfortunate student they'd had to kill at Cornell. In his mind he played scenarios, of Washington vaporizing, of them being led away by the FBI, or killed by the CIA. At such times he wanted to run away and be alone. Run where no one could find him. Run to where he couldn't find himself. The juices of puberty still coursed in his veins. He was barely twenty years old, and what had seemed like a terribly noble, romantic and heroic thing had sobered the intoxication of adolescence, made him a trifle more mature, thoughtful.

His eyelids gained weight, got scratchy. He hopped off the table, passed through the airlock and walked past the plutonium nitrate drums, under the chain hoist which would lift the drums of radioactive liquid in the concrete filled and shielded containers weighing nearly five hundred pounds each.

He put out all the lights in the barn and stepped back out into the frigid night air. He breathed deeply, knowing that he could fall asleep easily now, his doubts smothered, the commitment he had made rekindled.

CHAPTER NINE

Christmas Eve in Syria found a CIA operative disgruntled because he had been denied permission to return to the states for the holidays for the third year in a row. In retaliation, he decided to take a two-week Christmas vacation in Syria. He would simply stop making the rounds to his dead drops and cancel the live meetings with his operatives. His was a grubby little operation, and its insignificance made him even more angry. They had tried to tell him he couldn't come home because his job was too important, but that was bullshit and he'd prove it. Things would get along quite well without him for the next two weeks. It would damn well have to be that way, he told himself. He wouldn't be there.

*   *   *

Christmas Day was ushered in by border flare-ups between Syria and Israel; a self-immolation in New York City; three suicides from the Golden Gate Bridge; and the killing of nine police officers around the world, their lives snuffed out in the line of duty.

Peace. Good will toward men.

* * *

The well-kept Victorian home on Lake Street in Dryden was the scene of a happy Christmas for Leslie Atkinson, his wife and two children. One of the kids was home from college, the other was only eight.

It was an older house, built in the 1940's, but the former owners had maintained it well and so did Atkinson. He and his family enjoyed the full grown pines and oaks and shrubs out front, and the shade and fruit from apple trees in the back yard, while friends who had purchased new homes in the new developments were still tending saplings which would provide neither shade nor fruit for years to come. Atkinson could never understand why people would select a home site, bulldoze and scrape away all the topsoil before building the house, then spend thousands of dollars planting shrubs and skinny trees, buying tons of topsoil to replant that which would have been free, had not some cretin with heavy machinery become weird with all that power at his fingertips.

Atkinson was bothered by the list Richard Flowers had given him. He spent the morning with his family, watching them open presents and letting them watch him open his, and then came the inevitable phone calls from relatives and friends to fill up the pre-dinner hours. He was silent during that time, and managed meaningless banter as he stuffed himself with turkey and the trimmings, paying tribute to his wife's long day in the kitchen. But he excused himself before dessert and retired to his small study to concentrate on the list again. He read and reread the list, becoming more agitated with each reading. All logic told him it was just vandalism, stupid rip-offs.

It wasn't logic that turned him around, but a wild, crazy hunch that just popped into his head almost unbidden. Did those thefts somehow tie in with the missing plutonium? And if so, how? Also, why? Almost instinctively, Atkinson strode toward his bookshelves.

Atkinson had always loved books, and once he acquired one, he never gave or threw it away. He had textbooks, books friends had given him, castoffs from the public libraries, and substantial numbers of books, hardback and paperback, which he had bought brand new. There was knowledge in the words within those covers, and so much that he wanted to learn. His wife told everyone that once her husband became interested in a subject, whether sports or American history, or a biography of someone, or whatever, he would buy everything he could find on that subject until he lost interest. But he never gave the books away.

As his hunch materialized, like opaque precipitate from a clear solution, he knew which book on atomic energy he wanted. It was McPhee's *The Curve of Binding Energy*. He flipped through the pages of rather large type and found what he was looking for in a matter of seconds. It started on page 153 and went on for several pages.

There it was before his eyes, about half of the stolen materials on the list given him by Richard Flowers.

So that was it! Some radical group, right there in the Ithaca area, was building an atom bomb! Furthermore, if the subject of McPhee's book, one Ted Taylor, was right, any group of half-smart people could succeed.

But what proof did he have? A list of stolen goods matching a list in a book? A hunch? His superiors would ask questions, such as:

"Did you go to the FBI on this?"

"They checked the plutonium theft. They said to forget it."

"Did the FBI go to the Atomic Energy Commission?"

"The AEC said there was little likelihood anyone would build an atom bomb here in America."

"If the FBI isn't worried, and the AEC isn't worried, why should we worry? Forget it, Atkinson, just do your job."

Atkinson decided to say nothing, at least not until he got to the office the next day. He played

Chinese checkers with his eight-year-old daughter and finally went to bed early, hoping to get a fresh start in the morning. He dropped into sleep and found a nightmare awaiting him, He dreamed of giant mushroom clouds and maimed people, and himself and his family caught in the cloud, gasping, cindering before his own free-standing eyes. That dream and its variations would be an almost nightly occurrence for the rest of his life, and would become even more vivid in a few short weeks.

* * *

On the night of Christmas Day, Alexander paid an obligatory visit to his mother, although it was the last thing he wanted to do. She was solicitous enough, even offering him some of the substantial insurance money his father had left her, so that he could continue to study without financial worries. But Alexander assured her that he was just fine, he had a part-time job he really enjoyed and really didn't need the money. His mother sobbed some, that it was her first Christmas in many years without her husband, but the tears failed to register on her son, who felt no remorse for the part he had played in his father's murder. He patted her hand, gave her a hug, and as soon as practicable, he left to join his fellow conspirators in the Pub at Ithaca.

Tom and Amhed were in a corner booth drinking beer, while Jean was with a saucy young

cafe-au-lait wench he had picked up at the bar.
They sat on stools facing each other, her very, very
short denim skirt hiked up almost to the crotch of
her pantyhose. As soon as Jean saw Alexander
enter, he waved cheerily, then took the girl's arm
and marched her out the door.

Amhed, Tom and Alexander would later crawl
out of the Pub, knee-walking, commode-hugging
smashed, and would wake up the next morning
with a monumental hangover. For Jean, it was, as
he put it, "A day of piece on earth."

*   *   *

The Christmas drinking bout had left Amhed
sick for a whole day, and it was December 27th
before he ventured out of the farmhouse. The
money, even the additional funds, was nearly
gone, and he was going to make the trip into
Slaterville Springs, to use an out-of-the-way pay
phone to call Amani.

He had to hitchhike since Alexander had taken
the van and wasn't scheduled to return until
evening. The traffic on the back country road was
light, and it took half an hour before he got a ride.
The driver of the rusty pickup jabbered continuously, until he dropped Amhed off at a drive-up pay
phone down the road from a general store on Route
79. Amhed reasoned that he'd earned his ride by
listening to the driver's drivel.

He stuck a dime into the slot and gave the
operator Amani's number, and the number of the

153

credit card Amani had provided him. The phone rang a dozen times, and Amhed was about to hang up, disgusted, when he heard his benefactor's voice.

"Uncle, this is your nephew again," Amhed said into the mouthpiece. "I wish to thank you for the financial assistance you have given me. I am truly grateful."

"That is all right," said Amani. "You are a deserving student and will bring glory to Palestine."

"Unfortunately, uncle, although you have been most generous, expenses are greater than anticipated. Yet I am close to being the most successful in my class. I shall, however, need additional funds to support myself."

"How much?"

"At least five thousand dollars more."

A note of irritation crept into Amani's voice as the conversation continued. Finally Amani said grudgingly, "Very well, I will have the funds transferred to your account. But, I warn you, I shall demand a full accounting."

"You shall have it, my uncle."

"And this is the last of it. You had better finish up or there will be hell to pay." The last phrase was a bit of American "slang" Amani liked to add to his conversation from time to time.

"Yes, sir."

"Good luck, my nephew."

"Thank you," Amhed said, and when he heard the click at the other end he added, "And may the fleas of a million syphilitic camels infest your beard!"

Then he started back toward the farmhouse, hoping it would not take another half hour before he got another lift. The cold crunched through to his bones. Damn! He'd even sit with that stupid old pickup driver if he'd only come back.

*   *   *

Even as Amhed stood on the shoulder of the road trying to hitch back, Lieutenant Leslie Atkinson paced the floor of his office, tired, angry, frustrated. He had spent Saturday and Sunday, the 26th and 27th, calling the homes of every hospital administrator within a hundred miles of Ithaca. He stared out the window, trying to summarize the exhausting events of the past two days. He had tried to do everything methodically, to build his hunch into an air-tight deduction.

His first call was to the Atomic Energy Commission with regard to the missing plutonium, under the guise of a request for information. Had they heard anything? After all, the theft had occurred in his area, and he had a right to know.

No, the AEC had heard nothing further. But they did tell him that one container of plutonium oxide had inadvertently been mixed with in with the plutonium nitrate, and the oxide was a very, very deadly poison. Atkinson had another hunch, that the bombmakers, whoever they were, might not be as careful with the materials as they should be, and sooner or later, one of them was bound to get a fatal dose of the floury powder.

He then called the FBI, and they didn't seem excited either. In fact they were downright condescending. Hunches, the agent in charge for the day told him, could not be used to re-open an investigation. But thank you for your concern.

"Thank you, my ass!" Atkinson muttered. He dialed his division commander, who promptly chewed him out for calling him at home. The commander's remarks were exactly as Atkinson had visualized them: if the FBI and AEC doesn't care, why should you? And why call a man on his day off?

The hospital administrators had been no more receptive. Atkinson had struck out on all counts.

But he was determined to ride his hunch. What else did he have going for him but gut intuition? Besides, in his years as a cop, he had apprehended just as many criminals through hunches as through scientific methods.

And so he paced his office, shaking his head, chewing on his lower lip, and thinking of his recurring nightmare.

*   *   *

During the first two or three days after the Christian Christmas, Anwar Yesseh, Syroco's president and largest stockholder, had not been a happy man. The first letter from his man, Amani, had kindled in him some hope, but that had been weeks ago, and since then, nothing. His consortium group, which met from time to time as the occasion demanded, had watched the Israelis defeat the Arabs in battle and in politics, and yet no brave, intelligent, scholarly person (or group) had come forward to claim the reward. In disgust, one of the consortium, a shipping broker on the Gulf of Aqaba, had withdrawn his pledge, and the others, grumbling, had increased their pledges to make up the difference. The consortium had seemed to lose its cohesiveness, and like much of the Arab world slipped into despondency.

Yesseh had been equally despondent as he had gazed down from the twentieth floor of the highrise his business had built. He looked down at the crowds flowing along the sidewalks, and thought to himself that a stroll across the street from the building was like walking through a time machine, back through decades of backwardness.

Once there had been an old market where the building now stood. When the skyscraper was erected, the market had been relocated at enormous cost. But the buildings across the street had not been razed, and one by one the merchants returned, the lure of potential customers working in the building with the steel and glass being too much of a temptation to resist. Yesseh's monument to progress was thwarted, as men in business suits mixed with robed figures wearing the traditional Kaffediyeh. Yesseh had had the police arrest them and carry away their stalls, and when the vendors persisted, he'd hired thugs to terrorize them. Nothing had worked.

But now Anwar Yesseh was much happier. This day, the 29th of December according to the Christian calendar, had brought good news from the communications officer at the United Nations, Syrian delegation. It was a progress report, telling him that the bomb was on the verge of successful completion, perhaps in only two months. Surely Abu Amani would not lie about something like that. Why, he'd have him butchered if it wasn't true! Furthermore, Amani knew it.

With that in mind he promptly sent a telegram of greetings to the members of the consortium:

"The best wishes for a joyous holiday season. It is blessed that we give to those who deserve, so that we may prize their work for all the Arab world. Our patience will be rewarded and bear fruit, which will be prized for years to come. I looked forward to seeing you in the Imperial Hotel in Damascus at the appointed hour. It will be a day you will prize, and never forget."

He wrote the somewhat cryptic telegram out in longhand on the textured eggshell white paper that was his personal stationary, and had his secretary send it to the list of men he handed her.

And it seemed to him that his secretary acted peculiarly after sending the telegram. It was nothing he could put his finger on, but perhaps she might bear watching. After all the years she had been in his employ, it would be a shame to discharge her now, but something in the way she spoke and avoided his gaze gave him the impression she could no longer be trusted. Still, perhaps it was his imagination. Time would tell.

Om Kalim read the telegram with curiosity. Never before had Yesseh shown the slightest sign that he even recognized Christmas holidays, which offended her since she had been raised in a Protestant home rather than as a Muslim, like her employer.

And the telegram piqued her interest in another way. She remembered the first letter from the former employee, Abu Amani, mentioning his nephew and some sort of prize. Only today, another letter had come, from the same Amani, mentioning the same nephew and the same prize. The word *prize* had been repeated several times in the telegram.

So, once again Om took a longer than usual lunch hour, taxiing to the airport, and putting a copy of the telegram, as well as a list of the people to whom it was sent, in the locker dead drop.

Fortunately, the CIA operative in Damascus had cut short his "vacation." There was this dancer in a nite club, you see, and she had caught his eye, you understand, and he had caught her's, and she had a lush body, and she was more than willing. Completely trustworthy, mind you, but oh, wow! she could screw like a wild mink, and three days with her were about all his masculinity could stand. Exhausted, dragging, he decided that he could get more rest performing his normal routines. By New Year's Eve he had cleaned out all his drops, and the Yesseh letter, the Yesseh telegram, and the Yesseh list were passed on to the operatives at the embassy.

*   *   *

Alexander had spent several days perfecting his technique with the separation process. He had succeeded in processing about a dozen batches a day, which used up two containers of the nitrate solution, picking up speed as his proficiency increased. He had to go to Washington soon, to find the spot where the bomb could be detonated, and it would not be long before all the separations would be completed, ready for the induction furnace, which would produce metal from the precipitates he had gathered.

He worked diligently, the metal was produced and safely stored, and by January 5th, Amhed drove him to the airport. There was no hint of any green in the countryside, only an occasional pine which had shed its mantle of snow in the winds. It was another typical, overcast, dreary upstate winter day. Had it been sunny, it would be a fine day for skiing, and Alexander imagined there were still plenty of people standing in line at Greek Peak, awaiting another opportunity to commit mayhem on their bodies, while rocketing down a slope. Alexander remembered his only attempt at snow skiing, and the spill, and the month of limping around that followed. Skiing, he decided, was not his sport.

Trying to avoid the slippery hills down into Ithaca, Amhed drove north along Route 366, passing a couple of local nite spots and the state police barracks. He grinned inwardly and thought, "Hey, you dumb shits, here we are, murderers, burglars, felons of the worst sort, atomic terrorists extraordinaire, and we've done everything but drive through your parking lot!"

The white van slowed at a yield sign and then took an acute left down Route 13 to the airport, where a humble Allegheny turboprop would meet Alexander in half an hour.

If Lieutenant Leslie Atkinson saw the white van as it drove by his office, he took no notice of it. Why should he? It was just another vehicle on the road. Besides, the days since Christmas weighed heavily on his mind and he was pondering his next move. The stinging criticism of his worries about the plutonium thefts were mild compared to the pitying looks that inevitably followed his statement that he was convinced someone was trying to build an atom bomb right there in Ithaca, New York. Even his wife had begun to give him static.

"Well, I'm sure as hell going to show them who's right," he muttered.

"Sir?"

Atkinson had forgotten that Trooper Hoover was sitting across the desk and had heard the words he grunted.

"Nothing," said Atkinson. "Just some of my thoughts I happened to speak aloud. My mind wandered."

"I understand, sir," said Hoover.

"You've heard this before, and maybe you've laughed at it, but I'm still thinking of the missing plutonium," Atkinson continued. "I'm convinced someone around here is trying to build an atom bomb.

"Now, everything I've read about, and not coincidentally, everything that's been stolen, according to the Cornell list, uses a lot of electric current. As far as I can figure, our bomb builders have two choices: either they've set themselves up in some kind of business or warehouse, or they've got the stuff stashed in some basement. You read me?"

"Yes, sir," Hoover sat impassively. Atkinson couldn't tell if Hoover was laughing inside or being serious. Damn, if he started laughing, he'd get his ass chewed out!

"What it all means is, somewhere, there is either going to be or there has been a new hookup for electrical use. It will be at an existing location, where the voltage needs will skyrocket. That's where you come in."

"Me, sir?" Hoover looked and sounded as if he would rather not get mixed up in his superior's folly. Well, the hell with him. What the trooper wanted or did not want was of no concern to Atkinson.

162

"Yes, you. I'm taking you off the road and assigning you to the BCI again. I want you to visit the electric and gas company, and ask for a list of new customers with a high wattage rating, and another list of existing customers whose power usage has taken a sudden rise. I'm talking about business and private use."

Atkinson noted that Hoover sighed, and did not look exactly ecstatic when he left the office.

* * *

"Gentlemen, we have a taker for our prize!"

Anwar Yesseh read the look of incredulity on the faces of the six well-dressed business men who had assembled in a suite at the Imperial Hotel in Damascus.

"Perhaps you think I am deceiving you?" he said, breaking the silence. "I offer proof." He waved a piece of stationary under their noses, and relinquished it to a hand across the room. The hand's owner was a huge man, whose obesity was so immense that he avoided sitting in armchairs lest he become immobilized. He scrutinized the letter, written on stationary bearing the return address of the Syrian delegation to the United Nations. The fat man finished, and after a period of eyebrow lifting, he passed it along.

Yesseh waited until all six had read the letter. Then he said, "Can I assume that we are still in the plan, that we shall honor our pledges?"

163

One man, an Egyptian, seemed overly thought-ful. "It has been a long time," he said. "Perhaps we should re-examine the reasons for our pledge, and the possible after-effects."

"Perhaps our colleague is right," said another, also an Egyptian, who had started the consortium originally, but, as the Suez was reopened and his business increased, had gradually turned over the leadership to Yesseh. "Is it not possible that this bomb might aggravate the situation?"

Yesseh was only slightly irritated, for he could not really blame them. He knew that rarely does any group, whether a company or a country, act altruistically. Regardless of stated ideological goals or humanitarian ideals, there is always a profit motive involved. The profit may be only a measure of good will, but in the end good will is good public relations, and can ultimately mean greater profits or new allies.

No, he couldn't fault the Egyptians. More than likely, were he in their shoes he would act the same way. There are no true believers in high places. Presidents, whether they be heads of corporations or heads of state cannot afford to believe the trash they speak, for to do so would mean destruction at the hands of those who can manipulate. Every effective leader must be able to exploit his true believers, who are the true pawns in any struggle.

"My friends," Yesseh said earnestly, "the situation as it now exists in Egypt is not a constant. There is no guarantee that Israeli warplanes will not once again grace the skies over Cairo or Alexandria, no guarantee that you may not wake up one morning to find a Zionist tank in front of your company, and a Jew for a boss. Things may be going well for your businesses now, and I can't blame you for your attitudes, but how do you know for a certainty what will happen tomorrow?"

"But Arafat has achieved some degree of acceptability," argued the Egyptian cotton broker. "Nations are supplying him and his men with weapons and money. Why should we, as businessmen, dip into our profits or our own pockets to prop him up with an atom bomb?"

"For several good reasons," Yesseh countered, "the primary one being control. First, no sane government is going to put a nuclear weapon into the hands of that maniac. He may talk moderately now, but rest assured, he is as insane as ever.

"Second," Yesseh ticked off the reasons on his fingers, "we must use his insanity for our own purposes. You yourselves have seen the way he reacts to the numbered accounts we set up for him in Zurich. As one man takes to law and another to business, he has taken to terrorism as his method of attaining power, fame, and most of all, wealth.

"Third, the nuclear device we give him will not be an immensely powerful weapon, certainly not powerful enough to completely level Tel Aviv. But its psychological significance, the power it will give to that one demented man, will assure us that he will do our bidding in the future. If he should ever succeed, it is *our* will that will be done."

The cotton broker stroked his chin. "How can you be sure he will continue to obey us?" he asked finally.

It was Yesseh's moment of triumph, but he was

a very reasonable man when he played his trump card.

"Why else would I have specified that one of us must co-sign any withdrawals he makes from his accounts? When it comes to money for *his own* use, he must turn to us."

"True, true," muttered the cotton broker. He held a whispered conference with his fellow Egyptian. Then he said, "Count us in."

In less than twenty-four hours, tapes of the conversation at the Imperial Hotel reached Langley, Virginia, headquarters of the Central Intelligence Agency.

A hotel is a marvelously easy assignment for a trained, professional man with electronic bugs. The CIA, which had monitored that suite before, had placed sensitive bugs in lamp bases, in telephones, under tables and beds, and behind the grills of ventilating systems, confident that the group did not know it was under surveillance. They were right.

It took almost no time thereafter for the CIA to collate all the information concerning Amani, Yesseh, the consortium, make sense of it, and figure out that the prize so frequently mentioned referred to the nuclear bomb. All the messages had been hastily but properly coded and sent out before midnight covered Damascus. Before midnight came again, a dramatic decision would be reached at an emergency meeting of the U.S. Intelligence Board.

CHAPTER TEN

While the conversations were taking place in the Imperial Hotel, an Allegheny Corvair turbo-prop crop-dusted its way down New York State, finally setting down at LaGuardia Airport in New York City. Alexander climbed down the steps and walked across the oil-stained concrete apron toward the concourse, his coat collar turned up against the biting winds of January. He entered the concourse, ascertained from an attendant where and when the connecting flight to Washington could be found and received directions. The passengers were already loading when he reached the DC-9, and he settled down into a window seat of the tourist class section.

In an hour Alexander was in Washington. He took his carry-on luggage from the storage area, left the plane and soon was in a taxi, which dropped him at Fifteenth and F Streets, where the Washington Hotel was located, across the street from the Treasury Department. His room at the hotel was not much larger than a broom closet, but it was clean and would serve nicely for his brief stay.

He hung up his suitbag, walked down to the coffee shop for a hamburger and coke, then returned to his room and retired. Tomorrow was going to be a big day.

* * *

But that same night was a big one for a group of men who had gathered in the White House, nervously assimilating a report received from the United States Embassy in Damascus.

"Gentlemen, this may be the gravest problem we have ever faced," said John Coleman, the head of the Central Intelligence Agency.

Listening to Coleman speak were: the heads of two Defense Department intelligence groups, the National Security Agency and the Defense Intelligence Agency; the soon-to-be-confirmed Secretary of State and his lame duck predecessor; the head of the Bureau of Intelligence and Research; the head of the Internal Security Division of the FBI; the Intelligence Division of the Atomic Energy Commission.

Also present were the President and Vice-President elect of the United States, and the lame duck President, who merely sat and listened without comment. After all, he'd be out of office shortly, and he had made it known it was the new boy's baby, he wanted no part of it.

The head of the CIA continued. "Basically, all we know is that this group of Arab businessmen, nearly all of whom are displaced Palestinians, have offered a large reward for an atom bomb. Apparently, the offer is the same one we have heard rumors of for some time. However, we heard of nothing concrete except the offer, and assumed it had expired simply from the lack of a taker."

"You assumed!" the FBI representative exploded. "We're at the mercy of a bunch of looney terrorists because you prima donnas won't put out the effort to stay with a case until it's closed." FBI chief Hawkins was still unaware of the inefficiency of his own bureau. "You might call us a bunch of dull gumshoes, but at least we don't drop everything on some half-assed assumption."

Coleman was not surprised at the outburst. Rather he was embarrassed at having his shortcomings so dramatically and painfully pinpointed in front of so many top echelon people. He struggled to maintain his composure, while the FBI chief resumed his chair.

"Now," Coleman continued, "information from several sources indicates that the offer has been accepted. The takers are here in the United States. Apparently, the coordinator of these activities is a man named Abu Amani, a member of the Syrian delegation to the United Nations. Our proof is a couple of letters, written by him to one of the businessmen offering the prize. It's half-baked double-talk, but as easy to see through as a cleaned window."

"Mr. Coleman," the voice was that of the President-elect, Howard Bentley, "what do you think the terrorists will do with the bomb, assuming they succeed in constructing one?"

"Sir, the indications are that they cannot succeed. They would require their own miniature Manhattan Project, with dozens of people participating, if only to produce a prototype bomb. That would be impossible to accomplish without our knowing about it. Such a bomb would be an unusually large, heavy object, conspicuous. It could not be placed into a suitcase, or perhaps even in a small truck."

"That does not answer my original question," President Bentley was obviously annoyed. Coleman feared him. This was a shrewd man, whose opponents—the out-going President included—had labeled him "as calculating as a computer." His thinking processes were cold, rational.

"Sir, we do not have as much information at this time as we would like," Coleman confessed. "The tapes of the conversation in Damascus discuss psychological advantages which would accrue to the Palestinians. Therefore, I assume that they intend to use the weapon for negotiation, if indeed they have it at all."

At the word "assume" the FBI chief snorted. The new President showed no outward emotion.

"Do you also assume," he asked calmly, "that there is a chance this weapon might be used in the United States?"

"Hardly," was Coleman's reply. "They would not want to waste their limited nuclear resources on us. I feel they would save such resources for use against Israel. I can see no real benefit derived by exploding it here."

"Ransom!"

All heads turned toward Hawkins of the FBI. "It's not unheard of, you know." He stared hard at the CIA chief.

The President-elect broke the silence. "Perhaps Mr. Hawkins has a point there. I would like to follow that avenue a bit more."

Hawkins rose to his feet. "I, for once, agree with Mr. Coleman," he said firmly. "It is unlikely that this group could build an atom bomb, there are too many odds against it without our knowing what is going on. But there is the possibility that they could turn over to the Arabs some device which could be further refined by Egyptian scientists. From that standpoint, it threatens the tenuous peace that exists in the Middle East.

"And yet, it could be an important tool in the United States, if they sent us bomb plans, or perhaps delivered a sample of their core material. In such case they could put up a good bluff, that unless we delivered X-amount of money, or acceded to political demands, they would flatten, let us say, New York City. I feel we must be alerted that this situation may actually occur, and if so, we must be prepared to call their bluff, risking the fact that they may indeed have built a working bomb.

"And, about the bomb, sir, once it reaches the Middle East—which it shouldn't—that is not my responsibility. Mr. Coleman has let me know the lines of demarcation in responsibility often enough."

Hawkins was talking Bentley's language. The new President had made his fortune by taking chances, backing up his assessment of the odds, and he had attained the Presidency the same way. As a precision gambler, he liked the way the FBI man spoke his mind.

"What you say sounds reasonable," Bentley said. "Since the activities of this group seem to be focused somewhere in the United States, I think it reasonable that you be in charge of the investigation in this country. That is, if you agree, Mr. Coleman."

Coleman nodded, tight-lipped.

"Good. Then your job, Mr. Coleman, will be to concentrate on locating the delivery spot in the Middle East. I want you to do two things:

"First, I want you to intimidate the businessmen involved. Tell them we know who they are and what their plan is. If a bomb explodes in the United States, we will wreck their businesses and harm them as well.

"Second, I want you to take possession of the bomb at its delivery site and hand it over to the Israeli Foreign Ministry. There will be nothing official about this second act. In fact, I suggest

172

that you try to arrange for the Israeli Security to effect the actual capture of the bomb.

"Peter," the President turned to Secretary of State designate Sawyer, "I want you to let the Arab nations know the consequences of their supplying atomic weapons to the PLO. You know the sort of things that have been said in the past. I want them concerned enough so that they will actively discourage any of their nationals from supporting the move, and that might wipe out the financial support of the project.

"As for the rest of you gentlemen, this meeting is to be kept secret. No one not in this room has a 'need to know,' and all problems, all information concerning this situation, will be referred directly to me.

"Unless someone has something to add, perhaps we should adjourn."

The meeting broke up. The representatives of the Defense Department and the Atomic Energy Commission walked over to Hawkins, to pay their respects to the man who had obviously fallen into the President's favor. It never hurt to curry favor.

"I take it you're familiar with the plutonium nitrate theft last fall," said the AEC man.

"Yes," replied Hawkins. "Truthfully, I need all the help I can get, and I'd appreciate it if you'd send me anything you have. It might help us track down the bomb builders."

"You can depend on it," said the AEC man.

Hawkins excused himself in order to speak a word in private with Coleman.

173

"Look, I'm sorry about the problems that exist between our agencies," Hawkins said, extending his hand. "We must cooperate on this one."

Coleman ignored the hand. "I'll send you what we have," he said icily.

The President-elect had noted the brief exchange. He walked over to them.

"I'm sorry that relations between you two aren't better," Bentley said. "But don't get the idea that I'm favoring the FBI over the CIA. I'm going by the book. The FBI is responsible for domestic problems, the CIA for those in foreign countries. The assignments I handed out tonight seem to be the most efficient way of attacking the situation. I don't want any intramural warfare. I expect you to cooperate. You both know what's potentially at stake." His voice was neither friendly nor hostile, but emotionless, as if issuing a command he expected to be obeyed at all costs.

Well, Hawkins thought as the President-elect and his entourage left the room, he won't get any flack from me. Coleman had other thoughts as he left the room.

As Hawkins' chauffeur drove him home to his house in Chevy Chase, radio station WTOP, the all-news broadcaster, was predicting another cold day in January.

* * *

The bed at the Hotel Washington proved surprisingly comfortable, and Alexander did not wake up until almost nine-thirty. He shaved and dressed hurriedly, went downstairs to a ham-and-eggs breakfast, then took a taxi to Capitol Hill. The sky was grey and crying upon the city, an obvious oversight by the radio weather reporters who had failed to predict the unexpected rain. The cab driver, a Nigerian student who delivered a lecture on the internal problems caused by the Ibo, dropped him off at the east entrance to the Capitol Building. Alexander gave him two dollars on the eighty-five cent ride, told him to keep the change, and splashed across the sidewalk under the massive front steps.

A guard at the door checked him to see that he had no suspicious packages, and Alexander made his way to the subway tram that went to the Dirksen Senate Office Building. There he began to wander through the corridors, his footsteps echoing through the cavernous stone halls. He found no place a bomb could be concealed.

He tramped through the Russell Building with no better results. After two subway rides, he found himself in the Rayburn Building, walking through the underground garage. There would be no problem getting the bomb delivered here, he thought, but the blast would be muted because it was underground. For maximum effect the bomb had to be placed above ground, the higher the better. He wandered the spacious halls of the Rayburn Building; it was as devoid of nooks and crannies as the Senate Building had been.

He walked out of the Rayburn Building and up

Independence Avenue to the Longworth Building, where he was politely greeted by a friendly guard with a southern accent, who also checked him for packages. He took the elevator up to the top floor and began his search. The top floors were cluttered with boxes in the halls, but none so big as the desk-sized crate the bombers would have to use to deliver the atomic device. A crate that large would be noticed.

Alexander walked through another tunnel in the basement of the Longworth Building, past another guard, into the Cannon Building.

On the fifth floor, he found his spot.

The elevator system in the "Uncle Joe" Cannon Building was poorly designed, especially in the northwest corner. Several elevators went only to the fourth floor, and only two all the way to the fifth. The arrangement of elevator shafts left a great deal of wasted space in anterooms and corridors that gave access to the elevators traveling up to the fifth floor.

It was outside the elevator on Independence Avenue that he found what he was looking for, a cubbyhole next to the elevator, about five feet by eight feet, made even more ideal by the presence of a set of filing cabinets and a desk stored against one wall. The guards were evidently accustomed to some furniture in the area, and certainly would not become suspicious of another piece, even if it was in a crate. Another fifteen minutes of walking brought him to the rear delivery doors of the Cannon Building on C Street. Alexander had to jump away repeatedly as delivery men raced through the basement corridors with their fork lifts and motorized carts. It would be a simple matter to borrow one of those, to deliver the bomb to the fifth floor. Putting the bomb on a wooden skid would make it above suspicion.

Alexander walked out of the C Street delivery entrance to New Jersey Avenue and up to Independence, where he caught a cab back to the Washington Hotel. It was barely past two o'clock; he had accomplished his mission in less than three hours of actual work. He checked out of the hotel, paying his bill in cash. He stopped into the coffee shop and had a leisurely ham-and-cheese on rye and coffee, then took a cab back to National Airport. It was just past two-thirty.

He pressed his cheek against the cab window and stared at the Jefferson Memorial as the vehicle skirted the edge of the Tidal Basin on the way to Route 95 and the airport. From a map he had purchased, he knew that the location of the bomb, when it went off, would be scantly more than three hundred yards from every ranking member of the federal goverment.

The flight back to Ithaca was entirely aboard a twin-engine turboprop whose vibration and noise combined with the rough rainy weather to tinge Alexander's stomach with nausea by the time it finally put down high above Lake Cayuga that evening. He was met by Jean and the white van for the ride back to the farm. As they rode home the rain turned to snow.

*　　*　　*

Lieutenant Leslie Atkinson left work early because of a migraine headache, the result of the pressure of his investigations. His superiors were on his neck, demanding that he forget about stolen plutonium, which was the root cause of his debilitation. But he couldn't walk away, it wasn't possible, too many devils were driving him.

He had left the barracks some time after four o'clock, when Hoover had arrived back at the station with his list of electricity customers who might be suspects. The BCI rooms were crowded with arrests from a drug bust, and he had given Trooper Hoover his office to work in if he wanted to stay late.

Once again, two of the conspirators passed him on the road, but he didn't know it. How could he? It was just another van on the road.

Hoover's list contained more than four hundred names, a list seemingly impossible to sort through. Finally, after much mental effort, he hit upon the idea of listing the businesses and homes in a sort of priority, encompassing those who might be reasonably more likely bomb builders than others. A couple of friends dropped by at quitting time to find out if he was still there. "Atkinson's Folly," they called it, and asked slyly if he too might be losing his mind. Hoover dismissed them with a shrug and promised to join them later.

Now, as he went over the list, he decided to put all the commercial customers in the first list.

Among the top were those scientifically oriented, followed by engineering firms, schools, machine shops. The rest were arranged alphabetically.

He had checked with the county clerk's office regarding the four dozen private homes without a basement; those automatically went to the bottom of the list. The rest he arranged in order of electricity usage.

By seven o'clock he had finished with the arrangement list and left to join his buddies, hoping they were still there. Tomorrow he would ask the electric company for proper identification in order to pose as a repairman or meter reader, so that he could check the businesses and homes without arousing suspicion.

The Federal Security Agencies did not know it; the police at Ithaca did not know it; but the net was being cast out, hoping to seine out the big fish they were looking for. A lot was riding on their ability to find the big fish in time.

If they failed—ARMAGEDDON!

CHAPTER ELEVEN

CIA Chief John Coleman summoned to his office a select group of his top agents, and, one by one he parcelled out assignments, taking care that no one agent had enough information to grasp the overall mission.

One agent was to follow Anwar Yesseh and see that his movements were monitored around the clock. Another was to work with the Damascus embassy's CIA operative, to install permanent taps on all the communications facilities of Yesseh's company. Still another was to oversee the Damascus operative and encourage him to promote more contact with Yesseh's secretary, to ascertain his travel plans, who he saw in his office, his business rates.

Coleman decided against moving against the

Syrian U.N. delegation in New York or their embassy in Washington. He knew the FBI would be bugging their offices and he didn't want to get caught stepping out of bounds. He did, however, order one of his agents to question some of their student operatives in various GUPS groups (the infiltrators). For many years the CIA had recruited foreign students and paid them informers' stipends. The CIA agent was specifically told to ask only about unusual activities, nothing more.

Coleman knew no specifics about building an atom bomb, except that one required a great deal of high explosives. Thus one agent was instructed to contact every legitimate explosives firm, and several undercover ones, to find out if there had been thefts or purchases of unusually large amounts or types of explosives.

Finally, after the last agent had been assigned, he placed a call to what he privately referred to as the CIA THUG division. The term was no acronym; these men were pure thugs, working out of the Division of Special Operations under the Director of Operations (Clandestine Services). These were the paramilitary men, the ones who would carry out the threats against Arab businessmen backing the bomb. They were crude men, the animals of the CIA. Coleman hated to use them because when he did, he had the feeling he was sinking to their level. But they could also be extremely useful, especially in desperate situations.

The head of Special Ops looked like a sedate

college professor, very unlike the men he controlled, but Coleman knew he had a sadistically warped mind that could wreak horror upon an enemy. To him Coleman gave the list of Arabs, and instructed him first to destroy their businesses, and then to destroy the men themselves. The man left gleefully, Coleman could tell the man had been looking forward to the opportunity to cause pain and suffering.

As Coleman had guessed, FBI Chief Hawkins did tap the Syrians in New York and Washington, and also had bugs planted in Amani's private residence. Hawkins even considered having Coleman's agents tailed, to make sure they didn't encroach on his assignment, but shelved the idea. Knowing how the President felt, he wanted to be super cautious.

As he pondered further moves, Hawkins heard a soft knock at his door. It was Alan Perry, the young probationary agent.

"Sir, may I have a word with you?" Perry seemed tense.

"Yes, but make it brief," Hawkins said brusquely.

"Sir, perhaps you might think I'm imagining things, but I think someone in the United States is trying to make an atom bomb to sell to the PLO," Perry came right to the point.

Hawkins felt as if someone had slapped his face. How did this kid find out?

"What makes you think so, Perry?" Hawkins kept his voice calm.

"This report you gave me, the one from the CIA. If you recall, it was a bunch of papers sent over from the Agency, and you handed some of it out as a training exercise."

"Go on."

"Well, sir, I ran a check on the names and subjects found in the letter, and it turned out the author of the letter mentions some kind of a prize. Well, I nosed around, and I remembered that just recently one of our student informers mentioned the rumor that a group of Arabs offered a prize for an atom bomb. It got me to thinking, maybe the prize in the letter and the prize the student mentioned are the same prize."

Perry was somewhat frightened by the way his boss replied.

"I can't say anything, but you are to photocopy all your files and bring me the copies. Return all the original files to their places, but make sure nothing concerning the most recent letter gets into the files."

"Yes, sir."

"Don't mention this, don't even hint that you have talked to me. Not to anyone. Do you understand that? Not to anyone. It could mean the difference between a brilliant career for you as an agent, or never seeing the inside of this building again."

"Yes, sir." Perry was bewildered.

"Be available. Don't go out of town for the weekend."

Perry walked out of the office a very troubled

man. Soon afterward Hawkins left for the day.

* * *

The white Pontiac ambulance screamed through Ithaca, dodging cars, trucks and cyclists stupid enough to be out riding after dark, wailing its way toward the Tompkins County Hospital. In the back lay a Cornell University student gasping for breath; even the oxygen being administered didn't ease the difficulty.

They had picked up the student in front of Willard Straight Hall, after receiving a telephone call. Obviously he hadn't made the call, but he had been alone on the steps when they found him.

Halfway up the glacially-carved slope to the hospital, the driver turned off the flashing lights and siren. The student was dead. The resident on duty pronounced him DOA, and asked the ambulance attendant to wait until the coroner could come. The circumstances were suspicious, and no doubt the coroner would want to ask some questions of the attendant. To the resident eyeing the black face of the dead student, it looked very much like a drug OD.

But a quick autopsy left the coroner puzzled. This young man had died of acute fibrosis of the lungs. The coroner had been a physician for thirty years, fifteen of them as a pathologist, and he had never seen the condition he saw in the thorax of the young black man. He looked at the picture of the student on his ID card to make sure of the identification.

On the death certificate he wrote the name: Jean Lafayette.

The coroner decided to contact the school that night so that they could notify the dead man's family. Meanwhile, he thought the death curious enough to send a copy of his report to the head of the state police in Ithaca.

As the coroner was washing up, three frightened conspirators were huddled around the kitchen table in a farmhouse not far away.

"Where did you leave him?" Tom asked.

"At the Straight," Alexander replied. "I called the ambulance and helped him to the steps."

"Shit!" snorted Amhed. "If they do a detailed autopsy, or bring a geiger counter near his body, they'll find out what caused it, and they'll know the plutonium is in this area. They might come looking for us."

"Why the hell didn't you tell us that stuff was there?" Tom demanded. "You said the only thing on that truck was plutonium nitrate."

Alexander was tired of defending himself. After all, Jean was his friend more than the others.

"I told you a dozen times, I didn't know it was there. How the hell did I know there would be oxide mixed in with the shipment? Besides, why didn't you notice the container was different from the others? You could have used a little common sense."

Amhed raised his hands for calm silence. "Look, it happened, we can't change anything," he pointed out to the others. "We've got to decide now how to finish the job and move out before we get caught."

Amhed's words had the desired effect. The recriminations ended abruptly.

"The question is, how fast can we finish up?" Alexander offered.

"I doubt I can finish my work in less than a month," Tom answered.

Amhed said, "My work should take about three weeks. After that I could help either one of you."

"We'll get it done," Alexander said firmly. "I know Jean would want us to do our best."

"Right!" Amhed knew he had the group back on the right track.

"We'll make up all the components we have material for," said Alexander. "We can construct the two bombs and ship whatever components may be left to wherever the Mid-East people tell us to."

"I'll take care of that," Amhed said, knowing that if for some reason the consortium changed its mind and refused to go along with their plans for the Washington bomb, he would sell it to another buyer, perhaps Morocco or Algeria.

The three fell silent. Then, "They've got Jean's ID and other papers," Tom said. "They know who he is by now. Alexander, what home address does he have on his driver's license?"

"His old one at the dorm," Alexander told him. "But I'm sure they'll check and find out he hasn't been living there for months. He got his mail recently at a post office box in Ithaca."

"The fewer people who can connect him with us, the better," Tom remarked.

"The only people he knew around here were a few chicks he picked up," Amhed smiled. "I'll bet none of them got his last name."

"I'd suggest," Alexander said thoughtfully, "we don't show up on campus any more. Maybe somebody saw one or more of us together with Jean at some time."

"Wouldn't that arouse suspicion?" Amhed asked.

"Well, maybe we could hang around the Straight once or twice," Alexander conceded. "But not too long."

Alexander also suggested they wall up the door leading to the cellar. They could cut a hole in one corner of the floor and use a ladder. The hole could be covered by a chest of drawers. He made a mental note to destroy all Jean's belongings. He was dead now, out of the project. Goodbye, Jean Lafayette.

Now they set to work in earnest.

A plutonium drum was hoisted into position where its syrupy yellow-green liquid could pour into aquarium-like battery jars, set on a table formed from plywood and saw horses. About half the drum could be emptied into the jars, which were then covered with window glass to keep out impurities. Each jar had an opening at the bottom, to which was affixed some Tygon tubing, to draw out a bit of solution as needed.

The chemical processes were straightforward enough so that a freshman chemistry student could perform them.

Alexander filled a large beaker half full, and poured into it a measured amount of oxalic acid. The reaction produced plutonium oxalate, which is insoluble in water. The solution and precipitate were then poured through a millipore filter and crystals heated to drive out any bound molecules of water. What resulted was a cake of anhydrous plutonium oxalate. But the oxalate required further drying, and was placed in a sealed crucible connected to a container of hydrofluoric acid by a quartz tube. Quartz was necessary, since hydrofluoric acid is so corrosive it even eats away glass, something almost unheard of in the world of chemistry.

The container of hydrofluoric acid was heated, producing hydrogen fluoride gas, which was then passed through the tubing to the sealed crucible, where the oxalate was being heated to five hundred degrees centigrade. Plutonium fluoride was thus produced.

The next step was the reduction into metal form, and Alexander decided to wait until he had processed all the nitrate into fluoride before starting the reduction process.

It took less than a week for Alexander to finish

converting the nitrate solution to plutonium fluoride. Now he could reduce it to metal and determine the critical mass, and machine the final cores.

For the next two weeks Alexander made metal, building a stockpile of fluorid and storing it in 250-millimeter beakers, to avoid too much of it coming together at one time. He approximated that the critical mass of the metal would be about five to ten kilograms, but he had no idea how the fluoride reacted.

In one crucible he mixed a paste of magnesium oxide until it had the consistency of clay. Then, working it carefully, he fashioned a liner for the crucible out of the paste. The imprint of a brass sphere he had machined for that purpose made the surface inside the crucible smooth. The crucible and its liner were placed in one of the clay-kilns in the outer workshop to dry.

The reason for the liner was apparent the first time men had tried to work with the plutonium. It was highly corrosive, and as a molten metal would eat all but the most resistant materials. Without the lining, the ceramic crucible would have been severely pitted, resulting in contamination of the plutonium. Alexander wasn't sure how pure his samples would be. But he knew for certain that because of the large amount of alpha radioactivity of the plutonium, even light impurities had to be eliminated, since they contributed greatly to the neutrons available for spontaneous fission, making an accidental explosion more likely. That risk was raised because of where the plutonium had come from in the first place.

The longer a fuel rod remains in a reactor, the greater the percentage of heavier and less stable isotope, PU-240. This form of plutonium fissions spontaneously very easily, and could provide the trigger for an uncontrolled chain reaction. Plutonium destined for nuclear weapons remains in a reactor a relatively short time, but power companies want to get maximum mileage out of their fuel before sending them to be reprocessed and leave the fuel rods in a much longer time. Thus the percentage of 240 would be fairly high in the solutions Alexander was working with. The two compounds were essentially impossible to separate, and Alexander knew he would just have to work around the problem.

One good thing about the PU-240 was that the extra neutrons it produced made it unnecessary to add an initiator to the bomb, thus simplifying the task immensely.

The initiator in the original plutonium implosion bombs was a device that emitted an intense burst of neutrons when it was compressed, furnishing the "seeds" of the nuclear reaction. The initiator was usually a two-part device, one part composed of lithium, the other, polonium. By themselves, the neutron flux was negligible, but when brought together suddenly, the lithium and polonium emitted the neutrons that started the wild fission of atomic explosion.

In the first bombs, it was necessary to package the two elements in a small capsule, which was then placed in a hollowed out area at the center of the plutonium core. When the core was imploded, the capsule was broken, allowing the contents to mix. This was the detail eliminated from the conspirator's bomb.

Alexander took 500 grams of plutonium fluoride from the beakers and mixed it with 170 grams of finely grated metallic calcium. To this mixture was added 50 grams of iodine that was crushed with a mortar and pestle. Alexander stirred the granular mixture with a glass rod and poured it into the prepared lined crucible, which was placed in the hood of the induction furnace and the gas-tight front closed. Then he fed the heavy, inert argon gas in the top of the chamber, to force out any oxygen which could oxidize the metal during the melting process. Alexander hit the switch and watched as the temperature gauge reached 750 degrees, then turned off the current. Fascinated, he watched the temperature needle continue to climb. In less than a minute the exothermic reaction of the mixture had heated the contents of the crucible to a little more than 1,600 degrees. Then, after reaching its maximum after fifteen minutes, the mixture started to cool, dropping to less than 800 degrees. And while the mixture was cooling to room temperature, Alexander turned his attention to preparing successive batches for processing. From that point, he would run four batches at a time into the furnace.

It took more than an hour for the material to cool, but when Alexander finally opened the furnace to see what he had baked, he felt a surge of pride.

There was a hemisphere of metallic plutonium, its top surface scattered with bubbles and covered with the remnants of the reaction, mostly junk made of calcium and iodine, which could be washed off with nitric acid. After drying it, Alexander held the little lump in his hand, savoring the warmth, caused not by the heating in the furnace but by the alpha radiation.

Of the three main forms of radiation given off by radioactive materials, Alpha radiation is the least potent. A single thickness of a person's skin is sufficient shielding to prevent injury. Alpha rays aren't really rays at all, but highly excited pieces of material ejected from the nucleus: two protons and two neutrons, something akin to a helium atom stripped of its electrons.

Another type, Beta radiation, is caused by excited electrons, and is a bit more potent than Alpha, but neither of these comes close to the deadliness of Gamma rays.

Gamma rays are not particles, but true rays, with a phenomenal ability to penetrate matter. Gamma rays easily penetrate several feet of concrete and water, and are impeded only by substantial thicknesses of lead. It was this radiation the workers in the fuel rod reprocessing plants needed protection against. Such radiation is produced in great quantities only in a chain reaction situation. It would be toward the end of the month before Alexander had to worry about Gamma radiation.

Meanwhile, Tom Flaherty worked feverishly to produce the molds for the high explosive lenses. He was confident that his solutions to the partial differential equations of the implosion hydrodynamics, combined with the Greenglass drawings, would help him bypass the difficulties experienced by the original experimenters. They had worked from less sophisticated calculations than he had; their IBM computer was crude compared to the one Tom used at Cornell. They had obtained erratic results from their multipoint detonations, and were plagued by jets of the explosion that had jumped ahead of the spherical converging explosion wavefront. Much of this was aggravated by the high pressure points where the detonation waves collided. Tom knew that his lens system would produce the necessary converging waves to begin with, which would eliminate the jet problem.

But, a system working on paper does not mean it can work in reality. Errors on his part in constructing the lenses and assembling them could cause flaws in the explosion, which in turn would produce a dud.

To eliminate these imperfections, he was casting and machining the lenses, which involved the use of risers and overcasting techniques which had become a well-developed art at the "S" site at Los Alamos. By overcasting the lenses, the imperfections could be concentrated in the top

193

section of the casting. Because the casting had more than enough material, the top part was machined off, taking with it most of the imperfections. Tom had made his risers as small as possible, to reduce the amount of necessary machining. This was the most dangerous part of the entire maneuver, and would be done after the core and detonating devices had been finished and moved out of the barn, where they could not be destroyed by an accidental explosion.

Meanwhile, Amhed was tinkering with the electronic portion of the bomb, the firing mechanism.

Tom had selected electric spark-gap detonators to use with the high explosive lenses. Hercules Powder Company had produced the first detonators to Los Alamos specifications, and their design was no longer a secret. The ones Hoskins had supplied were an improved version.

The detonators had to be fired within a few microseconds of each other, and Amhed knew that mechanical switches were incapable of this. The firing was to be accomplished by discharging a bank of high voltage capacitors through some sort of low inductance switch. At Los Alamos, an explosive switch was tried first. In this type of switch, electrical contact was made by the detonation of an explosive charge, which broke through a thin dielectric layer between two metal discs, between which the voltage then passed. This switch had a grave disadvantage, because, like a match, it could not be tested before use, making it impossible to ascertain its realiability. The group switched to an electronic switch, using a device called a thyratron. This switch operated between two electrodes, the discharge being triggered by charging a third "probe" electrode to a suitable high voltage. These switches were able to pass very high currents in the order of a microsecond.

However, the thyratron was a bulky vacuum tube device, and had yielded its supremacy in high amperage, microsecond switching to a small semiconductor device called the silicon controlled rectifier, or, SCR. These were the devices stolen from the building near which the old wino had been killed.

It was a straightforward matter, Amhed thought, to connect enough of them with sufficient capacitors to fire 36 sets of detonators at once. There were a total of 72 detonators with each bomb, but they were arranged two-per-explosive-lens, connected together to be fired as one unit. The primary purpose of this arrangement was to make sure the lens fired, even if one of the detonators failed.

Amhed would complete his task in less than two weeks, producing three calibrated units.

The bombers' task was nearing completion.

CHAPTER TWELVE

January passed into February, and the intensive search for the bombers continued.

Trooper Hoover, in his guise as an electric company employee, trudged from one business establishment to another, carrying his small geiger counter, trying to detect the presence of radioactive material. Always finding nothing, he too began to suspect that his boss was just the slightest bit looney.

Atkinson had seemed to settle down after handing Hoover the house-hunting assignment, but then he nearly went berserk after finding out about the death of the black Cornell student. Of course the death was strange, but Atkinson seemed to be going overboard, insisting that the body be exhumed, in order to examine the lung tissue for radioactivity, on the theory that he had been exposed to the one container of plutonium oxide the AEC had told him about. Hoover knew the court fight might take weeks, and by that time everyone in the barracks would be driven up the wall. It would take weeks for Hoover to check out the four hundred names on his list of places to be inspected for radioactivity, so there was no surcease there.

To Trooper Hoover, it looked like a long, hard, cold February.

*　　*　　*

Anwar Yesseh was a worried man. The American CIA was taking action against the consortium. They had destroyed facilities that belonged to members of the consortium, and each time a warning was sent, promising worse to follow if they did not call off their agreement to pay the prize for the bomb.

But, from whom could these businessmen seek protection? Not from their own governments, who would have been truly horrified at the thought of an illicit atom bomb, to be used not by themselves but by terrorists. Afraid of digging themselves deeper, afraid of eavesdroppers, the consortium had ceased meeting or even calling each other. Yesseh had even cut off all communications with Amani in New York.

Finally, Yesseh took some oblique action. He contacted several ministers of Al Fatah and informed them of the situation. He found them sympathetic.

"There was a leak somewhere," said one of them. "Find that leak and plug it up." He made a mock pistol of his thumb and forefinger.

"But no one else in my business knew about the agreement," Yesseh protested. "Only the other businessmen in the consortium, and they are suffering from attacks as much as I am. I have had oil pipelines dynamited, refineries sabotaged, offices mysteriously burned to the ground. Similar things have happened to all of us. But I have done the bulk of the work, and only I have a complete picture of what is involved. No one who works for me could have found out about the prize and the bomb."

"But obviously, my friend, someone has," the Al Fatah man said reasonably. "Now think. A secretary, perhaps? Someone who relayed messages for you? We know that this pressure is coming from the Americans. It must be that they are afraid we might use the bomb against them."

"And it *will* be used against them," sighed Yesseh.

"Fool!" the man spat. "If that bomb is used against the Americans, it will either start a nuclear war between them and the Soviets, or, far worse, they might come after us with nuclear weapons."

"But we had to agree. The builders insisted," Yesseh whined.

"Stupidity!" snarled the Al Fatah man. "We can

do without the bomb if getting it means we must be wiped off the face of the earth.

"However, the situation is not impossible. Fortunately for you, I have an idea which will not only take the heat off your companies, but also serve to smoke out your security leak."

The plan was unfolded. Yesseh was to send a telegram to the other members of the consortium, saying that the prize was to be brought straight to the Middle East without first being tested. No one would find out about it until it was "unveiled" against Israel. Of course, the CIA would find out about the telegram, and think that at least America was safe from nuclear explosions. That would ease the sabotage caused by the Americans.

"You are to write out the telegram as usual, and place it on your secretary's desk for the usual processing."

At this point Yesseh protested. "Surely you don't suspect she is the leak. She has kept my company's most important, delicate secrets. She is above reproach."

"My dear Anwar," the man said patronizingly, "if you trust her so implicitly, why don't you go along with my idea and prove her innocence to me?"

"Very well," Yesseh mumbled.

"Good. You will also contact your man in New York, and have him make sure nothing is exploded until it reaches our hands. Naturally, your telephones are bugged, and so is your contact's, so that your conversation will be relayed to the FBI and the CIA. This conversation will serve to reinforce the telegrams you have sent. However, wait a few days after your telegram before calling New York."

The entire conversation had taken place in the Al Fatah man's limousine, which he knew contained no bugging devices. He dropped Yesseh at his office and sped away. Yesseh elevatored to the twentieth floor and wrote out the telegram, which he placed on his secretary's desk.

One day later a copy of the telegram was presented to the President of the United States (his inauguration had already taken place) by CIA Chief Coleman.

"I think this proves that our actions are working," Coleman said proudly, emphasizing by the words "our action" that he was referring to the CIA.

"Not necessarily," said FBI Chief Hawkins quietly. "It might be a ruse to get your agents off their backs. I've heard no confirmation of the action via their contact in New York. Until then, the jury is still out."

"I think you both have an element of truth in your appraisals," said the President diplomatically. "We will cease actions against the consortium for, say, ten days. If after that time, you have no confirmation of this message, we will resume activities against them."

The seldom heard member of the National Security Agency spoke. "Respectfully, sir, I think we should continue the attacks on them until they also agree not to use the bomb against Israel."

"No," the President reluctantly shook his head. "At the moment that is a problem Israel must face. We shall continue to give the Israelis as much help as we can, but top priority now is the protection of the United States." He turned to the FBI Chief. "Hawkins, if we receive a confirmation of the telegram, you will contact Israeli Intelligence and brief them fully. If they desire assistance," he swung around to face Coleman, "Coleman can send in some of his men. But, at the moment, I want no further action taken against the consortium.

"If that's all, gentlemen, I have appointments to keep."

*   *   *

Anwar Yesseh and his consortium were not the only businessmen in a jam. Thousands of miles away, in Connecticut, U.S.A., Eric Hoskins realized that his number was up, too.

It all began when he received a letter from the Interstate Construction Company in Virginia, the outfit building the stretch of Interstate in western Virginia. The letter stated that they had conducted an auditing of all materials at all their subcontractors, and had found that the quantity of explosives on hand was about ten percent less than it should have been. Their investigations indicated that the error lay with Hoskins' firm, and would he kindly respond so that they could get the matter straightened out?

Hoskins' first reaction was to write a letter to the construction company, telling them that he would personally check into the bookkeeping, to see where the error lay. Then he tried to contact his man who worked for the company, his "stipend man," only to find that his contact had been transferred to another work site. Hoskins realized that the shortage, which had been covered only on paper, had been unmasked by the new man in charge, who had taken a very careful inventory and noted a substantial quantity of explosives which could not be accounted for.

The mollifying letter Hoskins had sent to the construction company had not been sufficient. Furthermore, an investigator from the FBI had paid them a visit. The company had been required to report the shortage of high explosives, and had indicated that possibly they might talk to the man from Connecticut.

Eric Hoskins had always been a prudent man. When he started in business for himself, as a "skimmer" of explosives, he always knew that a slipup was possible. He had taken two precautions: one, to purchase a small house and some land in Costa Rica. Two, he bought a small Beechcraft, built up his flying proficiency and obtained a commercial license, and instrument and multi-engine ratings.

Most of his revenues were put into high interest

certificates of deposit at several local banks, since securities were not liquid enough.

Hard on the heels of the special delivery, registered mail letter from the construction company came a call from the investigating FBI agent. Hoskins had answered the agent's questions with equal politeness; indeed, the man's voice seemed tinged with embarrassment when he learned that Hoskins had once been attached as a consultant to the FBI while with DuPont, had worked on the Los Alamos project in a specialized way, and had long ago been given top FBI clearance.

But Hoskins knew the game was up. A double check would reveal his kickback operation, that he had been fired by DuPont; it was only a matter of time. He had to get out, in less than forty-eight hours, or he might not get out at all.

He immediately set about cashing in his certificates of deposit. They had varying maturity dates and he lost some interest, but, as he put it, what the hell. The cash-in was finished by noon of those two remaining precious days.

At one o'clock he called up the real estate agent who had sold him the house. The man was most cordial.

"I've got to sell my house quickly," Hoskins tried to put a note of reluctance in his voice. "I've been offered a consultant's position with the government, and I don't know where I'll be in a few days. You know how they are in Washington."

"Some kind of top secret stuff?" the real estate

broker was intrigued. How often did a man like him come in contact with the hush-hush operations of the federal government.

"No," Hoskins chuckled. "But I'll be traveling around for maybe a year or so, and it'll be almost impossible to contact you after that."

As Hoskins had hoped, the real estate broker saw a chance to make a quick buck for himself.

"Look, Mr. Hoskins," he said, "the market's sort of down now, and I don't know about a quick sale. But, I'll tell you what, I'll take the house off your hands myself. I'll take the gamble. After all, I sold it to you in the first place. That shows you were dealing with an honest broker, right?"

"That's very generous of you," Hoskins steeled himself to keep from laughing aloud.

"How much did you pay for it?"

"One-hundred thousand. But that was almost ten years ago. It's worth at least fifty percent more by now."

"Maybe," hedged the broker. "But it'll mean a cash outlay for me, and I'll have to hang on to it until I find a buyer. That'll tie up a lot of cash. I could offer you, say, a hundred and ten?"

"Oh, come now," Hoskins replied. "Surely you can do better than that."

The final price agreed upon was one hundred and fifteen thousand. The broker promised to draw up the papers immediately, and hand him a certified check the next morning if he'd drop around to his office. He hung up rubbing his hands briskly. Hang on to that house, hell! He already knew a buyer who'd gladly pay $175,000 without blinking. A sweet sixty-thousand dollar profit within a week!

Hoskins hurriedly packed his suitcases, taking with him only the bare essentials. He would be sorry to leave the house, but all good things had to come to an end. Damn that Tom Flaherty anyway! And damn himself for being so eager to help!

Early the next morning he threw his bags into his car and drove into Greenwich where he signed the necessary real estate transfer papers and pocketed the certified check. He went straight to the bank on which the check was drawn, where it was readily cashed. Hoskins kept ninety-five thousand in cash, and with the rest opened a new checking account, accepting the temporary blank checks until sets with his name could be imprinted.

One last step. He stopped at a used car lot and sold his car, taking a thousand dollars less than its true worth, as long as it was in cash. It was, he explained, a "jinx" to him, needing nothing but repairs ever since he got it. The lot owner started the engine, listened to it purr, and transacted the sale on the spot. Hoskins took his bags out, taxied to a car rental agency, and rented a Maverick.

Within twenty-four hours he had squeezed out the last possible nickel of his assets. In two attache cases rested slightly less than one million dollars in good, hard American currency!

Then he drove to the local airport and picked up his Beechcraft Bonanza. He left the rented car, placed his clothes and the money in his plane. Twenty minutes later, the V-tailed plane was climbing, to level off at 8,000 feet, leaving behind its home at Westchester Airport forever, its destination, according to the flight plan filed by its pilot, Washington, D.C. But that was only the first leg of a long series of gas-up jumps which would take Eric Hoskins into permanent but safe exile.

By the time Hoskins had already left Dulles Airport in Washington, four special agents arrived at his former home, armed with a search warrant and a warrant for his arrest. They had to smash the lock to get into the house. A neighbor across the street saw the four well dressed men doing violence to the door and phoned the police, thinking perhaps they were Mafia. The police would attempt an arrest at gunpoint before finally learning that the men in the house were from the Federal Bureau of Investigation.

Finding that their quarry had flown the coop, the agents went straight to Hoskins' warehouse in Greenwich. That too was empty. But on the desk one agent noticed a slip of paper with numbers and letters, evidently the license number of some New York State vehicle. Perhaps, he thought, it might be a clue, somebody who could steer them on to the trail of the fugitive.

It was the license number of Alexander Greely's white van, which Hoskins had thoughtfully written down a few weeks ago.

*   *   *

Anwar Yesseh was amazed, relieved and extremely worried. He was amazed that the American intelligence network was so swift, relieved that the attacks on his business had stopped, and extremely worried, since the telegram ploy instigated by the Al Fatah man had worked, completely implicating his secretary of so many years as the unmistakable leak.

Now he was on his way down in the elevator to be picked up again by the unbugged car of the Al Fatah minister. Oh, how everything had changed! Once they had groveled for his support, his money, his prestige, and now they were ordering him around, and he had no choice but to obey.

"Are you convinced now?" the minister asked when Yesseh got into the car. "Was it not your secretary who was the leak?"

Yesseh nodded miserably.

"Then you must also know she must be eliminated."

"But that's murder!" Yesseh blurted. "I haven't the stomach for that."

"My friend, her actions have endangered your life, caused much loss of property, and have, indeed, threatened the entire Palestinian movement. Why do you begrudge her death, after she has done so much to help your enemies?"

"I can't help it," Yesseh shook his head. "Call me a coward and a weakling if you will, but I cannot do it."

"Then we shall do it for you," the minister said simply. "Now, go ahead and place your call to your man in New York. This will give confirmation to the Americans regarding your last telegram, which we now know they have intercepted. They must be waiting for your call to him. Make it crystal clear to your New York contact that he is to get in touch with the prize group and order them not to explode their bomb, for a test or otherwise. It must be sent directly to us."

"I will do that," Yesseh nodded.

"As added confirmation for the call, send another telegram to your consortium. Its contents do not matter. Perhaps you can indicate that the new approach to the prize seemed to be working, now that attacks on your businesses have stopped. What counts is that the Americans must believe us."

After Yesseh left, the minister placed a call from the telephone in his limousine.

"She works for Yesseh, she is his secretary. The old man is too squeamish about it. In fact I suspect he might want to protect her somehow. Follow her. I want her out of circulation immediately," he ordered.

Indeed, escape was exactly what Yesseh had in mind for his secretary. He wrote out the telegram and summoned the woman. He handed her a check made out to her, in the amount of more than ten thousand dollars by foreign exchange, and told her to take a vacation starting immediately. She resisted, but he won her over by assuring her that her old job would be waiting when she returned. Now, he felt satisfied, he had obeyed Al Fatah and also his own conscience.

Next he telephoned Amani, who was greatly relieved to have finally made contact with his true employer. He stressed the importance of making sure the group would not explode the bomb, and was upset to hear that Amani had neither their address or telephone number, that he would have to wait to be contacted. But he was sure contact would be made soon. The group was always running out of money.

The dead drop at Damascus was now being checked daily by the CIA agent in Syria, promptly at two o'clock every afternoon. He knew that Yesseh's secretary could only make her drops during lunch hour.

Approaching the locker, he inserted the cylindrical key, and as he opened the door he was greeted by a numbing, nerve-shattering sight. He managed to stifle a gagging in his throat and the overwhelming urge to bolt and run.

He saw a plastic bag which, at a quick glance from a distance looked like hamburger with clothes. A closer look revealed the dismembered body of a woman, with her face wedged in the upper corner of the bag, which was filled at the bottom with red, clotting blood.

The agent slammed the locker shut, leaving the key inside. It was of no use to him now. In a barely controlled walk he made it to his parked car, and then he collapsed on the front seat, retching.

A couple of days later, airport security guards, led there by the stench, would open the locker to find this grotesque sight. Only then, after it was reported in the newspapers, would Anwar Yesseh learn that his secretary had not enjoyed a vacation after all.

CHAPTER THIRTEEN

Dawn of February 7th found Lieutenant Leslie Atkinson tossing in bed, unable to sleep. The night had been a fitful one. In fact the whole previous week had been one long hassle. In the end he had prevailed, but was it really worth it? If he was wrong, if he had been chasing ghosts, his whole career as a police officer might well be down the drain. He would be a laughing stock, the target of sneers and pointed fingers, considered a nut, who, once he got hipped on a subject wouldn't let go until something gave in.

For days he had been on the phone, pestering, demanding, requesting, cajoling, almost begging to have the body of Jean Lafayette exhumed from its resting place near his parents' home in White Plains, New York. In the end the district court had agreed. One judge, his patience exhausted, had signed the necessary papers, over the objections of Jean's parents, with the warning to Atkinson that if he was wrong, the consequences would be dire indeed.

Before six o'clock Atkinson was out of bed, out of the house and on his way to the barracks. There was no use lying in bed next to his wife, turning, awaking her, listening to her grumble, half asleep. Besides, what if his office phone rang while he wasn't there? Who knew when the autopsy would be performed? Perhaps they were at work already. He had to be there, ready, waiting.

He sat at his desk all morning long, consuming innumerable cups of coffee, wishing that he smoked so that his restless fingers would have something to do. He shuffled papers, got up, sat down, got up, paced, walked to the window, his nerves all but gone.

Precisely at noon his phone rang. Atkinson almost tripped over tangled feet reaching for the instrument. He hesitated only momentarily, praying, then picked up the instrument.

"Atkinson here."

"Atkinson, this is Walters, the County Coroner. I hope I haven't caused you trouble making you wait so long."

"It's okay, doc. What have you found?"

"I couldn't call you before because we had a lot to do on the body. You were right all along. Radiation. Big radiation."

Atkinson almost wept, his shuddering sigh took

almost ten seconds from long inhale to longer exhale.

"Thanks, doc," he managed to say. "I'm not happy about the man's death. Or, maybe I am, that is, if he was what I think. I can't thank you enough. Please keep me posted, doc. Thanks again, and goodbye."

He slammed down the receiver and managed to restrain the heartfelt YIPPEE! straining to tear from his throat. So he was a nut, was he? So he was a maniac, was he? Who's nutty now, who's a maniac now?

"Hoover!" he shouted through the open door. "Get in here!"

The trooper sauntered into Atkinson's office, tired. He was not wearing a normal uniform, but nondescript work clothes; a badge identifying him as an employee of the local electric company was pinned to his windbreaker.

"Yes, sir?"

"The pathologist's report on the dead boy at Cornell will be arriving in the mail in a couple of days," Atkinson said, without crowing. "But I just received a telephone call that told me the gist of it."

"Which was, sir?"

"The gist is that the lung tissue from that dead boy was so radioactive, it did everything but glow in the dark. He died of lung fibrosis, caused by plutonium oxide dust. Any questions?"

Hoover stared. "Did they say it was plutonium oxide dust?" he asked.

"No, they didn't. All the coroner said was great

radioactivity. All I did was put together a lot of information, and don't bet your next month's pay it wasn't plutonium oxide, because you'll lose." Atkinson was almost pugnacious in his elation.

Hoover's tone was most respectful now. "I'm glad you were right, sir. I never doubted you for a minute."

"I know." Atkinson was suddenly very tired. He had proved a point, but that wasn't important. There was still the missing plutonium, and the potential that an atom bomb was being built right under his very nose. *That* was important.

"How's the electrical check coming?" he asked.

"I've covered about two hundred and fifty out of the four hundred on the list, chief," Hoover replied.

Atkinson nodded. "Good. Keep at it. You'll come up with something sooner or later."

"I believe you're right, chief," Hoover said. And for the first time he meant it.

* * *

That same dawn, while Atkinson was messing up the bedclothes, three conspirators were already hard at work in their labs, in the final stages of completing their home-made atom bomb.

Tom had already finished the high explosive lenses, and had X-rayed them for imperfections in the castings. When the job was completed the night before, Tom found 113 good lenses, more than enough to make three bombs. He had already decided to glue the charges on the surface of the

213

tamper, and he told Alexander his thoughts.

The tamper was an inch-and-a-half thick sphere that had been used to protect oceanographic instrumentation. They also had three of these. The areas of the sphere that had been used to pass through electrical leads, and the large port that was used to insert the instruments themselves, had been machined to accept a tapered plug, larger at the outer surface, and tapering to the hole's original diameter at the inside. In this way the implosion pushed the plugs into their tapered slots, allowing a tight seal against neutrons.

The tamper in the original implosion bomb had been made of Uranium-238 because it was such a good neutron barrier, since the purpose of the tamper was to prevent neutrons from escaping the nuclear reaction. The more neutrons properly channeled, forced into participation in the reaction, the more efficient the explosion. Steel was not as dense as the uranium, but Alexander thought it would function quite well.

And now, this was the morning Alexander would finish the process he called "tickling the dragon's tail." He would determine the critical mass of the uranium bomb.

One of the original experiments involved fashioning a nearly critical mass with a hole through it. A machined slug of the same material was dropped through the hole, making it supercritical for just a moment. A variation of the experiment involved bringing two sub-critical hemispheres near each other and measuring the radiation output as they got closer.

As he sat behind his protective concrete block barrier, Alexander reviewed his procedures once more. He had, in his mind, dispensed with the late Dr. Slotkin's experiments, since he knew the critical mass of plutonium to be approximately five kilograms, or about eleven pounds. However, the problems were complicated by the tamper. The better the tamper, the smaller the critical mass. Therefore, *now* the actual size of the nuclear core would have to be determined experimentally, by placing the bomb in the tamper. The thickness of the explosives would also make some difference, but Alexander's calculations told him he could ignore it.

Alexander's own experiments called for him to first fashion hemispheres of different sizes, until he found the mass that was barely subcritical. Then a sphere slightly smaller than this was placed in one half of the tamper, while the other half was slowly lowered on top of it. The instrument probes, located inside the tamper shell, gave an indication of the density. Alexander expected an S-shaped curve of neutron density from which he could "read" the critical mass.

Now the "tickling" began. Alexander had a dozen plutonium hemispheres of varying sizes, and he tried out different combinations. Each time he would put two hemispheres together and drop the assembly in the bottom half of the tamper, he held his breath, hoping that each testing combination would be the last one. He watched on the television screen as he slowly lowered the top half of the tamper by means of a rope and pulley. It was not exactly a sophisticated procedure, but it worked, and he saw no need to complicate matters. The more complex a system, the more things could go wrong with it.

It was dark now. The starred sky was clear, cold, lung-chilling, but inside the lab it was warm and still as Alexander started to lower the tamper top. Even before he had it all the way down, he knew he had it, the critical mass!

The previous sphere had been 7.35 kilograms. This one was 7.50 kilograms. Working from the neutron densities measured from the two spheres, and the table of cross sections of the steel cylinder, Alexander decided that the final core would weigh 7.42 kilograms. He attributed the larger size to impurities in his plutonium.

Alexander arose and rubbed his eyes wearily. Somehow, he felt a kinship with Einstein, Oppenheimer, Slotkin, and all the great scientists who had a hand in fashioning that first murderous atom bomb. No, he felt superior. Think of all the equipment, the facilities, the money, the assistance they'd had, and look what this rag-tag foursome had gone through! Look what they'd accomplished in an incredibly short time. Impossible! It could not be done! But it had been done!

At that point fabricating the final cores was the only obstacle between this small group and their own Day of Trinity. There was still some work to be done, of course. The spheres had to be machined, and the easily-corroded surface had to be replaced with nickel. The original implosion bomb had problems with pitting of its nickel coating, but it hadn't affected the explosion. Alexander figured it would not affect theirs, either. Soon—very, very soon—they would have succeeded in constructing a working, destructive atom bomb.

Entering the final stages, Alexander prepared the crucibles to accept the plutonium that would become the core of the bomb. Using the density of 19.7 grams per cubic centimeter of plutonium, he had determined that the core of his bomb had to be 9.6 centimeters in diameter. He machined a brass sphere that size to be used as a mold for the crucible liner, and he had six crucibles lined and dried in the kiln, each liner retaining the polished smoothness of the spheres. Into the six prepared crucibles, he intended to place about three and three-fourths kilograms of plutonium, which would melt and assume the hemispherical shapes of the crucible liner. The hemispheres would then have their flat surfaces machined smooth on the milling machine to assure a tight fit and bring the combined weight of pairs to exactly 7.42 kilograms.

It was long past midnight when the exhausted Alexander decided to quit for the day. As he walked into the kitchen, he heard Tom and Amhed arguing.

"I say we shouldn't jeopardize the five million. Let's just pack everything and get the hell out of here," Tom was saying.

"Look, we don't even know for sure it came from

my contact," Amhed said. "It might have come from the CIA or some other source." Amhed was lying, but he was also convincing.

"In that case, all the more reason to get the hell out of here," Tom said forcefully.

"What's going on?" Alexander asked.

"Our brave man here wants to chicken out and take everything, and run, without doing any testing, and without bombing Washington," Amhed explained tersely.

"No dice," Alexander was firm. "That's the only reason I agreed to this stupid caper in the first place, and I'm not about to give up now. We can explode our thing soon, and I want one of the explosions to hit Washington. What started this thing in the first place?"

Amhed recapped his activities of the past few days. As usual, he had called his contact to ask for a little more money. His contact had refused, demanding that Amhed give him his address. And Amhed had refused. In the end, Amhed had written a letter, giving a rented post office box as a return address. By return mail, he had received a letter instructing him to ship all materials directly to Damascus, without the Washington blast.

Alexander pondered this bit of news. "Looks like somebody got to him. If so, it means that maybe they're right on our tail, and you can bet they're out trying to find us."

"That's what I think too," Tom said. "So what's our next move?"

Alexander thought for a moment or two longer,

then said, "From now on we use the van as little as possible. We'll have to dispose of it sooner or later so nobody can trace us. For all I know, maybe they've got a start tracing us through Jean's body, I don't know. But I agree with Tom, we've got to finish up and cut out, quick. I can be ready to leave in a couple of days at the most. Any problems?"

"How about Washington?" Amhed asked.

"We bomb it," Alexander said with finality. "Tell that to your contact."

"I'll tell him," Amhed grinned, "but he won't like it."

Amhed couldn't have cared less.

CHAPTER FOURTEEN

Abu Amani opened the plain white envelope and withdrew the sheet of paper within. He recognized it as his own stationary instantly. It was the letter he had sent to Amhed, ordering him not to detonate the bomb in the United States. At the bottom of his neatly typed letter, which he had mailed to a post office box in Ithaca, was a reply scrawled with a red felt-tipped marker pen. He recognized Amhed's handwriting. The note read:

"No way! Will continue my academic progress as I have previously reported it. See you in Damascus. Signed, Your Nephew."

Amani promptly put in an overseas call to Yesseh. "My nephew is hard-headed," he said. "He insists on doing things as originally planned. Please advise me."

Yesseh was agitated. He knew that Amani's phone was tapped by the FBI, and now he had a suspicion that his phones were tapped too, probably by the CIA, and not impossibly by the Egyptian GIA and the Russian KGB. By Allah, was there anyone in the world who *didn't* know about the bomb being built in the United States? No doubt the Israelis had gotten wind of it too.

"I will get back to you as soon as possible," he told Amani. "I shall see what can be done from this end."

He broke the connection, sat back and began to wring his hands. Then he took a deep breath. He was, he thought, acting like an Egyptian rather than a Palestinian. Those Egyptians could never do anything right by themselves. The Israelis, as much as he detested them, were able to build their own arms, some of their own planes, and could even build a nuclear weapon, which they would do sooner or later, despite the deterring efforts of the Russians, and sometimes even the Americans. But those fumble-fingered Arab Egyptians? Nothing!

He recalled the show put on by their armed forces during Farouk's corrupt reign, and that was all it was, a show. The forces Nasser tried to build were likewise paper armies, equipped with the best hardware the Russians could provide but unable to make them function. Oh, those Egyptian generals talked big, and were as proud of their Russian tanks and MIG jets as a child was proud of his first two-wheeler bicycle. But, eventually the child learned to ride his bike because he had the motivation and the courage to get up after a spill. The Egyptians couldn't seem to learn anything. Even though they improved somewhat under Sadat, it was still the Russian "advisors" who had to pilot the planes and aim the missiles. How natural that the Egyptians had to call on four American college students to furnish the Fedayeen with an atom bomb!

Then Yesseh knew what he had to do. He left his office, rode down in the elevator, went out into the street and walked until he found a pay phone in the lobby of an old office building, one he knew was not tapped. After all, those damned foreign agents couldn't tap every telephone in Damascus, could they? Even he didn't know which phone he would use until he found this one.

He placed a call to Abdul Samir, the PLO minister who had disposed of his secretary, and asked to be picked up in the limousine. In less than half an hour he was sitting beside Samir.

"What can I do?" Yesseh implored after he had explained the situation. "I am not as experienced at this as you are. Obviously, we want the bombs intact, but I fear what will most assuredly happen if they succeed in their plans."

Abdul Samir had known Yesseh for a long time, even before the disaster of 1967, after which the idea of building the bomb had been brought up. He had taken Yesseh's money gladly, and been overjoyed at the idea of financing a nuclear weapon. But in his heart, Samir had nothing but contempt for this frightened weakling. Yesseh feared for his business more than anything else.

And yet, was he any worse than the top leaders of the PLO? No, not really.

Once, before they had gained a measure of respect, the PLO had been a daring, fanatic group, bound together by a common hatred of Israel, dedicated to action regardless of the cost. Now, the organization was concerned only with the idea of obtaining power and wealth for each individual at the top. They had forgotten about the ideal—to regain a country for the Palestinian people.

What had they become, these PLO leaders? Petty politicians, nothing more. Since being admitted as an observer at the United Nations— that rectangular blob on First Avenue in New York, that quagmire of useless windbags and diplomatic paraplegics, whose idiotic pomp and circumstances were an insult to decent citizens of the world—since being admitted, the PLO leaders had gradually moderated their stand. Now they lusted after the acceptance, which would bring them personal riches, personal prestige, personal power. They moderated until, Samir thought, they were no better than the Jews. Sure, the Jews moderated, negotiated, but at least they had the balls to fight. Negotiations alone were a weak man's game, which was why Samir liked working with the project to obtain nuclear weapons. But now, although they didn't want anyone to know it, there was a chance that, in their rush to moderation, if the weak ones in the U.N. had their way, the bomb might not even be used against Israel.

Still, the nuclear bomb was there now. But what to do with it? The thought of turning over the weapon to a jellyfish like Arafat was too much, too much! However, even as a double-pronged idea was building in his mind, Samir knew he had to exercise caution. The time would come, and very soon, when he would transfer as much of the PLO funds as possible to his own personal accounts, and to those of the more radical Black September Group. In the meantime, he had to play his cards close to the burnoose. It would involve a few harmless lies to Yesseh, but that was of no consequence whatever.

"I think I can help you with the problem," he said to Yesseh as the limousine purred along. "Understand, we would not want to damage our observer status at the United Nations."

"We must locate those bomb builders and stop them," Yesseh said urgently.

"Have they been told they will receive no money if their bomb is exploded in the United States?" Samir asked.

"Of course. They were *ordered* not to explode the bomb there."

Ah, thought Samir, this was a group after his own heart. Zealots, like himself. But he must not let on to this frightened businessman, sweating in spite of the limousine's air conditioning, that he, Abdul Samir, *wanted* the bomb exploded in the United States, needed that, his very soul demanded it! No, he must play along. For now.

"You say Amani does not know where they are. Is it possible to trace them somehow?" Samir nudged his friend.

Yesseh thought in silence for several minutes. "Perhaps there might be a way," he said slowly. "When this group accepted the challenge to build the bomb, Amani said they needed a method of paying for incidentals, such as restaurant meals, gasoline, incidentals. I sent him an American Express card, issued to a fictitious employee of my company. Perhaps their path can be traced by the notations on their charge slips." He gave Samir the name in which the fictitious card had been issued, and the name of an associate of his at American Express who would cooperate fully.

"My friend, I doubt that anything except death can stop this group from exploding the bomb in the United States. Therefore, I shall give you the name and address of a man who can be of service to you in that regard. He is called Muhammed Khaddam. Tell him what you have told me. Mention my name. Introduce him to your associate at American Express. His fee will be moderate, considering the task he must perform." Samir wrote rapidly on a piece of paper and passed it to Yesseh.

He dropped the businessman near a taxi stand and left him to find his own method of communicating with the hired thug named Muhammed Khaddam. Let him think that mediocre hired thug could stop the college group from carrying out their plan. In a little while he would make another

225

telephone, to make sure that they *would* carry out their plan to bomb America.

*   *   *

Alexander used the remainder of the argon gas to fill the induction furnace for melting the plutonium into hemispheres of the right size. By ten o'clock in the morning he took the first of the hemispheres out of the furnace. In the lathe, he took off layer after layer of the flat surface until the hemisphere was exactly the right weight. He repeated the process five times more, so that when dusk fell all of them had been machined. He placed the hemispheres in separate battery jars, each filled with aqueous nickel salt solution. The hemispheres were placed flat side up on a tiny wire stand, which supported the round surface and also served as the electrode. The plating process would take several hours, and Alexander turned on the DC current, setting the timer for nine hours. He then offered to help Tom with the process of securing the explosive lenses to the tamper sphere, but Tom was nearly finished.

For all intents and purposes, the atomic weapons had been constructed!

*   *   *

The phone on Lieutenant Leslie Atkinson's desk rang. Almost absently he picked it up.

"Atkinson here," he said into the mouthpiece.

"Les, this is Rusty Liss." Atkinson recognized the voice at once. It belonged to an old Marine Corps buddy, now an FBI agent in Connecticut.

"Rusty, you old S.O.B.," Atkinson laughed. "Good to hear your voice again. It's been a couple of years. What can I do for you?"

"I need a favor, Les," said the agent. "You can save us a lot of time and trouble if we don't have to go through channels. I need the ID registration of a license plate number, which seems to be in your area. Can do?"

"Sure," Atkinson pretended to be miffed, "but how come you only call me when you need a favor? Okay, let's have the plate number." He wrote down the license plate ID, which he knew had been issued in Tompkins County.

"I'll have it for you in two shakes, Rusty," Atkinson said, waving in one of his troopers and asking for the make quickly. "Meanwhile, mind telling me what it's about, or is it classified?"

Atkinson listened with increasing interest and excitement as his friend told him how the number had been found on the desk of an explosives expert, now fleeing from charges of having stolen a quantity of very potent high explosives.

"A ton of the stuff!" Atkinson exclaimed. "That's enough to blow us to hell and back!"

Even before he told the Connecticut agent the name and address of the registered owner of the vehicle with that license number, Atkinson's mind was already in high gear. Where had he heard of pentolite before? Back in the corps, yes, but more recently than that. Then it hit him.

"Look, Rusty, I've got something important to do right now. I'll have the trooper in charge of DMV give you the number. Won't take more than another minute or two. Just hang on." Atkinson was already out of his chair.

"I'll be back in an hour," he told the trooper manning the desk. "If anyone calls, take the message. And have that license number make called in to the guy that's waiting on my line." He had his jacket half on when he strode down the hall and into the biting air. Half an hour later, he knew where he had heard of pentolite.

From the shelves of his snug den, Atkinson pulled first one book and then another, hastily leafing through each one before he found what he was looking for. Actually, it wasn't a book; its cover was a yellow title sheet, with another yellow sheet on the back, a series of photocopied sheets stapled together.

The information was on page 224 of *The Manhattan Project History, Project Y, The Los Alamos Project.*

Although "Composition B" was the most commonly used explosive in the first implosion bombs, others were experimented with, including torpex, *pentolite*, baronal and baratol. Evidently the conspirators had selected pentolite, since there was not a great deal of difference between it and Composition B, only they had a supplier for pentolite.

Returning to the station, Atkinson asked who

that vehicle was registered to, the one that had been requested by the Connecticut FBI agent.

"Alexander Greely, Junior," he was told.

"Oh, dear God!" Atkinson choked. It was the son of the guy who'd been knocked off in the plutonium highjacking! The circle had come full swing.

*   *   *

Amhed arrived back at the farm with a crated desk he had purchased at an office furnishings store on State Street in Ithaca. He found that Tom and Alexander had finished the final assembly of two halves of the bombs.

They wrestled the desk out of the truck and removed it from the crate. In the outer lab they used the crate as a repository for a bomb's components: the bomb itself, the firing device and the batteries that would power it, the timing device that would make it an atomic time bomb. The sheath of wires, thirty six of them, each with two plugs on the end, lay bundled at the bottom of the crate. The detonators would not be placed in the explosive lenses until just before they were ready to fire it.

The assembly in the crate took little time, since all the components were already assembled, and only needed to be fastened to the pallet under the crate and plugged in. The other bomb was already assembled on another pallet, and would simply be covered with a tarp in the back of the truck.

The truck itself, and the police's ability to trace them through it would prove no problem, they thought. It would be vaporized by the atomic blast emanating from within it.

The van was driven into the ceramics shop, and with the aid of the chain hoist, they manhandled the two 3,000 pound bombs into the rear. Around them they packed their clothes, tools needed for adjustments and repairs, and lastly, the makings of a third bomb which was packed in a wooden box they had built for that purpose. It contained forty-two high explosive lenses, core material, a tamper, a firing device, detonator and timer, and the blueprints and technical material they had used. The box would be shipped to a Morocco address.

They finished before nine o'clock, and decided to take turns guarding the old van with the sagging springs. Before daylight they would pull out and head for the Adirondacks, stopping only long enough to pick up another rented van for their getaway.

Tom took the first watch. Alexander and Amhed went to bed.

*   *   *

As Alexander and Amhed were sacking out, Lieutenant Leslie Atkinson was knocking at the door of the widow Greely in Ludlowville. She saw the police uniform and cringed.

"Something wrong, officer?" she asked tremulously. "Another accident?"

"No, Mrs. Greely," Atkinson said politely. "May I speak with your son?"

"He isn't here," responded the woman. "Why do you want him? Is he in trouble?"

"I don't know yet. I'd like to ask him some questions. Have you any idea when he'll be home?"

"He doesn't live here," Mrs. Greely told him. "He rented a farm somewhere outside Ithaca, but he never told me exactly where. You know how boys are when they reach that age. Always so secretive."

"Does your son own a 1969 white Ford van?"

"Yes, he does. Was it stolen? Is my son in trouble? Please tell me, officer." Mrs. Greely was getting worried.

Atkinson grimaced inwardly. Trouble? I'll bet a year's pay that sonofabitch son of yours is helping to build an atom bomb! Is that trouble enough for you?

But all he did say was, "If your son contacts you, will you have him call me at this number. Or, you can call me." He wrote down the office telephone number and left.

Now what, he thought as he drove back. Put out an APB for the car? On what grounds? The license number on that white van had been found in the office of a man who was fleeing because he had stolen some explosives. But that didn't mean Greely Junior was involved in the theft, although Atkinson was dead sure he was connected somehow. But he had no proof, nothing tangible.

Where was that Ithaca farm? There were a

hundred farms outside Ithaca, one not much different from another.

Wait! Greely Junior's farm *might* be different. If it was using more electricity than a normal farm would use, it sure as hell *was* different.

Back at the office he dialed Trooper Hoover's number. No answer. Damn, he was probably out bowling and drinking beer with the boys, or on a date, or in a movie. No way to find him now. He'd have to wait until Hoover reported in at work in the morning. Atkinson resolved to be there when Hoover walked in.

He phoned his wife and told her he wouldn't be home that night, but if something came up she could reach him at the office. He took a canvas folding cot from the closet, a blanket from the shelf, opened the cot and lay down. He was tired, but couldn't fall asleep. And morning seemed a long time away.

CHAPTER FIFTEEN

The drone of the turbine engines of the L-1011 and the rushing of air past its metal skin were the white noise that sleep was made of, and Hamid Saad wavered alternately between a half sleep and an excited awareness of the body of the Air France stewardess. She was demure compared with the woman he had just left at the Carlton Hotel in Cannes, but attractive enough to be exciting. As he asked her for another glass of white wine, and she smiled prettily while serving it, Hamid's mind drifted over the past twenty-four hours.

There had been that girl he met at the Carlton bar, young, voluptuous, jet-haired, a Lolita who would have driven Nabokov to the brink. Dinner, a few drinks, and he could see that the passion in her eyes matched his own. He steered her to his suite, past the discreet concierge, who, although he was past sixty, looked at Hamid with undisguised envy.

Then came the telephone call. Why, oh why, had he told Abdul Samir where he was staying? Well, of course there was every reason to tell Abdul Samir whatever he wanted to know. Hamid Saad, one of the youngest, most expert assassins in the Middle East was in the direct employ of Abdul Samir. Considering how much he was paid every month, whether he killed anyone or not, Hamid was only too willing to tell where he was going on a brief vacation.

Hamid was about to fall asleep when the telephone rang; once, twice, three times. The vixen at his side stirred. Hamid reached for the instrument reluctantly.

"Yes...?"

"Hamid? This is Abdul Samir. I have an assignment of the utmost urgency for you. You are to leave immediately for the United States."

Swiftly, Samir briefed Hamid. There was a group in the United States building an atom bomb for the PLO. They wanted to use it against the United States. Those who had put up the money for the bomb were chickening out, and did not want the bomb used against the United States. But he, Abdul Samir, wanted what the bomb builders wanted. To placate the financial backers, he had given them the name of a clumsy killer he sometimes used when no one else was available, one Muhammed Khaddan. Hamid was to intercept

Khaddan, and, if necessary, kill him. Muhammed Khaddan would attempt to track down the bomb builders via their American Express card, issued to a fictitious employee of the Syroco Company. All Hamid had to do was follow that dolt Khaddan, who would undoubtedly find the group before too long.

Silently, Hamid had dressed, packed his bag, left the suite and paid his bill downstairs, with instructions to awaken the lady in his suite in the morning, serve her breakfast in bed and send her on her way. Oh, yes, and be sure to give her his undying love.

He drove his rented car to Nice, where he caught the first plane for Paris, then on to Kennedy Airport in New York. Once there he would visit his gunsmith—he had them in various cities throughout the world, since he could no longer smuggle weapons through customs now—pick up suitable hardware, find Khaddan, and let nature take its course. Nothing he couldn't handle, routine, really.

He finished the wine and handed the plastic glass back to the stewardess. A pity, he thought. Nice girl. If only he had the time—but he didn't.

Half an hour later, the huge jet lowered its wheels and glided onto the runway.

*   *   *

As the Air France L-1011 was taxiing toward the terminal at JFK Airport, a white Ford van turned left onto Route 28 in the Adirondack foothills town of Forestport, about twenty miles north of Utica. They had been traveling for well over three hours, heading for their destination, Lake Placid, the Adirondack Mountain community whose overpriced resorts, surly merchants and lack of courtesy were nearly as legendary as its Winter Olympics fame.

Route 28 wound its serpentine way through ski resorts, mountain lakes and dense forests, interspersed with the vacation homes of millionaires and the hunting shacks of those cursed with being merely middle class. For sixty miles more it wrapped its way around peaks, and towns called Raquette Lake, Big Moose and Thendara. Finally, at Blue Mountain Lake, a town even smaller than Forestport, they turned onto Route 30. The bright sunlight made the white layer of snow on the ground glow like fire, and even through dark glasses Alexander squinted. Beside him, Amhed slept; Tom was perched on a pile of clothes in the back.

The tedious drive continued, onto Route 3 which took them into Saranac Lake, then Route 86. Along the way, they had stopped to rent another van, and then, turning off onto a side road, had stopped to manhandle everything out of Alexander's van except for the single atom bomb which would be exploded. The load was now more evenly distributed between the two vans.

Finally they reached Lake Placid, and both vans crept through the glut of cars jamming the narrow main street. Alexander sneered. All those people who had fled New York City to get away from traffic must be right at home here. At the traffic light in front of the old ice skating pavillion they made a right turn and moved up the steep incline in first gear to the Holiday Inn. While Alexander and Tom parked the vans, Amhed checked them into three rooms he had reserved with the Syroco credit card.

Alexander helped Amhed take the clothes into their rooms, while Tom, behind the closed doors of the white van, set about arming both bombs. He insisted on doing it alone; it would only take him about an hour or so. By the time he finished, it was nearly dark, and he looked with satisfaction at the monster he had just armed. The explosive lenses looked like deformed breasts, the conical shapes pointing out in all directions, each one with two nipples sticking out of it. The wiring harness snaked its way from the firing device, dividing like a Hydra's head into 36 wires, which led to the twin detonators of high explosives.

After supper they headed out of town in the two-van convoy. Fortunately, there had not been too much snow the past few days, and the road up Moose Mountain was passable most of the way. When they were unable to go higher, Tom turned the white van off the road, jounced it fifty yards into the brush, and turned it over to Amhed.

The entire firing device was to be powered by nine automobile batteries connected in parallel. The voltage was converted by a vibrator, transformers, rectifiers and filters into the high voltage DC needed to charge the capacitors that would fire the detonators. Amhed tightened all the connectors and checked the neon lights to see that the capacitor bank was charged. He set the timer for eleven o'clock that night and left the truck. He closed and locked the doors and turned a key under the rear bumper. The key activated microswitches in the doors, which would detonate the bomb if the doors were opened. The group wanted to take no chances on some stray, nosey passerby foiling the blast.

Hands numb with cold, Amhed joined his two comrades in the rented van and they drove back to the Inn. They figured, if the blast went off, most of the windows in town would be shattered, but not much more damage than that. As for casualties— well, they were not concerned with that. Stupid American pigs! Who cared? They intended to watch the happenings through multiple layers of welders' lenses.

Reaching the Inn, they retired to the game room, and killed some time playing the pinball machines.

*   *   *

Lieutenant Leslie Atkinson had managed only a handful of winks when Trooper Hoover reported for work in the morning. He rubbed the bleariness from his eyes and called the young policeman into his office.

"Hoover, were any of those addresses on your

high voltage list for a farm or a barn?" he asked.

Hoover nodded. "Sure. I mean, for a farm. I don't recall a farm and a barn together. But I haven't checked them all. That's a big list, sir."

He showed the list to Atkinson, who looked at it briefly. The ceramics studio nearly leaped out at him. It fit! A farm in Slaterville, out in the boondocks, not far from Ithaca. It had to be there.

Half an hour later, Atkinson saw how right he had been all along. He and Hoover, both in unmarked patrol cars, and accompanied by two additional cars each with three troopers, drove out to the farm. One car drove around the house, another stopped at the exit road to block it while Hoover and Atkinson pulled into the driveway. The house was obviously empty. Atkinson and Hoover walked over to the barn. It was padlocked.

"Cut through the wood and take that lock off," Atkinson ordered. "I'll take full responsibility."

Using a hammer and screwdriver, one of the troopers chipped through the wood surrounding the lock. It took almost twenty minutes. They swung the barn doors open and went inside.

It looked like a ceramics shop, all right, with the kilns and the samples of pottery. They walked around to the rear of the barn forced open the rear doors and were confronted with a wall of hay bales. Atkinson pondered them for a moment; something about the setup bothered him, but he couldn't put his finger on it.

"Tear down those bales," he ordered. Fifteen minutes later, they found that the wall was only two bales thick. They went inside.

And there was the laboratory!

"Hoover, get the geiger counter," he said. The young trooper returned from the patrol car, and as the instrument warmed up he yelled out.

"Lieutenant, I wouldn't stay here too long. Just about every part of this place is hot. They must have spread the stuff all over."

Atkinson thought, if that's the oxide, we're all in trouble. He ordered everyone out, took a camera from one of the cars and snapped several pictures. The rest of the investigation would have to be carried out by those competent to deal with radioactivity.

He assigned one car to guard duty and drove off back to the barracks, then telephoned his FBI friend in Connecticut.

"Good Lord," breathed the agent, "I didn't expect you to find all that. Any explosives left?"

"Not much, but some," said Atkinson. They must have used most of it for their bomb. Rusty, call Washington on this. The FBI and AEC have a cooperative system to deal with this kind of situation." He gave his friend the proper numbers and hung up.

He leaned back wearily in his chair, and now he knew, for the first time in months, that he would be able to fall asleep. But it was all so stupid, so heart-breakingly stupid. The FBI had given him a royal run-around, the Atomic Energy Commission had been politely condescending, everybody thought he was some kind of a nut, a hick cop out in the sticks who needed help to tie his shoelaces.

He folded his arms on the desk to make a pillow, put his head down and closed his eyes, gave out one long, shuddering sigh and was asleep.

Trooper Hoover walked into the office, saw his chief was out like a light, shook his head, smiled affectionately, and softly closed the door.

*　　*　　*

The meeting that night at the White House was tense. The men argued, tossing the blame about like a medicine ball. Finally the President of the United States restored order.

"Gentlemen," he spoke firmly, "you have all put forward your best efforts. But it wasn't good enough. Had it not been for the stubborn deter-mination of a New York State officer named Leslie Atkinson, we would not have progressed this far. Now we must capture those people, and if we have to step on a few civil rights to do that, so be it. What is at stake may be the lives of hundreds, possibly thousands. We will waste no further time arguing. I want action, and I want it immediately!

"This meeting is adjourned."

*　　*　　*

Snow had started to fall heavily. The three men stood in the bitter cold, up on the hill near the Holiday Inn, looking down at the town, and across at the hill they knew would light up brighter than the sun. They were behind a row of cars, ready to duck down at the first stab of light, which would be followed by the shock wave. Each glanced nervously at his own watch, following the ticking second hand as it languished its way around the dial.

Eleven o'clock; nothing. Another minute; nothing; five minutes, then ten; nothing.

Ahmed spoke softly, the words spilling out in white wisps. "Shit! Shit! Shit! Shit!"

Even in the darkness he could sense, even see the expressions of disappointment on the faces of Tom and Alexander.

"It has to be the detonator firing mechanism," Amhed said. "Had it worked, at least the high explosives would have been set off. It's my fault, my fault! I must go and fix it."

He started to move away, but Tom reached out a hand and restrained him.

"Not now," he said. "Tomorrow. You're tired now. You could screw it up for good. Tomorrow."

Amhed nodded. The three men walked down the hill and back to the Inn. Amhed kept repeating, "Shit! Shit! Shit! Shit!"

CHAPTER SIXTEEN

The Tudor Hotel on East 42nd Street in Manhattan was a far cry from the Carlton, Hamid thought, as he drove the new rented Caprice across the Tappan Zee Bridge, some twenty-five miles north of the modest brick hotel. He had slept well, breakfasted early, paid cash for meals and lodging, then went upstairs to check the arsenal he had picked up the night before.

He loaded the .44 magnum handgun with hollow point cartridges and screwed the silencer onto the barrel threads. What resulted looked like a miniature cannon, and would be about as effective. The hollow point slugs would explode on impact and completely mess up whatever they hit. The silencer would effectively muffle the roar of the heavy bore weapon.

Hamid closed the blue suitcase containing three other weapons; including a folding rifle with scope, and an assortment of incendiary explosives, garrotes, poisons, and other instruments of violence. They were the tools of his trade, he had been trained to use them, first as a soldier in the Iranian army, later as an officer in the fierce, sadistic secret police of the Shah, and now as a mercenary, employed by one of the more militant splinter groups. And there was no doubt in his mind, or in the minds of everyone whose paths he had crossed, that Hamid Saad was the best.

But now, as Toll Route 87 turned north around the western border of Harriman State Park, Hamid was concerned with *saving* lives. He had to find those bomb builders as soon as possible, for their own safety, because another hired killer was loose, stalking them.

Hamid had arrived in New York too late to pick up Muhammed Khaddan's trail; he had already left on his mission. But Hamid got all the necessary information from the contact at American Express, who, while puzzled as to why he had to give the same information to two different people, nevertheless did as bidden.

According to the latest information, two slips had very recently been signed at the Adirondack village of Lake Placid, both bearing the name of the Syroco employee. Well, that was where they were staying, at the Holiday Inn. To check, he called the Inn just before leaving the hotel to see if they were still registered. They were. The trip from

New York to Lake Placid was about three hundred miles, which would put him there by late afternoon.

*   *   *

By the time Hamid had reached the Tappan Zee Bridge, the three conspirators had reached the foot of the road that climbed Moose Mountain, where they had parked the van, only to find it impassable due to the heavy snow of the night before. Hastily they drove back down and into town, where, at a Texaco station on Route 86 they could rent a couple of snowmobiles. Again Amhed used his credit card, and soon they were going back up the mountain, their tools in bags strapped to the vehicles. The noise they made sounded like a chain saw gone berserk, but they made it up the slopes and soon were at the van, almost invisible in the snow drifts. Amhed turned off the booby trap switches, then unlocked the rear doors and stepped in.

Tom watched through the windows as Amhed tinkered and prodded the electric circuits. A half hour later, Amhed poked his head out, all smiles.

"Know what the trouble was? The timer froze in the cold. Nothing wrong with the rig," he said proudly. "It was twenty below, and the lubricant in the mechanism got hard as parrafin. It shut off about ten o'clock. All we have to do is keep the engine running so the van stays warm enough."

They checked the gas tank. It was nearly full.

Just idling, the engine would run for hours. They cleared the snow from the tail pipe, re-set the timer, started the engine, turned on the heater and took off. The exhausts of the two-cylinder engines drowned out the gurgle of the vans as they sledded down. They ate a late lunch.

*　　*　　*

Abu Amani left his apartment to attend a meeting at the United Nations. He never made it. Waiting for him in the underground garage where he parked his car were two burly special ops from the CIA—part of the section Coleman referred to as "animals." Too late he felt his arms pinned, too late he saw the white gauze pad smothering his nose, saturated with ether. He was unconscious in half a minute.

Eight hours later; four of those hours spent stripped naked in a tub of ice water; two hours in a bin of human excrement; two hours more in that same bin with electrodes clipped to his genitals and nipples; Amani told them the name of his contact in Ithaca as far as he knew it, the name on the American Express card he had been given. He begged for mercy.

One of the special ops shot him in the back of the head and watched him sink into the brown ooze. Ooze that would be dumped by the city, along with a veritable mountain of other sludge, far out in the Atlantic Ocean.

*   *   *

That same afternoon, while Hamid Saad was speeding north toward Lake Placid, while the bombers were re-setting firing circuits, while Abu Amani was in a tub of excrement, a Beechcraft Bonanza came in for a smooth landing on the Yucatan Peninsula to take on fuel for the last leg of a flight to Costa Rica. The bill was paid in most welcome American dollars.

Eric Hoskins was home free.

*   *   *

Another plane, a commercial jet, was just lifting off from Washington, D.C. Aboard was FBI Chief Hawkins. He had just left the Attorney General, who had told the top agent that he had simply made legal all the President's instructions. In an attache case was material which the President of the United States had ordered him to show to an obscure lieutenant in the New York State Troopers, the man who had been able to bust open the case where the FBI and the CIA had failed. Perhaps, to another man, it would have been galling. In his heart Chief Hawkins knew it was only right and proper.

*   *   *

The afternoon had passed slowly for the conspirators as they waited for their second try with the bomb. Would it simply be a high explosive burst with no nuclear reaction, or would it be enough to convince the United States and the world that the PLO was a force to be respected, to be reckoned with?

The sky had grown dark with the winter sun, and the snow-laden clouds had gathered again, to the delight of the skiers. Hamid watched the three men walk up the hill from the main street. His attention was focused on them. In a few seconds it would not be.

As the three men reached the doors at the entrance to the left of the three-story motel, a hand steadied itself on the roof of a nearby auto; the hand gripped a large bore handgun with silencer, similar to the one carried by Hamid. The hand was cold from lack of a glove, but the feel of flesh against the steel trigger added precision. Tom had reached for the aluminum crossbar of the door and pulled it open. He stepped in, followed by Alexander. Amhed reached for the door.

The hand holding the gun tightened the grip and the index finger squeezed the trigger. The faint click of the firing pin striking the center of the cartridge was lost in the barely louder sputting sound as the silenced bullet erupted from the muzzle. It was doubtful that Amhed heard the muffled sound, and if he did, it was the last thing he ever heard. The hollow core slug of lead made a round hole behind his left ear, disintegrated and fanned out as it passed through Amhed's thoughts. A terrible fireball of white pain filled his head, and perhaps he thought he heard music as a small fragment stimulated the appropriate synapses. Another fragment produced the memories recorded in his pre-natal days, until now hidden in deep, unremembered places. A feeling of returning to the womb, of inky blackness and then a bottomless void, and then—nothing.

Tom had reacted reflexively when he saw Amhed fall, saw the horror of the spreading wound in his skull. Alexander had watched numbly. But Hamid acted with stunning swiftness.

He had heard the soft sound of the gun firing, spotted its source. He raised the .44 magnum, and, holding it with both hands, sighted down the barrel and squeezed off three rounds in rapid succession. The barrel leaped upward slightly with each report of the silenced bullets, and the slugs ripped through the neck of Muhammed Khaddam, the impact threw him against the hood of the car behind him, his gun clattering to the ground.

Hamid had been watching them all day long. And he had grown careless. Perhaps it had been the ball-numbing cold, which he was unaccustomed to, or the importance of his mission, or his contempt for Khaddam, whom he knew to be a clod of no importance. He would have to explain that to Abdul Samir, but he knew he could.

Stuffing the handgun inside his belt, knowing his shots had found their mark, Hamid sprinted toward the door through which Tom and Alexan-

249

der had entered. He stepped over the body of Amhed and raced inside. Tom rose to fight him, but stopped when Hamid stood still and held out his empty hands.

"Quiet!" Hamid hissed, thankful that no one was around besides this pair. "I just saved your lives. Let's get to your room before somebody finds us."

Hamid extended his hands to Alexander and Tom, both of whom shook gladly, and they went up to Tom's room.

When the door was closed and locked, Tom asked, "What the hell happened? Who the hell are you?"

"I am Hamid Saad," he said, "and I have been sent here to look after your health. Judging from what just happened, I am needed. The man who killed your companion was sent by the group offering the prize for your bomb. He was ordered to stop you from exploding the bomb in the United States. Although I have no proof of what I am about to say, it is not impossible that he would have killed you, delivered the second bomb himself, and collected the entire prize for himself." The last was a lie, but Hamid was expert at mixing truth with falsehood in just the right proportion to make his words sound convincing.

"How did you find us?" Tom demanded to know.

"Your companion's credit card," Hamid replied. "He left quite a trail. How do you think I found you? How do you think that assassin found you? And how long do you think it will be before others—the American authorities, specifically—find you?"

Alexander and Tom were taken aback. "What do we do now?" Alexander managed to get out.

"How far along are you? Why are you here?" Hamid asked. Tom explained about the test bomb cached on the mountain overlooking the village, and the time it would detonate.

"We must leave this place at once," Hamid instructed. "Gather up everything you have and follow me. In a few minutes the Inn will be crawling with cops."

Five minutes had passed since the shootings. Tom and Alexander grabbed their suitcases and left their rooms, just as a guest discovered Amhed's body. The guest was on the telephone in the lobby, calling the police when Tom, Alexander and Hamid walked out of the Inn. Tom and Alexander got into the rented van and drove off, following Hamid. They went northeast on Route 86 until they came to the toll road that wound its way to the top of White Face Mountain, about forty miles from Moose Mountain by road, but only five miles as the crow—or shock wave—flies. The snow was melting on the salted and sanded road as they pulled off on the side of the road at the top and parked.

At this point, the last two hundred feet of the peak shielded them from Moose Mountain and would protect their vehicles. They trudged up the slope and took the elevator to the summit, 4,867 feet above sea level. Below, to the southwest,

Mirror Lake and Lake Placid reflected the lights of the towns which glimmered like stars in the valley. There were few lights on Moose Mountain itself, directly to the west.

There were about a dozen other people on the summit, but they were couples, wrapped up in each other, and they paid no attention to the three men.

The shooting had occurred at 9:38 p.m. and it had taken them forty-five minutes to make the drive up the mountain. The approximate half hour they spent on the summit was made interminably long by the intense cold and the wind raging at that altitude. The snow had subsided, and the clouds had lifted somewhat.

Five cops from the Lake Placid police department and half a dozen state troopers looked at the two bodies and scratched their heads. The eleven law enforcement officers, and five times that many onlookers, were speculating over what had happened when their heads were turned by an eruption of light, like the rising of a hundred suns, coming from the northwest.

CHAPTER SEVENTEEN

The huge fireball momentarily looked like a giant luminous brain, covered with convolutions, and then grew into a mammoth glowing giant in the night. The fireball turned reddish-yellow and then blood red. The hues of the monster were of every variety, and like a garbled spectrum, glowed an eerie yellow-green-peach-purple-violet, erupting like an insane display of fireworks, only far, far more deadly. It was beautiful nature run amok.

Seconds later, the shockwave bowled over the townspeople who watched with furtive glances through slits between their fingers, fighting the pain of a light whiter and brighter than any they had ever known. The next day, hospitals in Plattsburgh, in Burlington, and in numerous small communities would resound with the kind of stories not heard since Hiroshima and Nagasaki.

Most of the initial victims were from rural areas outside Lake Placid who lived in widely separated homes in the hollows. Most of the injuries in town included blindness—temporary and permanent—for those who looked directly at the fireball, or were cut by flying shards of glass. And there were the self-inflicted wounds: a woman on Canandaigua Street, convinced that World War III had started, pointed a pistol at her head and pulled the trigger. The .22 caliber slug missed a vital spot and she would recover. There were suicides: one person jumped from the top of White Face Mountain to an instant death, screaming hysterically about the end of the world. There were accidents: a skier, zooming down a slope full tilt, his attention distracted, rammed a tree and died of a fractured skull.

Before the explosion had pushed its flaming gasses to their apogee, three of the spectators, smiles of savage satisfaction on their faces, took the elevator back to road level and drove away, over Route 9N to Keeseville where they caught Interstate 87, and then they sped on for six hours, stopping once for food and gas in Albany. They reached Manhattan early that morning, checked into a downtown hotel, retired to their rooms and slept most of the day of February 14th.

It was 11:30 p.m., a half hour after the blast when the President of the United States learned what had happened. By midnight he was presiding over an emergency meeting with the Joint

Chiefs of Staff, his Cabinet, and the Chief of the CIA. The head of the FBI had already been called in central New York State, with the instructions that he return to Washington instantly, and bring with him the police lieutenant named Leslie Atkinson.

"So it has happened," said the President, his voice strained. "An atomic device has been exploded on American soil. How ironic! We have prepared all these years against a massive nuclear attack, and have ourselves stockpiled an immense strike force, but now we stand mute, stunned, helpless, because we do not know where to strike back. All our plans, all our missiles, are useless.

"I have talked with the Soviet and Chinese premiers a few minutes ago. Both have assured me it was not their bomb, a fact I already knew. Both have offered whatever assistance we need in tracking down the culprits. We know who the bombers are—a small group who intened to collect a reward for turning over the bomb to terrorists in the Middle East. Unfortunately, we do not know *where* they are."

"I can't understand it," said the Secretary of State. "Why should they have exploded a valuable part of their arsenal here? Why didn't they save everything for use against the Israelis? It doesn't make sense."

"Terrorists are at their most effective when they make no sense," said the President. "Senseless killings are their most powerful psychological weapon."

"We know that one of the people involved is a Cornell University student named Amhed Ismael," offered Coleman of the CIA. His goons had elicited that information from the late Abu Amani.

"And Mr. Hawkins has informed me that another member of the gang has been identified," said the President. "His name is Alexander Greely, Junior, the son of the truck driver who was murdered when that plutonium was highjacked last November. He was traced through the death of another conspirator, an immigrant from Haiti, named Jean Lafayette, who died from inhaling some of the material the group was working with. It seems that a Lieutenant Leslie Atkinson of the New York State Police at Ithaca, uncovered the bomb factory. I should add that Lieutenant Atkinson had been pestering practically the entire federal government about this matter for months, but no one would listen to him. He was put down as a crackpot. Mr. Atkinson is being brought down to Washington. He should be in transit now."

The meeting continued for seven hours. A nuclear strike at Syria, from which much of the financial support for the bomb had come, was discussed but dropped. The Secretary of State pointed out the possibility of Soviet intervention, and also the fact that the Syrian government per se had nothing whatever to do with the plot. The President agreed, and instructed Coleman to destroy the rest of the companies involved in supporting the bomb. Coleman was also to divert men from other areas, to discover where any other nuclear device would be delivered in the Middle East. At least half of the FBI would comb all areas of the United States.

Although he wasn't sure what it would accomplish, the President ordered a general alert of the armed forces, and a partial call-up of reserves. It would be a good psychological and political move. At least the electorate would think their leader was reacting swiftly.

*   *   *

The atomic blast at Lake Placid set off still another kind of chain reaction:

Item: The entire Lake Placid area was evacuated to avoid further casualties from radiation fallout.

Item: Meteorologists all over the world began tracking wind currents and rainfall patterns, to determine where and when the radioactive cloud would settle.

Item: All the news media concentrated on the atomic explosion, almost to the exclusion of all other news.

Item: New York City panicked.

Broken down in detail, the events that followed the explosion were a bizarre mixture of the controlled and the chaotic.

Five hundred people had been killed and three thousand injured by the Adirondack blast. As reports of radiation sickness filtered in, health authorities estimated that more than ten thousand people would contract the disease to varying degrees. Some authorities estimated a higher number.

New York City was the scene of mass confusion and near-riot as many people, convinced that they were the next target, tried to get out, without knowing where they were going. Air, train and bus terminals were besieged, roads, bridges and tunnels were clogged with cars and trucks, all unable to move an inch in the massive traffic tangle. People began taking up residence in subway stations, using them as bomb shelters, further snarling transportation. Civil Defense volunteers, finally put to some sort of test, were totally unable to cope with the situation. Medical services were helpless, simply because ambulances could not get through anywhere, and people in physical distress could not reach hospitals. Fires raged unchecked because fire trucks were immobilized. There were muggings, sluggings, druggings, in Manhattan's Central Park, in Brooklyn's Prospect Park, in Harlem, in Bedford-Stuyvesant, in fashionable Beekman Place. Bars and liquor stores were broken into, the shelves emptied. There were lootings, of appliance stores, clothing stores, supermarkets. Radicals in Washington Square Park made impassioned speeches, demanding immediate disarmament by the United States. Blase pleasure seekers took to their beds, fornicating the day away, convinced it was their last on earth.

In the United Nations, delegate Hafez Khalim

denounced the United States for what he said was the covert explosion of a nuclear device by the Central Intelligence Agency. He spoke to an empty chamber; other delegates were frantically burning papers in embassies, trying to get through to their home countries, further jamming overloaded telephone lines.

Strangely, by six o'clock that same evening, order had been restored.

The governor of New York called out the National Guard, using the media to inform the troops to report to their respective armories. Guardsmen, with fixed bayonets, fanned out, prodding, begging, ordering people to return to their homes. With the cooperation of the police, auxiliaries, uniformed firemen and Civil Defense personnel, the streets were slowly cleared of massed humanity, vehicles began to inch along, public transportation began to function, and an attempt to clean up the incredible damage was begun.

While all this was happening, three men were fast asleep in a downtown Manhattan hotel, exhausted after what they considered a good job well done. When they awoke, Hamid Saad obtained some blank stationary, rented a typewriter in the hotel and wrote a note. He directed the original to the White House; carbon copies were addressed to the *New York Times* and the *New York Daily News*. The letter read:

We are the Army of Palestinian Liberation. We

have rejected moderation of weak pigs and apologists like Arafat and his band of cowardly weaseling negotiators, whose diplomatic groveling before the world has only enriched them and exploited the Palestinian people.

We have taken up the cause of the Palestinian people, for a return to their homeland and the destruction of the illegal State of Israel with our nuclear strike force. We have demonstrated our capability to the world with the detonation of our first bomb in the Adirondack Mountains.

We chose that area in order to minimize the loss of life and property. But we have additional bombs, and will not hesitate to use them, to destroy the warmongers who threaten us. The United States was chosen as our first target to prove that we are not afraid of so-called American power, and because the United States has stood by Israel in its Zionist attempt at genocide of the Palestinian people.

We warn that another major American city, with its millions of people, will be struck by our next bomb, unless the following conditions are met:

(1) The United States must withdraw all its military support of Israel and break diplomatic ties.

(2) The United States must free all Arab

prisoners in its filthy prisons, including our black brothers who have accepted Muslim faith.

(3) The United States is to force its Zionist lackeys in Israel to free all Arab prisoners and political prisoners.

(4) The United States must pay an indemnity of one billion dollars to the bank accounts of the Army of Palestinian Liberation, in Rabat, Morocco.

These demands are not negotiable. There will be no compromises. We would prefer to save our nuclear bombs for the stinking Jews in our homeland, but if necessary we will use them against Zionist allies.

(Signed) Muhammed Muhammed

The copies of the letter sent out by Hamid arrived at their destinations the following day.

* * *

Alexander, Tom and Hamid reached Washington a few hours before their letter. They had abandoned the rented Caprice and the van rented in upstate New York, and loaded the extra bomb in its desk crate, the crated parts of the third bomb, and their luggage into another van Hamid had purchased for three thousand dollars in cash at a used car lot in Flushing, Queens.

To avoid renting multiple rooms, Hamid rented a suite at the Guest Quarters on Shirley Highway in Alexandria, south of Washington. He registered with the clerk while the others waited outside in the truck. It was a spacious, two-bedroom apartment, with a sofabed in the living room, glass and chrome furniture, framed modern art on the walls and a small but efficient kitchen. Tom clicked on the television set, and the trio watched an in-depth rehash of the previous day's events, which was still the feature on all three networks. Finally Hamid clicked off the set and suggested lunch.

"But first," he said to the builders, "we've got to get rid of that wooden crate with the components. And we can't send it to Morocco any longer, at least not directly. Anything destined for Rabat would be suspect."

"We can always re-address it," said Alexander. "Where do you want it?"

"My contact in Rome. He'll know what to do with it."

With a new name and a new destination, the crate was sent off via Braniff International, prepaid with Hamid's seemingly endless supply of cash. Like all his ilk, he never left a trail of credit cards or checks if he could avoid it.

Then they drove into nearby Old Town Alexandria for lunch at a small restaurant which Hamid often visited on trips to Washington. It was just down the road from a business he often dealt with, Interarms Company. Interarms was a CIA front, specializing in supplying arms to revolutionaries supported covertly by the U.S. government. The arms were often used to "destabilize" a foreign government, in order to have installed other leaders more sympathetic to American interests. Ostensibly, they supplied arms to police departments, but Hamid had discovered their true business while employed by the Iranian secret police, when his commanding officers had ordered him to work with the firm to help funnel arms to various groups in the Middle East. The restaurant Hamid chose, the Kings Landing, was just a block from the big brick Interarms warehouse. Hamid thought it the best eating place in or near the Washington area.

While they were lunching, Hamid's ransom note arrived at the White House. Neither the *Times* or the *News*, who had received their copies a couple of hours earlier, had published the letter, but were frantically trying to confirm the fact that the President knew about it. Press Secretary Ron McDonald was trying desperately to stave off the barrage of questions.

The President, meanwhile, had called Coleman and Hawkins into the Oval Office to discuss the matter. Accompanying them was Atkinson, strangely uncomfortable without his uniform. He had returned to Washington with Hawkins. He shook hands with the President, much in awe.

"It's an honor to meet you, sir," he said softly.

The President smiled and nodded. Then he said, "What's the next move, gentlemen? Does that group have us over a barrel? I want to know what substance there might be to that letter. Do they have other bombs? Can they carry out their threat?"

"I doubt that very much," said Coleman firmly. "The plutonium was stolen late in November. They exploded a nuclear device in mid-February. It was an incredible feat to have built one bomb, let alone additional ones. I think they shot their load."

"I agree with Coleman," said Hawkins.

The President looked at Atkinson, who squirmed in his chair. "How about you, lieutenant?" he asked. "What's your thinking?"

"I'm afraid I must disagree with Mr. Coleman and Mr. Hawkins," he said apologetically. "After going over the lab, and auditing the amount of material they had to work with, I'd say they surely had enough supplies and equipment for at least one or two more bombs. It's just a hunch, Mr. President, nothing I can prove, but it strikes me that if they could make one bomb that fast, it's just a matter of keeping going to make the others."

There was silence. The President looked at him. Coleman looked at him. Hawkins looked at him. Atkinson felt naked, stupid, sorry he had opened his mouth.

The President said, "Assuming they do have another bomb, lieutenant, where would they explode it?"

"I don't rightly know, sir," said Atkinson. "It would have to be somewhere in the east. Obviously, New York or Washington are the logical target cities, since one is the population center, the other is the seat of government. If I was part of that group of nuts, and I wanted to do as much damage as possible, I'd hit Washington."

"Indeed," said the President pensively, making Atkinson feel as if the top of his head had been opened and his innermost thoughts were exposed. "I'm inclined to agree with you. New York City panicked without having a bomb explode in the vicinity. If a bomb exploded in Washington, not only New York, but other cities would undoubtedly react in similar fashion. One bomb here would get inestimable mileage. Why waste others?"

As all three men nodded, the President knew that this man Atkinson, who had risen in life to become a lieutenant of a state police barracks in a small New York city, was the only one of the three with any grasp of the situation, and probably the only one in the room, himself included, who had a chance to unravel the Gordian knot. But he had to test him just a bit more.

"Suppose we pay the ransom, lieutenant," the President passed the demand letter to Atkinson. "What then?"

Atkinson read the letter carefully and shook his head. "I'm sorry, sir, it won't wash," he said. "I think the group intends to explode their bomb here in Washington, and they will try to do so whether their terms are met or not. Our only chance is to stop them before they can carry out their threat."

"And how do you propose to do that?"

Again Atkinson shook his head. "I'm afraid I don't know that yet, sir. Most likely they'll try at a time when they could do the most damage. It needs more investigation."

The President dismissed Coleman and Hawkins, and to their chagrin he asked Atkinson to remain behind.

"Leslie," he said, putting the trooper on a private first-name basis, "you're in charge. You will have at your disposal all the manpower and resources you need, including the Treasury Department, the Secret Service, and any other agencies you think may be of assistance. You are to report directly to me. If Coleman or Hawkins give you any trouble, call me immediately."

The President arose from his chair, walked around the desk and shook Atkinson's hand.

"Good luck," he said. "We've got to find that terrorist group."

"Yes, Mr. President," Atkinson said.

They left the Oval Office together.

CHAPTER EIGHTEEN

It was three o'clock when the conspirators finished lunch and walked out of Kings Landing. They had been the only patrons in the room on the second floor of the restaurant, and they had discussed the final phase of their mission in hushed tones. They decided that the sooner they got the bomb positioned, the better. They knew that photographs of Alexander and Tom would soon be in the hands of every cop in the country, and indeed, millions of copies had already been printed, and the pictures had appeared in newspapers all over America—indeed, all over the world. But perhaps they might get away with it.

Hamid Saad never trusted "perhaps." From one of his suitcases he produced a brown wig and dark tinted glasses.

"Try these on," he said to Alexander.

The disguise altered Alexander's appearance appreciably, although anyone who had known him for a long time and had seen his actual appearance frequently, would see through it in a few moments. But a stranger would not look twice, regardless of whether or not he had seen Alexander's face the previous day in the papers.

Taking a circuitous route, they drove out Washington Street to the George Washington Parkway, past National Airport to I-95. They turned north and crossed the 14th Street Bridge, and exited before reaching the Washington Channel. They turned into a deserted area of East Potomac Park and stopped by a group of trees.

Tom crawled back into the interior of the van to arm the bomb. He carefully inserted the detonators in the holes he had drilled in the high explosive lenses weeks before. The wiring harness was gingerly connected to the metal-tipped ends of the detonators. Then Alexander took over.

Alexander was familiar with the firing devices, and besides, Amhed had written out detailed instructions for the electrical work.

There were three detonation devices in the desk crate. One was the timer like that which had set off the first bomb, the same model, and Alexander made the same connections. The second was a radio-controlled switch that could be used to detonate the device from a distance of forty miles. They had tested the device by placing it in the basement of Clark Hall on the Cornell campus, and then keying the transmitter from various distances. They had no reason to doubt that the device would not work inside the stone edifice of the Cannon Building.

The third firing device was a series of four mercury switch arrangements, with each of the arrangements composed of three mercury switches. These devices consisted of small glass tubes, into which a small drop of mercury had been enclosed. When the tube was tilted properly, the mercury flowed to the end of the tube and surrounded the electrodes. Since mercury is a metal and conducts electricity, the mercury droplet completed the circuit. Three switches had been used to make the assemblies sensitive to move-ment in all three possible axes: up-down, side-to-side and longitudinal. If any of the switches in the four assemblies was tripped, the bomb would explode. It was a kind of fail-safe idea, so that in case the bomb was discovered, it would be extremely difficult to disarm.

The power switch was left in the *off* position. The switch was situated behind one of the letters in the manufacturer's name on the side of the crate. When they wanted to turn on the juice that would run the radio equipment and the firing mechan-ism, all that was needed was a quick poke with a sharp instrument through the letter, to strike the flattened toggle on the switch.

The top of the crate was resealed and a label attached, indicating that the desk had been or-dered for the personal use of Congressman Barnes, whose office was on the fifth floor of the Cannon Building.

The last step was to affix plastic signs to the sides of the van, telling the world—and, they hoped, the guards—that this truck was owned by the Congressional Transit and Storage Company.

They left Potomac Park and headed toward the Cannon Building. Alexander, complete with wig and glasses, was dropped off a few blocks away, for two reasons: first to see if anyone would recognize him in his disguise, and also, to set up the fact that a delivery was expected in the Cannon Building.

No one on the street gave him a second glance.

Alexander walked up the steps of the Cannon Building, took the elevator to the basement, and walked through the corridors to the rear of the building. He turned left and walked over to the photoelectric device that opened the grey fire doors, and continued into the auto passageway that led under the building to the parking garage below. Several trucks were being unloaded outside with a forklift. Alexander walked up to one of the guards standing next to the entrance.

"Seen a truck from Congressional Transit?" he asked. "It was supposed to be here with a desk for Congressman Barnes. It's two days late already, and he's getting pissed off."

"Too bad, buddy, things are tough all over," the guard smiled. "Those congressmen are a bunch of jerks anyway."

"Yeah," Alexander agreed. "But Barnes isn't so

bad. He's better than most."

Alexander hung around for another ten minutes, and then, on schedule, Tom appeared with the van. Alexander heaved an exaggerated sigh of relief. He secured the services of a forklift operator who wasn't busy, went over to the truck, pretended to sign a bill of lading and handed it back to Tom. The forklift was maneuvered under the pallet and the crate was lifted out of the truck, which was promptly driven away.

The forklift carried the crate to an elevator, where it was transferred to a hand-pulled carrier, since the forklift was too heavy for the elevator. The operator helped him shove the crate into the lift car, which then went up to the fifth floor. Alexander dragged the crate out at a small alcove in the southwest corner of the building. He pulled it through a corridor lined with boxes and crates, and soon reached his destination, an open alcove among the welter of boxes. Twisting the hydraulic mechanism of the carrier, he watched the pallet drop to floor level, then pulled the carrier free.

From his pocket he took a small bubble-level, which he used on all the plane surfaces of the crate. Good! It was resting perfectly, with no tilt anywhere. Had there been an appreciable tilt, he could not have activated the toggle switch, for the mercury would have started to flow through one of the tubes and the bomb would have gone off then and there.

Now he took a long nail from his pocket, which he jabbed through the proper letter, and after

271

fumbling and feeling around a bit, located the power switch. He hit the nail, heard the soft click.

The beast was armed!

Casually, Alexander ambled back to the elevator, rode it to the first floor and walked out of the Cannon Building. The truck, with the signs now removed, was waiting for him. Alexander got in. He looked at the innocent-looking transistor radio, which was really the transmitter that would broadcast the destruction of the American government.

* * *

All three networks interrupted regularly scheduled programming simultaneously at nine o'clock in the evening. Three different announcers said:

"Ladies and gentlemen, we interrupt this program to bring you a special address by the President of the United States."

President Howard Edward Bentley was seated behind his desk in the Oval Office. He began to speak.

"Good evening, my fellow Americans.

"Today, I received a note from a group of demented people, amoral terrorists, who have killed or maimed thousands of people in New York State. Their action, in exploding a nuclear device on our soil, is one which will be avenged. And it will not happen again.

"This group of maniacs has had the temerity to

send a letter to me, and to several newspapers, making a number of demands. Of course, these demands will not be met. The American people do not frighten easily; we are tougher than this senseless group thinks.

"Over the past decades, the United States has been benevolent, patient with the nations of the Middle East, even when they unilaterally decided to hit us with an oil embargo. We have remained passive, turning the other cheek while our detractors derided, belittled us. Our passivity has now come to an end.

"The terrorists have indicated that they have another bomb and will use it. My information indicates that they will do so whether or not we accede to their demands.

"It would have been morally repugnant to bow to this band of cutthroats and murderers. We will never pay ransom blood money. As for prisoners in our institutions, they are there because they have committed crimes against society, and there they shall remain until they have served appropriate sentences. And we have no hegemony over our Israeli allies, and cannot, we will not, force them to make any release from their prisons.

"Undoubtedly, those who perpetrated this violence are listening to me now. Let them know, then, that we shall not surrender to blackmail. Let them know too that we have dossiers on them. They are financed by a group of Middle Eastern businessmen, who have engaged in this conspiracy with the full knowledge of their governments.

And their governments have failed to halt their insidious plans.

"For this reason, I make this solemn promise, if another atomic device strikes American soil:

(1) The capitals of the following nations, who have tacitly supported the conspiracy, shall be struck by American nuclear missiles: Syria, Egypt, Lebanon and Libya.

(2) The United States will annex as territories as much land and materials as deemed necessary to protect its supplies of petroleum.

(3) The United States hereby gives the United Nations and its terrorist sympathizers a period of two years to find another location in another country.

"I realize that these measures may seem harsh. Yet, for decades, the United States has freely given of its food, money and technical assistance to other countries, who use this wealth to thumb their noses at us. We have restrained our might in the interests of world peace and fairness, even when such actions did not coincide with our national interests. But, no longer.

"As my first policy in office, I urge that we embark on a program of self-preservation. Not a program of imperialism or military might for the sake of revenge, but in order to make sure that our own resources are devoted to our own self-interests, before lending assistance to others. I shall present a more detailed proposal to Congress in my State of the Union address.

"Good night, my fellow Americans."

The speech was followed by the inevitable analyses over all the networks, by all the savants of the networks. They only served to confuse the situation more.

*   *   *

Sitting self-consciously in a corner of the Situation Room of the White House, looking at the instant analysis but failing to hear them, Lieutenant Leslie Atkinson leaped to his feet. The last line of the President's speech had lodged in his brain and refused to move.

Of course! The State of the Union Address! What better time to strike with the atom bomb?

With that one stroke, the entire federal government of the United States would be wiped out! Attending would be the Presdient, the Vice-President, the Speaker of the House, all the members of the House and Senate, the Cabinet, the Supreme Court Justices, the Joint Chiefs of Staff—everybody!

But he also knew that the President would not postpone his address until the terrorists were caught, for that would belie his own words, show weakness in the face of a lesser enemy, weakness at a time when he demanded toughness from himself and his countrymen. And he would also insist that every member of the Cabinet, every Congressman, every Justice, every ranking official, attend the speech, to show the world that the United States feared no one, anywhere, at any time.

Atkinson steeled himself with the realization that he had to set up a net through which the bombers could not pass. He summoned the head of the Secret Service, and the two of them began to prepare the unprecedented security operation which would cause Capital Hill to become impregnable.

Starting the next day, no vehicles of any kind would be permitted into the area bounded on the south by the Southwest Freeway, on the north by Union Station, by Robert F. Kennedy Stadium on the east, and Eleventh Street on the west. All deliveries would be transferred to army vehicles at the perimeters, and they would take them to their destinations. Around the perimeter, twenty thousand troops would be stationed, on round-the-clock sentry duty. Air space was to be patrolled constantly by helicopters, armed to the gunwales, and, on the day of the address, heat-seeking missiles would be wheeled into position.

This perimeter, the planners figured, would serve as an effective barrier. Defense Department scientists had studied the Lake Placid blast site, and determined that the bomb had the equivalent of twenty-five kilotons. Thus the Capitol would be safe, could withstand a blast of that size if ground zero was outside that perimeter.

The beefed-up security system went operational immediately. Additional guards patrolled garage entrances and building corridors, under the impression that anything already delivered was considered safe. Thus they took no notice of the welter of boxes and crates on the fifth floor of the Cannon Building.

At four o'clock in the morning, Lieutenant Leslie Atkinson could no longer keep his eyes open, and he went to bed, not knowing that an armed bomb was already in position, needing only the touch of a button on a transmitter to open the floodgates of disaster.

* * *

Eight time zones away it was midnight. A Syrian air force jet, carrying a full complement of weapons, including a quantity of napalm, streaked toward the top floor of the Syroco Oil Transport Building.

Anwar Yesseh, almost sick with worry, was looking out the window. In the distance he saw something white floating through the air, gently downward. Then he saw the oncoming plane. He almost fainted in terror.

The jet crashed into the building, and an intense fire erupted immediately, destroying five floors immediately, and igniting the rest of the structure as flaming napalm seeped down. No one would ever know that the pilot who ejected and was never found was a member of the Israeli Intelligence, who had infiltrated the Syrian armed forces.

At almost the same time, cotton warehouses in Cairo were blown to bits. Simultaneously, an attractive villa in Giza, Egypt, was ripped from within by an enormous explosion that killed its cotton-broker owner and all his staff of servants.

Before the day was ended, all members of the consortium would have met similar fates at the hands of John Coleman's CIA agents.

CHAPTER NINETEEN

February 20th, the day of the State of the Union Address, dawned under a cloudless sky. Unable to sleep despite the sleeping pill the White House physician had given him, President Bentley was already pacing through the White House, first through one room then another. He watched the sun come up; the winter days were getting longer, morning came sooner. He went down to breakfast at seven, and was joined by the members of his Cabinet. The scene was one of forced lightness, unsuccessfully blanketing the fear, the apprehension felt by everyone. This would surely be a State of the Union message unsurpassed by any that had gone before.

                              *   *   *

    Not far away, Hamid Saad drained the last of
his coffee and pushed away from the table. He
walked over to the telephone, dialed some digits
and waited for the phone to be picked up at the
other end.
    "As-salaam alaykum," he said into the mouth-
piece. A voice echoed the traditional greeting.
    "Are all the arrangements made?" Hamid
asked.
    "Yes."
    "We shall meet at National precisely at 9:30."
    "Yes."
    "We must be airborne no later than 10:30."
    "Yes."
    "Good. *An-naar,*" Hamid said, giving the Arab
word for victory.
    Alexander and Tom smiled, grateful that
Hamid had taken proper precautions. By this time
every airplane ticket with an international destination had to be checked against the names of
Alexander Greely and Tom Flaherty. And there
was the fingerprint check, along with applications
for tickets. And photographs of the two men.
Disguises would work only to a point; it would be
totally impossible for Tom or Alexander to board a
commercial jet and escape the country. Hamid had
thoughtfully arranged for them to fly to Cuba in a
chartered aircraft, piloted by one of his associates.

*　　*　　*

Lieutenant Leslie Atkinson, like the President, had spent a sleepless night. He was plagued by nightmares of exploding atom bombs and the inferno they caused. He too was pacing, wondering, cudgeling his brain. Security had been tight. But what if...

What if the bomb were already in place?

The day before, he had contacted the firm called Aerial Radiological Measuring Surveyors on the west coast, and requested that they send their units to the Capitol to help with the search. Their special aircraft were equipped to detect even slight radiation levels on the ground. If the bomb weren't too well shielded—if indeed it were there at all— they could find it. The owner of the firm promised that his pilots would fly through the night, they would reach Washington the next morning.

"What time in the morning?" Atkinson asked.

"Maybe eight or nine o'clock."

"Make it eight o'clock," said Atkinson. The President was due to begin his speech precisely at 10:30 in the morning.

He was waiting for the pilots at National when the plane landed. He walked over to introduce himself.

"Gentlemen, I'm Les Atkinson. Happy to meet you. Please refuel quickly so we can get started."

"Hey, how about breakfast?" protested the co-

281

pilot. "Don't we get time for that? We've been flying all night, we're bushed."

"Time is something we have very little of," Atkinson said grimly. "The life of the President of the United States, the life of this country may be at stake. I pray God that this is all for nothing."

"Okay," said the pilot soberly. "We'll make do with some coffee and donuts. I'll see to refueling."

"We've got special clearance for this trip," Atkinson told the pilot. "Ordinarily, aircraft are not permitted to fly over the Capitol or the office buildings, but we've got all the clearance we need. Just identify yourself to the tower as *Critical Mass One*. They already have your flight plan filed. What we'll do is just eyeball it. I'll tell you which areas to cover."

By 8:55 in the morning they were taxiing and then lifting off. The plane banked around Washington Monument and soon began its passes low over Capitol Hill. They started with the northern perimeter, making east-west swoops, working toward the south.

With the last pass over Independence Avenue, the needle on the recorder in the plane almost leaped off the scale.

"Hey, we've got something!" yelled the co-pilot. "Go back over that last run."

The pilot slowed the plane to near stall speed and made his way back up Independence Avenue after swinging around over the General Services Administration Building. As they passed over the office buildings, the needle jumped again.

"There's your target, Mr. Atkinson," the tense pilot pointed down. "One of those buildings down there has your bomb."

They made several additional passes, but were unable to determine which of the three House Office Buildings the source of radioactivity was emanating from. Atkinson thought of radioing instructions to all personnel to begin searching the buildings, but then he realized that there were no frequencies available through which he could reach the President, or the Secret Service, and he had to keep everything in low profile to avert a panic or cause utter confusion.

"Get this thing down as fast as you can without crashing it," Atkinson barked. The plane sped back toward National, and the tower routed them ahead of a dozen commercial planes stacked up over Arlington and Springfield.

It was ten o'clock by the time Atkinson was down and could get to a telephone. He dialed the White House.

"I must speak with the President," Atkinson almost shouted. "It's urgent!"

"I'm sorry, the President is at the Capital, Mr. Atkinson," said the operator.

"Can't you get a message through to him?"

"No, sir. Not right away. But I'll send a messenger. What shall I say to the messenger, sir?"

Atkinson gritted his teeth. And what could he

tell to this operator, the messenger, to anyone? That a bomb was probably ticking somewhere, set to go off at any moment? All he'd get would be a scream and a faint.

He hung up and dialed the Secret Service. It was a full ten minutes before he could be located. He was not at his desk.

"It's in one of the House Office Buildings!" he shouted into the mouthpiece.

"Which one?"

"If I knew I'd tell you! Get your men over and find it! Take a lot of geiger counters with you!

"And for God's sake, get the President and everybody else the hell out of there!"

Even as he spoke, Atkinson knew that was impossible. The President, maybe; everybody else, no way.

It was 10:12 when Atkinson raced through the terminal pell mell. He almost knocked over three men, two of whom were wearing disguises. He kept running.

*   *   *

The President was running late. He had spent more time than he intended, speaking with the Senate Majority Leader in the cloakroom. Secret Service agents jammed nearly ever corner of the building, looking calmly around. No one, including the President, knew of the frantic search taking place across the street. And one other agent, who did know, was having a hell of a time

284

wedging through the throng of people, trying to locate his Chief of State.

Now President Bentley walked out into the House Chamber to deliver his State of the Union message.

CHAPTER TWENTY

Inside the House Chamber, every seat was taken.

The Speaker of the House and the Vice-President had already taken their places on the top dais, with the Vice-President, as President of the Senate, sitting in the right-hand seat under the field of stars of the great flag, hung behind the dais with its stripes running vertically.

As the Speaker surveyed the throng, he was not thinking of this momentous occasion, nor of the important proposals the President would make, nor of the terrorists' blackmail threat. His mind was on his mistress, a striking girl from Venezuela, who was his constant companion. He thought of her supple young body, and he thought also of his alcoholic wife, who had nearly burned down their last three residences after passing out in bed with lighted cigarettes between her fingers. He remembered too that moment two hours ago, when he had to leave his mistress's apartment, and her words, "Speakie, be careful."

He hated when she called him that, but she enjoyed teasing him.

But the Speaker was an exception to the rule. Everyone else realized the importance of the coming speech, just as they understood the direct words spoken by the President a couple of days earlier. Reaction from most members of Congress had been favorable, but some columnists had called it "The New Imperialsim," and several of the more "liberal doves" openly opposed him. The State of the Union Message, they knew would contain an ultimatum to the Palestinians, to shape up—or else.

Had the conspirators been able to take a head count, they would have been disappointed by their failure to score a complete wipeout. One senator was in a drying-out tank in an exclusive sanitarium, another at his sick wife's bedside. One senator, a bitter enemy of the President, was in his Alexandria apartment, a tribute to the hostility that existed between him and the Chief Executive Officer of the United States. For various reasons, some thirty-three assorted senators and congressmen were not present. Likewise, the Chief Justice of the Supreme Court was convalescing from coronary bypass surgery at Bethesda Naval Hospital.

Another five minutes passed. Joan Bentley, the President's wife, watched the double doors to the right of the dais through which her husband would soon pass. She gazed at the full length portrait of Lafayette that flanked the right side of the door, and at the equally imposing portrait of Washington that was to the left of the door on the other side of the platform.

The whispering and buzzing abruptly stopped as the Doorkeeper of the House announced, "Ladies and gentlemen, the President of the United States."

Everyone in the room arose and applauded as Howard Edward Bentley, the President of the United States, entered the chamber, walked through and mounted the platform. For an instant, his tall, lean stature and his dark suit made him seem like another of the four black marble columns that graced the rear of the platform.

He was followed by the Senate Majority Leader, who took a seat near the door. AND...

Secret Service men across the street frantically ransacked boxes and crates, racing through corridors like bloodhounds gone mad from the scent. They started with the basement corridors and rooms, not bothering with locks, simply smashing open locked doors in a mad search for a large box. They had reached the fourth floor of the Cannon Building, AND...

"Honorable Members of Congress, Honorable

288

Justices of the Supreme Court, members of the Cabinet, members of the Joint Chiefs of Staff, ladies and gentlemen, my fellow Americans," President Bentley began. He looked up at the gallery and caught his wife's eye. She smiled.

"I doubt that any President or Congress of the past has ever assembled for a State of the Union Address when the State was in better condition, but when that condition was in greater peril."

The room was pin-drop silent, AND...

The black Lear jet charged down the runway and lifted off. According to instructions from the tower, it combined a gentle climb with a port bank. The Pentagon passed below, as did thousands of markers in Arlington National Cemetery. Soon they were passing over the urban sprawl that was Washington, continuing its curving climb. Alexander spotted Falls Church below. AND...

"It's here!" shouted a Secret Service agent on the fifth floor of the Cannon Building, as his geiger counter leaped like a living thing. "Get a forklift! Let's get the damned infernal machine out of here!" He waited fearfully knowing that Satan's power of destruction was sitting in a desk crate only two feet away. AND...

"We must remember," the President said, "that in our strength lies the freedom of the world. Only through the defiance and firmness of American power can smaller nations survive the forces that would destroy them. We shall remain strong."

A storm of applause swept through the chamber, AND...

The forklift arrived, coming up the elevator, in spite of the operator's protest that it was too heavy. It came to the crate. The operator pulled levers, nervously, then tilted it backward slightly to make sure it stayed on the fork. Standard procedure.

Somewhere inside the crate four balls of mercury in different areas raced toward sets of contacts. They reached their destination. The combined capacitive forces, amounting to several farads of stored electricity, raced through the semiconductor network, and from there to the sparkgap detonators, where they leaped the space between two electrodes. One of the dual detonators in lens 34 failed to fire, but its companion did. AND...

Lieutenant Leslie Atkinson had just reached the Jefferson Memorial after crossing the Fourteenth Street Bridge when he saw the rainbow of hideous colors erupting to his right. He knew instantly that he had failed. He slammed on the brakes of his car, ducked down on the floor.

It was the same thing he had done in his nightmares. AND...

Alexander, Tom and Hamid, and the pilot, marveled at the monster that had been unleashed. AND...

Millions of Americans were puzzled when the

television image of the President of the United States suddenly turned black, and nothing appeared on the screen for more than five minutes. The truth that would come within a half hour would spread panic throughout the land. AND...

NEXT

THE TRINITY IMPLOSION—AFTERMATH

ROBIN MOORE,
Biographical Notes

Robin Moore, born Robert Lowell Moore, Jr., in Boston, Massachusetts, on October 31, 1925, has been writing all his life. After flying with the Air Force during the second World War, Moore entered Harvard College. He spent the summer of 1947 in Europe as a correspondent for the Boston Globe, and when told by a writing teacher that he was not a particularly promising student, Moore challenged: "You mean that scholarly writing is not my field. I intend to become a rich writer, not an academic." Since then, he regularly sends incribed copies of his best sellers back to Harvard.

Although Robin's first novel, *Pitchman*—on the early days of the television business—was not the best seller Robin had hoped it would be, his second book, *The Devil to Pay*—the story of Jack Youngblood, a notorious gun runner and adventurer in the Caribbean, and one of the pilots for the Tropic Air Charter Service that Robin had started—made a splash since Castro had taken over Cuba at the time of the book's publication. It was Robin's next work, though—*The Green Berets*—that was hailed as one of the most controversial books in years. In 1962 while in Jamaica, Robin found an old copy of a *New York Times Magazine Section* story about a group of men in the United States Army who wore green berets and were specialists in guerilla warfare. Moore obtained the Department of Defense's cooperation in the writing of the book, which included Robin's actually becoming a trained Special Forces man and spending six months with his friends in Vietnam. Although the Department of Defense was highly displeased with Moore's published results since he had revealed too much of the truth about what was happening in Vietnam, Moore was by now internationally known.

Moore followed with a novel called *The Country Team* and a biography of Arthur Fiedler, conductor of the Boston Pops Orchestra and an old friend of Moore's. Then, the public received *The French Connection*, *The Khaki Mafia*, *The Happy Hooker*, *The Fifth Estate*, *Dubai*, and *Valency Girl*.

Robin Moore lives and works in Westport, Connecticut.

THE KAUFMAN SNATCH

ROBIN MOORE

19128 ★ $1.95

Torn from today's headlines, a finely meshed novel, a bigger than life drama of IRA terrorists, CIA renegades and the $2,000,000 ransom that was to pay for the biggest bloodbath in history.

ANOTHER HARD HITTING BOOK
FROM THE BEST SELLING AUTHOR OF
THE FRENCH CONNECTION

BLIND SPOT

ROBIN
MOORE

19129 ★ $1.95

**Inside the clawing, frantic, driving life of big business.
This expose of corporate control of the lives of the men
and women who will do anything to get to the top will
get you thinking about who owns America.**

ALOHA
ROBIN MOORE

19133 ★ $1.95

*The war games and trial could turn into
a killing reality. What was a routine
maneuver took on a kind of fright that
seemed to be without end.*

IT DOESN'T HAPPEN EVERY DAY

ROBIN MOORE

AND PETER DANE

Against a background of Hollywood fighting for its life against the new medium, television, an aging star pits her past infamy and glory. Sex and success go hand in hand, but all she has now is her talent.

19134 ★ $1.95

19139 ★ $1.95

THE ESTABLISHMENT
ROBIN MOORE

A sweeping story of one man
caught up in an all consuming
drive for power, where love, hate
and murder conspire to make the
price of success too high.